# GOOD CHRISTIAN GIRLS

Visit us at www.boldstrokesbooks.com

# GOOD CHRISTIAN GIRLS

*by*

## Elizabeth Bradshaw

2024

**CREDITS**
EDITOR: JENNY HARMON
PRODUCTION DESIGN: STACIA SEAMAN
COVER DESIGN BY INKSPIRAL DESIGN

# Acknowledgments

I wrote this book for my younger self. I got you, kid. I also wrote this book for my life partner, Cass. You are my favorite person. Thank you to my parents, who did the best they could, and whom I love very much. I'm sorry if you read this. Thank you to my friend Jen, for believing in me. Thank you to my very first therapist Kelli, for saving my life. Thank you to my Pine Cove camp counselors. Thank you to the members of the LGBTQ+ community, who have bravely paved the way toward the kind of representation we all deserve.

For Cass, my only should have

# CHAPTER ONE

## *Lacey*

Nothing interesting ever happened at Camp Lavender. Of this, I was absolutely certain. Every summer was exactly the same—girls piled into camp, spilling out of buses and minivans or the occasional two-door convertible if their dad was going through a midlife crisis. They spread out over the camp grounds shrieking and giggling and ready for a summer away from their families. Six weeks of bug bites and Bible studies later, they piled out again, their hair a little lighter, their skin a little darker, and their shoes caked in the stubborn orange dirt that only Gladwall, Texas, could produce.

When I woke up on that particular June seventh, I felt a familiar pit in my stomach. My days of wandering the camp grounds unbothered were officially at an end and the seemingly endless days of avoiding sweaty campers and their irritating zest for life stretched ahead. The only thing that made this summer special was the fact that it would (hopefully) be my last one spent here. I pulled my faded Camp Lavender T-shirt from three years ago over my head and took a deep breath before descending the stairs to the kitchen, where I could hear my parents chattering with excitement. The only thing worse than feigning excitement, I had learned from experience, was the emotional torture of my parents' crestfallen faces when my enthusiasm for the first day of camp was lacking. Being the daughter of the founders, they reminded me every year, came with certain responsibilities, and mandatory enthusiasm was one of them.

This place was their dream, their livelihood, and the culmination of years of effort, and it seemed to me to be rude and unnecessary to express my disdain for the entire operation. It's not like they were pressuring me to take over the family business or anything like that. One more never-ending summer here and I would be permitted to move away to the college of my choice, provided I got in and received a financial offer stable enough to justify *the decision*. That's what my parents had taken to calling it—*the decision*—as if the words *college* and *move* and *future* were too jagged to pass their lips without cutting them open. They couldn't understand why I would ever want to live anywhere but Texas. I kept reminding myself that they didn't have to understand.

There was a giddy air to the way my dad handed me my plate of scrambled eggs and toast that morning. I stifled a sigh at the thought that this was the last breakfast my dad would make me in our kitchen until summer was over. If I wanted a hot breakfast for the next six weeks, I would have to eat it in the dining hall, teeming with other high school students, and not until after an impassioned prayer offered up by one of the counselors. I had noticed over the years that the prayers seemed to get more and more sentimental as the weeks went on and the camp counselors' heat exhaustion increased. If God could make Texas a little cooler in July, I would accept that as a definitive ontological argument for the existence of a higher power. St. Anselm himself would have had his doubts after the heat index hit 112 Fahrenheit.

"Are you ready for week one?" my dad asked and grinned across the breakfast table. I smiled back and shrugged.

"I guess!"

I didn't mean for it to come out in the breath of a sigh.

He tilted his head down and looked at me over his glasses with feigned disapproval.

"When did Lacey turn into such a cynical teenager?" he asked, as if I were not in the room.

My mom settled into her chair next to my dad with a bowl of her favorite bran from Buckwheat's. It seemed like everything she ate those days was some form of beige and brown mush.

"Please," she said. "Lacey was born a little old man. She came out of the womb with a pipe and a cane."

I paused mid-crunch on my toast and mumbled, "Get off my lawn, you crazy kids."

"I hope you're going to be nicer than that when the campers get here," my dad said. All I could offer him was a noncommittal shrug. He shook his head at me in half-sincere frustration.

"Remember," he said, "that this camp may be old news to you, but it is a place of transformation and miracles for the young women who attend. It's a place where they won't get distracted by boys and cell phones—and Slip or whatever that new app is called."

"It's called Slant, Dad."

"Well, you know what I mean." He waved away the invisible nuisance with a fork full of sausage. "This is a place for peace and human connection and *spiritual* connection. This is a place to escape from all the temptations and distractions of the secular world and be able to hear the *still small voice*, maybe for the first time for some of these young ladies. Perhaps this year you will witness to one of them and make a lifelong friend."

It was a good speech, and one that I had heard in various iterations since before I was old enough to understand it. He must be right, though, because I had seen so many girls break down in tears after worship on Wednesday nights, overcome by grace or faith, or whatever it was that made them close their eyes and put their hands in the air while Crowbar played his guitar on the worn down stage in the rec room. Yet somehow it was always those same girls who snuck to the woods after curfew with a bottle of Nate's Grapes Wine Blend they had stowed away in the bottom of their trunks. If I had cared, I might have told my parents that they needed to start checking the contents of trunks, but as far as I was concerned, it was better to look the other way.

And then there was The Prayer. This was the emotional event that would ideally happen for each camper before they left Camp Lavender that summer. The Prayer, as I understood it, would guarantee their salvation and absolve them of the burden of sin and death to which they were otherwise doomed. I, of course, had said this prayer long ago, when I was seven years old, repeating it after Silly Putty, my all-time favorite camp counselor, at the picnic table looking over the lake. Silly Putty (whose real name I had eventually learned was Chloe) had the biggest eyes and the widest smile I had ever seen. Her passion for All Things Jesus was hard to describe, except to say that it was the least-cringey I could ever remember witnessing. It was like Jesus was her best friend, and I wanted that. I didn't have a lot of friends back then. Not that I had any now.

My parents were in a hurry that morning, thankfully for me. If I were still seven, I would have run down to the front gates of camp to jump and cheer with the counselors as the girls arrived. But after a reasoned request when I was thirteen, my parents had allowed me to keep to myself throughout the majority of the summer weeks. For the first day, I had developed a system that (almost) always ensured that I would not run across a single jubilant soul on the first day of camp, which was inevitably the worst day of all.

First off—the dining hall. I put on my slip-ons and ambled down the path from our cabin to the dock. The heat from the asphalt radiated up my body and created the day's first pools of sweat in all my crevices. I swore to myself for the thousandth time that I would go to a university on the East Coast, NYU if all went well, where people wore boots and scarves in the winter and carried canvas bags full of poetry books to read at coffee shops. I was convinced that I had been born in the wrong place and quite possibly at the wrong time.

"Banana chocolate chip pancakes, two fried eggs, and turkey sausage?" Sidewinder asked as soon as I stepped into the dining hall. It was eerie when it was empty, but in a way that I loved. A dozen rickety round tables were set up in a zigzagging pattern across the frayed carpet, which was stained and threadbare after suffering thousands of caked teenager sneakers twice a day.

"No, ma'am! I just ate with my parents," I replied, pushing through the swinging metal door that led to the kitchen. Sidewinder was broad and red and had been at Camp Lavender as long as some of the pine trees. She stayed back of house as often as possible, coming out of the kitchen only when my dad decided to *bless the hands that had prepared the food* for one of the camp meals. I could tell that Sidewinder hated this ceremony, but she always smiled politely and bowed her head, keeping one eye on the kitchen while blessings were showered upon her.

I took a deep breath through my nose. The dining hall kitchen always smelled like coffee and boxed mashed potatoes and I loved it. There was always coffee available, in case the staff needed it, and I had come to love the ritual of starting off even the unbearably humid mornings with a steaming Styrofoam cup in my hand, sitting on the dock, watching the sounds and colors of the day start to stretch over the lake. My mother loved to tell me that drinking coffee was going to stunt my growth, but at five feet nine inches, I had no desire to grow any further.

I carried my cup to the dock, kicking aside some of the pine needles on the steps. The dock was lined with built-in benches that faced inward toward the dock. I sat backward, with my legs dangling through the gap in the bench a few feet above the water. I set my coffee on the bench and pulled a small olive green notebook out of my back pocket. I kept this on me at almost all times for three main reasons: one, my parents didn't let me have a cell phone; two, I didn't want my parents to find it; and three, you never knew when inspiration might strike.

If it weren't for watching the pages of this notebook transform from blank to covered in ink, I don't think I would have had any sense of time passing at all. I wasn't one of those delusional teenagers who think they are the next great American poet. In fact, I had decided that no one was going to read my poetry if I didn't turn it into lyrics and set it to music, so that was my plan. Eventually. For now, my plan was to stare across the same man-made lake I had been staring across for eleven years and see if I could conjure some kind of original thought. On this particular morning, my thought started to transform itself into some sort of mantra or prayer—a plea to God or the gods or whoever was in charge of the next six weeks—*Can something different happen this summer? Anything different. Please.*

Despite my bone-aching, earth-shattering boredom, I had to admit to myself that there couldn't be a better place to watch a sunrise than at Camp Lavender, but I hadn't been out of bed to see one of those since I hit my teens and suddenly lost two-thirds of my energy. Sleep was one of my primary strategies to decrease the time between now and college. I wasn't altogether sure whether I was excited about college— the transition from a university to a career as a renowned poet seemed tenuous at best—but it was by far the fastest way out of the flat circle of time Camp Lavender had created for me. In seventh grade, I read my dad a poem I had written about a mallard I had seen gliding across the lake that morning.

"I want to be a famous poet," I had declared with that broad young confidence small children have before anyone has ever hurt them.

"It's a beautiful thing to dwell on the glory of God's creation," my dad had replied. "But remember that this was given to you by Him—and you must give the glory back to Him."

Soon after, he had given me a biography of Isaac Watts, which inspired me to try my hand at writing a hymn. The glow on my parents' faces when I sang it to them in the living room was unmatched by anything I had seen before or since. They told me that God had given me a beautiful gift. My mom made copies and laminated one to put on the fridge, held there by a cross magnet that had been previously reserved for Christmas cards from immediate family.

But the green book was for something else.


I pushed open the door to the infirmary as hard as I could. I liked the way that Dr. Dan would always jump a few inches out of his chair and slap his hand onto his chest as if he were having a heart attack.

"Doc, I'm CRASHING!" I yelled as I stumbled dramatically toward the exam table in the middle of the room. "Get the smelling salts! I've got a desperate case of the vapors and a touch of consumption." I sank to my knees, clutching at the exam table paper.

Dr. Dan leaned back and crossed his tan arms. "First day getting to you already?"

I shrugged. "Honestly, it's not that bad. If I play my cards right, I think I can get through the whole day without seeing a single camper."

Dr. Dan swiveled back to his computer and shook the mouse to wake it up. This was the fifth year he had spent the summer at Camp Lavender, and I was no longer the buoyant twelve-year-old he had met when he first pulled up in his yellow convertible. I wondered sometimes what he thought about me, the girl who lived at camp all year long.

"What you need is just to make an *actual* friend," he said.

"You're my friend."

"A friend your age. A teenager. A girl."

"Why do I need to do that?"

Dr. Dan seemed to think that my reclusiveness was more a result of social awkwardness than verified introversion and that the only cure was a generous dose of human interaction. To be honest, I thought he might be right.

"Because you don't want to show up at college in the fall like a girl who just stumbled out of a cave and doesn't know how to adjust to human society."

"College isn't about making friends. It's about getting educated."

"Education is useless by itself, Lacey. You have to develop social intelligence, too."

I stared at him in silence, trying not to flinch at the sting of the words and the idea that he thought of me as some kind of antisocial freak.

"Besides, aren't seniors in high school supposed to play pranks and get up to reckless shenanigans before they graduate?"

Dr. Dan seemed like the kind of guy who was probably very popular in school. He had a sharp jawline and a confident laugh. He was compensated well to be the resident doctor at Camp Lavender. He said that it was a laid-back way to practice medicine with many perks and very few drawbacks. My parents loved him. My mom made him her world-famous chocolate chip cookies and my dad let him dock his Jet Ski at the lake free of charge. Most of his days were spent tending to minor lacerations and abrasions, sometimes with my assistance. He removed his fair share of splinters and treated a yearly outbreak of pinkeye and spent weekend nights in town. Once I asked him what he did while he was in town, but he told me that he would tell me when I was older. I never asked again.

I leaned against the edge of his desk. "Are you going to let me give any shots this year?"

"Are you going to say *whoops* when you give them?" Dr. Dan fired back.

I grinned. "I make no promises."

He shook his head and hid a smile. "Please don't go to medical school."

"That's a promise I CAN make," I retorted. "Also, don't you have to be good at science to be a doctor?"

"And math."

"Gross." I tapped my fingers on the edge of Dr. Dan's desk, my eyes roaming over his computer.

He sighed and stood up from his chair. "All right, have at it."

"Five minutes," I promised as I dropped into the chair in front of the computer.

"Remind me why you can't just use your computer at home for this?"

"Because then I'd miss my chance to come visit the world's greatest doctor," I said. "I just need to do a little research for an English essay." Dr. Dan pursed his lips, but said nothing. Over the past few weeks, I had become very efficient at logging into Slant, checking or posting a poem, logging off, and erasing the computer's search history. Not that Dr. Dan would care one way or another to read my anonymous online poetry, but on the off chance he should mention it around my parents, I did not even want to contemplate what the consequences would be.

I typed in my username and password while Dr. Dan flipped open his phone.

Twelve notifications.

Dr. Dan stood up to walk to the restroom and I switched back to a KnowAll page about Emily Dickinson. I kept my eyes trained on the tab in front of me until I heard the bathroom door click, then I switched back to Slant.

@MoonBoi11 liked your post.

@MoonBoi11 commented on your post: *This is one of the most beautiful things I have ever read.*

I quickly reread the poem I had posted, wondering who this stranger-on-the-internet was who had found, read, and taken the time to *comment* on my writing. I pulled the green book out of my back pocket and held it open with my forearm while I typed out my new poem as quickly as I could.

The walkie-talkie on Dr. Dan's desk let out a gravelly sound.

"Uh-oh," I heard from the bathroom.

I exited the Slant tab and cleared the search history as the toilet flushed. I was hard at work taking notes on Dickinson when Dr. Dan opened the bathroom door. He picked the walkie-talkie up from the desk and turned up the volume, holding the earpiece to his ear.

"Sounds like we've got our first camper injury down by the blob," Dr. Dan said, setting the walkie-talkie on the desk.

"That was fast."

"Wanna go pick the camper up and bring her back? Sounds like it might be a stitches situation."

"Are you gonna let me give her stitches?"

"I'll let you take the golf cart."

"Deal!"

I grabbed the key off Dr. Dan's desk.

"Don't go all Evel Knievel out there on me."

"Pedal to the metal!" I called back through the door as it swung shut.

# CHAPTER TWO

## *Jo*

I already knew it was going to be the worst summer of my life. I wasn't thrilled to be shipped off to Camp Lavender, but staying home was just not an option, so I resigned myself to the fact that I would spend six weeks making friendship bracelets with rich teenagers instead of learning about meteorology at Launchpad, the highest ranked youth science camp in the entire country.

My mom had given me the impression that there was a chance I *might* be able to afford Launchpad, with the help of her Tía Laura, but once Tía heard *the news*, she had better ideas. Tía Laura always had better ideas about what was good for you than you did, it seemed. *You* might think that learning about meteorology for two months would give you a head start at being the next Joanne Simpson, or at least a better chance of getting a scholarship at a four-year university, but Tía Laura was certain that going to an all-girls Christian camp would have a much more positive impact on your life. The problem was that what Tía Laura believed in was what Tía Laura would pay for, and my powers of persuasion could not surmount my powers of being snarky at the *exact wrong time*. Even a Hail Mary appeal about the Protestant leanings of the camp could not sway Tía Laura from her firm belief that I would come back at the end of the summer *cured*.

"Did you pack an umbrella?"

I hated it when my mom came into my room without knocking, but my door did not have a lock, so there wasn't much I could do about it. Somehow the thought of being trapped in a cabin with seven other high school girls and a toxically positive Texas A&M student was more palatable than the way my mother was settling herself on the edge of my bed. She peered into my duffel bag and pursed her lips.

"You don't need to take a sweatshirt, Josephine. It's going to be a hundred degrees every day."

She started to pull the blue hoodie out of my bag and I hurried over to snatch it out of her hand.

"Mom, don't do that. I'm packing for myself. It might be cold inside."

"Are you taking an umbrella?"

"I'm not going to need an umbrella," I said. I tried to keep an impatient tone from creeping into my voice. "Texas gets almost no rain in June and July. And I'm sure they'll have umbrellas there if I *really* need one."

"Well at least take that rain jacket I got you. Is it in your closet?"

My mom stood up and walked to my closet. She slid the door aside and started pawing through the hangers, running her hands over sleeves, and pulling out random items.

"Why don't you ever wear this sweater from your abuelita?"

"It's so…yellow."

My mom sighed.

"What does that even mean?"

I shrugged. I knew that my mom thought that I was being a difficult, rebellious teenager, who refused to wear clothes that my family bought me. The truth was that I meant exactly what I said, but I knew that there was no point in explaining it.

"Are you going to be ready to go in fifteen minutes?" I asked my mom.

"Ay, reyna, why do you need to be there so early?"

I also hated it when my mom answered my question with a question, but I had learned long ago to stick to a line of inquiry either until my original question was satisfied or until the chancla put an abrupt end to the discourse.

"The car has gas in it, right? You know it's like a ninety minute drive, and there might be traffic."

My mom waved a dismissive hand at me.

❖

Two excruciating hours later, I was gingerly lifting my duffel bag out of the trunk of the car while my mom spoke to a camp counselor at a higher volume than seemed strictly necessary. I checked my watch and saw that I had arrived just in time for the first activity—one that involved the lake and something called *the blob* and required me to come *dressed to get wet*. My mom had insisted on purchasing and packing an atrocious yellow tankini with pineapples in sunglasses printed on it, but I had kept the details of the schedule to myself to avoid being coerced into wearing it on the drive over.

"They are going to take your cell phone, but remember that you can write me a letter if you want to, reyna."

"Okay, Mom," I muttered, pulling the strap of my bag over my arm. A jubilant counselor in an aggressively purple shirt approached me and asked for my name.

"Jo Delgado."

"Okay!" The young woman nodded, her blond bun wavering precariously on top of her head. "You'll be in cabin six! I'll take your bag there, because right now everyone is headed to the lake. You can catch up with them if you hurry!"

She pointed to a mass of girls traipsing down the asphalt path fifty yards away.

I reluctantly slipped my arm out of the strap of my duffel bag as the counselor hoisted it over her shoulder. I glanced at the driver's side of the car, but my mom already had her cell phone up to her ear. She gave me a quick wave, mouthed, "Be good," and put the car in drive.


"ALL CAMPERS HAVE TO FOLLOW THE RULES OF THE BLOB!"

Another blond counselor was standing in front of a large wooden structure that towered over one side of the lake. Directly underneath it was what appeared to be a gigantic floating pillow striped with bright yellow, blue, and red and looking out of place sitting on the surface of the lake. I leaned out of the line to try to get a better look at it.

"One camper will *jump* onto the blob and *crawl* to the end and the next camper will *wait* until I *say* to jump."

A tall girl with long blond hair and a dark pink two-piece swimsuit stood with one foot on the ladder in front of me. She heaved a sigh and flipped her head over to pull her hair into a ponytail using the hair tie on her left wrist.

"This is the third year I've come here and they give this, like, *intense* speech about every activity," she said to no one in particular, or possibly to me. "And I bet anything Funfetti is going to come nag me about my swimsuit."

I gave one of those little quiet *ha* laughs that you give when you're not sure if someone is actually talking to you or just speaking into the ether. I looked up at the ladder, wondering if it was the highest place you could get easily at Camp Lavender. This might not be Launchpad, but that didn't mean I couldn't do a little science on my own. It all depended on how strict the schedule was, how much down time they gave me, and whether I could get high enough to set up my electroscope, assuming that it hadn't been destroyed when my duffel bag was carelessly tossed into cabin six.

"Hey." Funfetti walked up to the tall blonde and put a hand gently on her shoulder. "Just so you know," she said in a low-pitched voice, "two-piece swimsuits are actually against our dress code at Camp Lavender."

The girl scoffed. "You're kidding." She raised her eyebrows at me as if to say, "*See?*"

Funfetti smiled with her lips pressed together. "No, we have a modesty code here. That way we can focus on Jesus and no one gets distracted."

"Seriously? There aren't even any boys here to *get* distracted." The girl gestured around her, just missing me with her arm.

Funfetti laughed quietly. "This is about practicing modesty. We believe that *modest is hottest,* so next time we'll grab you a T-shirt, okay?"

Funfetti's eyes fell on me. I was, in fact, wearing a T-shirt, completely unprompted by rules and regulations.

"You won't be the only one," Funfetti said to the girl, but she smiled at me, and I felt my cheeks reflecting the full force of the East Texas sun. I gave an awkward nod, trying to acknowledge the comment without giving away the fact that I had tuned into the entire conversation. The girl's eyes fell on me and, once again, I felt my face inflame as the girl gave me the evaluative up-and-down glance I spent so much of my energy avoiding.

"So y'all want me to basically look like a boy?" she muttered under her breath.

Funfetti must not have heard this, because she was already climbing up the ladder to the high deck. She moved with the ease of someone who had done it dozens of times. She waved a hand for the girl to climb up after her, which she did, and waved for me to follow. At the top, I did a 360-degree-turn and took in as much of the camp as I could. The lake did not appear as expansive from this height. On the west side of the lake was a dock attached to a two-story building, on one side of which was a somewhat dilapidated assortment of canoes and paddle boats. On the east side, I could only see clusters of pine trees and a few asphalt paths and a small structure that looked like it might be a cabin. I actively ignored the mild twist in my stomach trying to reinstate my fear of heights.

"Okay, Hayley—JUMP!" Funfetti called. The girl's blond ponytail disappeared like a flame being blown out and her body made a solid *smack* hitting the blob below. I leaned forward just far enough to see her adjusting her dark pink swimsuit bottoms as she crawled on hands and knees to the edge of the blob.

"The trick is to land as hard as you can without falling off," Funfetti said, "so you can shoot her as high into the air as you can! Aim for the blue stripe."

Basic physics would indicate that I was not going to be able to launch anyone particularly high into the air, no matter how hard I landed, but I was determined to give it my best shot. I walked a few steps back and took a running start, leaping as high as I could and pulling my knees close to my chest. Instead of focusing on the blue stripe, I looked up at the sky as I jumped.

The moment my body hit the blob, I knew that I was off center. I felt myself roll backward and off the right side of the blob. I didn't know what my knee hit on the way down, but whatever it was—it hit hard.

I tried to avoid wincing as I sat on the bench holding a towel over my knee. I saw out of the corner of my eye that Funfetti was looking at me and speaking into a walkie-talkie. My mind started to spiral outward and down. Now I was the girl who cut her knee open on the first afternoon of camp, as if there weren't already enough factors to set me apart from the group. Was I going to have to fill out some kind of paperwork? Would they call my mom? Would they stop me from doing camp activities? If they took me off campus to some kind of doctor's office, were they going to charge me or ask me for insurance?

I kept my eyes trained on the orange dirt under my feet. I had never seen such vivid dirt in my life. An ant was inching its way across the ground in front of me. That ant had no concerns except to find some food. I wished I could be that ant. I wondered if the girls in line for the blob were looking at me. Everyone takes note of what people do on the first day of something new. There's the girl who's late; the girl who forgets her toothbrush; the girl who cries randomly. There was no avoiding it—I was going to be the girl who cut her knee open in the lake when she fell off the blob.

I saw a few drops of blood start to seep through the towel pressed tightly over my knee and I turned my head sharply to the left to stare down the dirt path, taking in a deep breath. Seemingly out of nowhere, a golf cart whipped into view. For a few moments, I felt sure that it was headed straight for the bench where I was sitting, but it screeched to a halt a few feet in front of me. A girl with a mop of sandy hair and a baggy purple Camp Lavender T-shirt took off her sunglasses and squinted at me.

"Are you the hurt one?"

I pointed to my knee and nodded. "Are you a counselor?"

"I'm Lacey. Hop in."

"Where are we going?"

Lacey put her sunglasses back on. "I'm kidnapping you. Gonna ransom you back to your parents for ten thousand dollars."

"*What?*"

Lacey grinned. "I'm taking you to the infirmary."

I glanced over my shoulder. No one seemed to be paying the slightest attention to this interaction.

"Do you want your knee fixed or not?"

I stood, wincing as the blood rushed to my knee. I kept the pressure of the towel applied the best I could as I limped to the passenger side of the golf cart. Lacey peeled off almost before I was seated, pulling a sharper turn than a golf cart was meant to.

"So what happened?"

A halo of frizz swirled around Lacey's head as she pulled another sharp turn. I took note that she looked young enough to be a camper, but that her camp T-shirt and access to a golf cart indicated otherwise. Her tan legs were swallowed by loose jersey shorts that pooled around her knees. The other counselors all wore khaki shorts with their T-shirts tucked in and brown or black belts.

"I fell off the blob and sliced my knee open on the way down."

"You fell off the blob?"

"Yeah."

"Like when another camper jumped?"

"No, I just...rolled right off."

Lacey smiled. She must have noticed my knuckles whitening as I gripped the metal bar on the side of the golf cart seat. She put more pressure on the gas pedal and watched me brace against the floor with my feet.

"We're not gonna get hurt, I swear," she said.

"If you say so."

We ground to a quick stop in front of the infirmary and Lacey jumped out and gestured for me to follow her. She held the door open as I limped through. My T-shirt was soaked through, since I was wearing it when I fell into the lake. It clung to me in a way that made me feel cold and uncomfortable. I felt self-conscious in my swim trunks. There's something oddly embarrassing about wearing swim clothes when you're not near a body of water.

"I've got a young female presenting with a case of severe clumsiness," Lacey said as she followed me through the door.

I gave an awkward little salute to the doctor. He smiled and indicated the exam table. I pressed my lips together as I moved toward it. My knee was starting to sting in earnest, but I swung up onto the table as gracefully as I could, trying not to let it show.

"All right, let's see what we're working with." He took the towel off my knee, and I took in a sharp breath. "What's your name, Miss Camper?"

"Jo Delgado."

"Nice to meet you, Jo. I'm Dr. Dan."

"You don't have a fake name?"

Dr. Dan let out a short laugh. "No," he said, "sadly the camp doctor doesn't get a camp name. This might sting a little bit."

I glanced around the room while he started to disinfect, and tried to focus on anything but the bright burning sensation concentrated in my knee. I watched Lacey settle herself into the office chair, observing the whole operation. I didn't know why, but I wished she wasn't seeing me like this.

"You're not going to have to send me home, are you?" I cringed at the faint wobble in my voice.

"No, you're going to patch up just fine. But you are going to have to keep this wound out of the water for about a week."

"That's going to make camp significantly less fun," Lacey piped up. Dr. Dan frowned at her over his shoulder. She shrugged. "I'm just saying—it's basically two months of snow cones, water activities, and Bible study."

Lacey was looking at Dr. Dan when she said this, but she seemed to notice the way I stiffened.

Dr. Dan threw Lacey a disapproving look. "Come on, Lacey," he said, "you're never going to become a nurse with that bedside manner. Say something encouraging to our patient."

"Did I mention the snow cones?"

"That does sound pretty good right about now," I said through gritted teeth as I pressed my palms into my thigh trying to keep still.

"Why don't you swing by the Snack Shack after this?" Dr. Dan suggested. He gave Lacey a wry smile.

I watched as she pursed her lips.

"Has your Lavender Loot loaded yet?" she asked me.

"Excuse me?"

Dr. Dan was taping gauze around my knee. "It's like camp money," he said. "Your parents load it onto your card and then you just tell them your name at the Snack Shack and you can buy snacks, sodas, and all that."

I froze. "Do you need it for meals?" I asked, trying not to convey concern.

"No, no," he said. "You get three meals a day. Loot is just for—extras."

"Got it." I sighed with relief.

The probability that Tía Laura had loaded my card—whatever that was—with extra fake money seemed slim at best, if she was even aware that such a function existed, the probability of which was slimmer still.

Both Tía and Mom made sure to remind me of how little money we had anytime I needed something that wasn't absolutely necessary.

"I'm going to give you some ibuprofen, but I want you to come back in a couple days for me to take a look, okay? You know where to find me."

I nodded.

"And remember, no—"

"—water activities," I finished for him.

Dr. Dan nodded approvingly. "Why don't you take her wherever she's going next?" he suggested.

I stood up slowly, actively resisting the grimace blooming on my face. Lacey held the door open for me and followed me to the golf cart.

She glanced at her watch as she settled into the driver's seat. Abruptly, she said, "They're going swimming next. Probably so the chlorine can kill whatever slimy diseases they pick up in the lake."

"Oh. Okay. Well, I can…um…"

"Do you want me to take you to your cabin?"

"Sure, cabin six."

"Do you need help getting in?" Lacey asked as she pulled up in front of the cabin.

I felt embarrassed by the offer. "No, I got it," I said, hearing the tight quality of my voice as I struggled to balance myself. I felt the blood rush to my knee as I stood and took my breath in sharply.

"All right, well, have fun and let me know if—"

"Actually, I have a question," I interrupted.

Lacey paused, her foot poised above the gas pedal of the golf cart.

"What's the highest I can get here?"

"What?" Lacey raised her eyebrows.

"Where's the highest point on the camp grounds?"

"Why?"

Why couldn't anyone just answer a question, I wondered. "I just… want to see it."

Lacey stared at me, and I tried to guess what she was thinking. Did she have an aversion to spending time with campers in general, or just me? Was she just curious about my intentions? Had I said something terribly wrong or broken a rule I didn't know about? Finally, and to my surprise, she opened her mouth and said,

"Meet me out here at midnight."

# CHAPTER THREE

## *Jo*

I stood outside cabin six in my dark blue hoodie with my hands shoved into the front pocket and the hood pulled over my head. I looked from side to side nervously until I spotted Lacey making her way up the slight slope to the porch. Lacey put her finger to her lips and gestured with her head for me to follow her. I crept down the steps and jogged to catch up with Lacey.

"No golf cart this time?"

"Technically, I'm not really supposed to be driving the golf cart. Besides, it would be too loud."

"Are we allowed to be doing this?" I asked. "I really don't want to get sent home on my first night of camp." I imagined Tía Laura's face upon learning that I couldn't behave myself well enough to last a single night. She'd lecture my mother about how I am irresponsible and wasted her money. I would never hear the end of it.

"You're not getting sent home," Lacey said. "They did bed checks at eleven, right?"

"Right."

"No one will be back until seven in the morning."

"But what if one of the other girls notices?"

Lacey gave me a sidelong glance. I wished I knew what she was thinking.

"Have you talked to a single one of the other girls staying in your cabin?"

"Well…no."

Lacey opened her hands, as if to say, "There you have it."

"But—" I began.

"Look." Lacey stopped abruptly, turned toward me, and folded her arms. "Do you want to see the highest point of the camp for whatever mysterious reason?"

"Yeah."

"This is the time I have chosen to show you."

"Okay, but—"

"*What?*"

"Can you just real quick tell me, like, who you are?" I felt like I was annoying Lacey. But I desperately didn't want to get into trouble with my family. Again.

Lacey sighed and continued walking. "I live here. My parents own this camp."

"Whoa."

"Yeah."

"So you get to be at camp like…all the time?"

"Yep. It's a pure delight."

I opened my mouth to ask another question, then closed it again. I did not consider myself a master conversationalist by any means, but I had the social intelligence to deduce that Lacey was not keen to discuss what it was like to live at summer camp. I could not imagine anything more satisfying than having endless access to these camp grounds and not having to mingle with *society*, but I kept my fascination to myself.

We walked in silence on the asphalt path, lined on both sides by enormous pine trees stretching toward a sky illuminated only by the first quarter moon. I gazed up at it and marveled at what the sky could look like without the contamination of streetlights and power lines. I hadn't seen it like this in years.

Suddenly, Lacey turned off the path and into the trees. I followed her without question, thinking that this felt awfully similar to the beginning of a lot of homicide unit procedurals. After another minute of stumbling through trees, we emerged upon an enormous clearing. On the opposite end of it was a giant tower. It must have loomed nearly thirty feet into the sky. It was like it had been made exactly for me. This might not be the quality of resource I would have had access to at Launchpad, but it would do just fine. Lacey started across the field toward the tower.

"What is that?" I asked, completely in awe.

"It's the zipline tower," Lacey said.

I followed Lacey as she started across the field toward the tower.

"Look up there," Lacey said. I craned my neck upward and saw two cables running parallel across the clearing, thrown into sharp relief by the moonlight. "You start at the top of that tower," Lacey continued, "and zipline across to that platform." She turned and pointed in the direction we had come from. I squinted, but all I could see were pine trees.

"I'm no scientist, but I'm pretty sure this is the highest point at Camp Lavender. Why did you want to see it, anyway?"

I guessed that Lacey's legs must have been about three or four inches longer than mine and I had to do an awkward walk-jog motion to keep up with her rapid pace. The first breeze of the day blew Lacey's frenzy of curls away from her face and I took a close look at it for the first time. She had soft features that all seemed to fade into each other, like an oil painting. Or maybe it was just the moonlight. Her monochromatic ensemble and quick gait gave me the impression of one of those inflatable tube men outside a car wash, all angles and motion.

"I want to run an experiment."

Lacey glanced over her shoulder with a small frown, but did not stop walking. "What kind of experiment?"

"Well," I started slowly, "How much do you know about the science of storms?"

"Not much."

"Well, I made something that attracts lightning."

"Go on," Lacey said.

We had arrived at the base of the tower. Looking up at it from this angle, I felt a strange knot in my stomach.

"How do we get up there?"

"The stairs, duh," Lacey responded. "But first, we need to put on harnesses."

Lacey pulled a large silver key out of the pocket of her jeans and inserted it into a padlock around the handle of a door that swung open forcefully. Inside this storage area was an array of straps, buckles, and helmets. With casual expertise, Lacey lifted two harnesses off a metal hook and closed the door.

"Let's go ahead and put these on down here before you get all dizzy and weird up there."

She handed a blue harness to me, and I began turning it over in my hands, trying to watch Lacey out of the corner of my eye for instruction. Lacey stepped into her harness effortlessly and pulled it up around her waist, cinching the straps tightly on either side of her hips. She looked up at me. I was holding the harness away from my body like a snake. A flicker of a smile crossed her face. She lifted the chaos of straps out of my hand and held it out for me.

"Here—step into it."

I stepped through the straps and stood as still as a deer in the middle of a road as Lacey pulled the harness up around my waist and cinched the straps.

"Too tight?"

"All good. Thanks." I was thankful to be in the dark. The experience sent all my blood straight to my face.

"Okay, follow me."

Lacey started up what looked like a thousand steps and I wearily followed behind her.

"So you want to attract lightning," Lacey prompted. "With your invention."

I let out a small laugh and took a long inhale before knowing I was about to sound extremely nerdy.

"Right. So I made this thing called an electroscope. A switch-activated electroscope actually. Mine not only measures the charge of lightning, it also attracts lightning. The switch activation turns on a powerful magnet that redirects lightning toward it."

I paused to catch my breath, but my words and steps did not slow down. "The lightning's heat is absorbed by a mesh of insulated wires that prevent the whole thing from overheating and melting. I just need a place to set it up and then I need to turn it on right when a storm starts so I can catch a bolt."

"You can't just leave it turned on?"

"I don't have a battery strong enough to charge this big a magnet for longer than twenty minutes."

"So you need a high place to set this up and then you need to get here to turn it on *while* a storm is happening."

"Exactly."

"Why?"

"Why what?"

"Why are you doing this?"

"Well," I said, "first of all, it could save lives. Renewable energy is the future."

"And?"

"And what?"

We were almost at the top of the stairs. I felt my chest tighten, whether from the oxygen level, Lacey's pace up the stairs, or this line of inquiry, I could not tell.

"Lifeguards save lives, too. And they go better with camp," Lacey said. She took the last step up the stairs and turned around to wait for me. I felt a twinge of irritation. This girl had told me basically nothing, but seemed to feel entitled to my entire raison d'être. On the other hand, she was also granting me access to a resource I needed for no apparent reason, so perhaps she was owed an explanation.

"I want to get into MIT's meteorology program. An original invention could make that happen."

"Stand still."

Lacey grabbed a carabiner dangling from the end of a cable and clipped it to the front of my harness. "This will keep you from falling to your untimely death," she said.

"Great, because I wasn't planning to die until at least tomorrow," I responded.

Lacey gave a short laugh as she clipped a carabiner onto her own harness. "The other side feels even scarier," she said.

"Fantastic."

"Well, we didn't come up here to zipline, we came up here so you could case the joint, right? If you want to zipline, I need to hook you up to that super long cable."

"No, no, I have no desire to do that."

I gulped and looked down. From here, I could see the dock and the lake where my untimely blob incident had occurred just a few hours ago. I saw the cluster of cabins where the other campers were sleeping soundly. I saw asphalt paths weaving through the pine trees and more structures too small to identify from here. As I looked down, I felt Lacey watch me take it all in.

"Why are you at Camp Lavender?" Lacey asked.

I shrugged. "Because I have to be," I said, trying to sound as dismissive as possible.

Lacey nodded. "Wanna sit?"

"Sure."

"Okay, I just need to reattach us to the zipline cables. These don't reach."

"Wait, but then if I fall I'll shoot across to the other side?"

Lacey let out a short sigh. I suspected I was annoying her again. "Look, I'll just hook us into the same one. Will that make you feel better?"

I thought to myself that it would not, but I said nothing.

Lacey hooked herself in and sat down at the edge of the platform with her legs dangling over the side. I walked closer to Lacey, hoping that she wouldn't notice the distinct tremor of my limbs.

"You'll have to sit close so I can hook you in."

"This cable can't reach."

"Right. Unhook it, sit down, and then I'll hook you back up."

"But—"

"Just unhook it and then grab my hand. I won't let you fall."

Lacey watched me fumble with the carabiner. I finally unhooked myself and immediately sat down, inching myself slowly toward her and the edge of the tower. A wave of nausea overtook me and I reached out and grabbed Lacey's hand. She gripped my hand tightly, almost reassuringly, and I was surprised by the strength of her grasp. In order for her to clip me onto the same cable, I had to sit close enough that I could feel the pressure of her thigh against mine.

"I should have brought the electroscope with me," I said, mostly to myself. "But I'll need something to secure it with."

"Like what?"

"Well, preferably, I would screw it in, but since I'm going to have to remove it, I could really just use duct tape. Do you think you could bring me back here?"

"Sure." Lacey laughed.

"So," I said, squinting out at the enormous field in front of us. "You live here."

"Yep—right over there."

Lacey pointed toward what I figured to be west. I could see a one-story house separate from all the cabins. I thought privately that it must be lonely to live in that cabin in the fall, winter, and spring when all the other cabins were empty.

"Where do you go to school?"

Lacey's finger did not move. "I don't."

"*What?*"

"I mean, I *do* school, I just don't *go* to school."

"Who teaches you?"

"Well, technically, my mom teaches me, but at this point I mostly just teach myself."

My eyes widened.

"You must have met a homeschooled person before," Lacey said, an icy tone in her voice.

"Well...yeah. But all the homeschoolers I've met are—"

"Anti-social freaks?"

"I was going to say...a bit awkward."

Lacey's laugh had a bitter edge to it that did not escape me. A hundred questions raced through my brain. Was she homeschooled for religious reasons, or just because her parents ran this camp in the middle of nowhere in East Texas? Had it always been this way or did they pull her out of school at some point? Did she get the same education as everyone else or did she follow some special curriculum? I stole a glance at Lacey, who was gazing into the middle distance with an unreadable expression. Before I could pick one of my burning questions, Lacey said, "Did you want to go to science camp?"

"Yeah."

"What happened?"

I shrugged. "My aunt decided I should go here instead."

"Are you nervous?" Lacey asked.

"What? No. About what?"

"About falling."

I laughed nervously. "Um, a little," I admitted.

Lacey put an arm around my shoulder.

"Thanks," I said quietly, wondering if Lacey could feel the pounding of my heart through my sweatshirt.

"Do you know the best way to overcome the fear of falling?" Lacey asked. A smile played at the corners of her mouth.

"What?"

I felt Lacey's hand tighten around my shoulder. A breathless moment passed.

"You jump."

Before I could take the words in, Lacey wrapped her other arm around me and pushed us both off the edge of the platform and into the dark.

## *Lacey*

"What the HELL!" Jo hollered as we swung up to the platform on the opposite side of the zipline field. For a moment, I thought Jo was going to hit me. Her hands were balled into fists and she was shaking from head to toe. Then her shake erupted into an earthquake of laughter. She doubled over, grabbing my forearm and gasping for air.

"Why...on God's green earth did you do that?" she panted.

"To help you get over your fear of heights!" I started to laugh myself. "And it just...seemed like fun."

Both of us were gasping for air, full of adrenaline and post-zipline shock.

"You are absolutely out of your mind," Jo said, and I was again taken by panic that I had made this stranger angry. I looked up to assess her expression and saw Jo grinning with her balled-up hands on her hips.

Sneaking into your house after curfew was something I had only read about teenagers doing, or seen in the occasional coming-of-age film. Creeping up to my own front door at three thirty a.m. did not feel like something happening in my real life at all. I felt my body pulsing from the backs of my knees to the sides of my neck. There was absolutely no way either of my parents were awake—they rose with the sun, which would be swelling over the lake not long from now.

The cabin was utterly peaceful when I turned the doorknob with the delicacy of a surgeon and shut it behind me. The stairs were merciful in their creaklessness and I made it to my bedroom without mishap. As I shut my bedroom door behind me, I felt an uncontrollable smile spread over my face. So...this is what those teenage films were all about. I wanted to get into bed as quickly as possible, not to sleep, but to replay every moment of the night in slow motion.

I stared at the ceiling with my blankets pulled up to my chin, making note that I should really take a shower in the morning and maybe change my sheets. My eyes unfocused as I conjured the rush of adrenaline I had felt as I and a strange camper had flown across the field, dangling together from a cable, in the middle of the night. I smiled up again at the ceiling and put my hands over my face, trying to calm down. Jo had freaked out again when we had to descend the metal staircase to the ground. She had kept reaching out to grab my arm to steady herself, then withdrawing it again, as if I would not notice her fear or her shaking legs. We had walked back to cabin six slowly, Jo describing in hushed and reverent tones the classes she had been going to take at Launchpad, and detailing her invention in technical jargon that I could not fully wrap my head around.

I wondered why her aunt got to decide where she went to camp. What about her parents? Was she sent here for religious reasons? Was she some kind of atheist or wayward teenager in desperate need of a daily dose of Bible reading? Was she going to have a meltdown and wreak havoc on camp activities? When we'd arrived at Jo's cabin, she'd halted and turned toward me, running a still-shaking hand through her hair.

"Well, thanks I guess, you maniac."

"You're welcome, science nerd."

"See you never, I guess?" There'd been a question in Jo's eyes.

"I'll be around."

I played her laugh in my head over and over until I eventually fell asleep.

# Chapter Four

## *Jo*

I was awakened a mere three and a half hours after I had fallen asleep to the resounding clang of a bell that was, as far as I was concerned, not distant enough. I was known in the Delgado household for functioning on no less than seven hours of sleep—preferably ten. I had crept into the cabin and curled up in the bottom bunk bed in the corner I had claimed earlier that day, still in my hoodie and shorts. This turned out to be an excellent choice, since the thought of showering and dressing after so little sleep was absolutely off the table.

I cracked one of my eyes open and counted my cabin mates as they bustled around in the unbearable light. There were five. One of them was the bikini girl, Hayley, from yesterday, who had given me an instant knot in my stomach at our encounter. I had attended enough schools to know exactly what type of girl this was and to dread the inevitable antagonistic interactions we would have.

I slid out of bed as cabin six began to file out and toward the dining hall. My knee stung and my bandage was starting to sag. I lagged slightly behind, taking in my surroundings and mentally calculating where I was from the vantage point of the zipline tower last night. One of my organs did a somersault at the memory of Lacey pushing us off the tower platform, and the sheer terror followed by exhilaration that rippled over me as I flew across the field.

In my opinion, the first day of *anything* was always terrible. You don't know anyone; you don't know where you are; no one has explained the schedule or how anything works. Basically, the likelihood of public humiliation is at its peak. What's worse—you can only make the first day go away by living through it. There is no shortcut to the second day. The only person I had really met so far was unpredictable and apparently unlikely to show up except to fly in on a golf cart or arrive for a secret mission in the middle of the night. And there was absolutely no way in hell I was going to agree to another night of truncated sleep in the name of science and adventure.

No way…well, probably.

The dining hall featured a disturbing moose head mounted on the wall above a worn-down and carpeted stage. I felt my vegetarianism kick into high gear as I made unwilling eye contact with the poor guy. I glanced around the room to deduce the order of operations and saw everyone lining up with paper plates in front of the breakfast buffet.

The camp food looked surprisingly fresh and appealing. I set my eyes on a chafing dish filled with french toast and a bowl of brightly colored berries. I piled my plate high and turned back toward the tables. I saw Funfetti standing by a table with a large number six on cardstock in the middle and I silently thanked whoever had the presence of mind to make it clear where I should sit. Funfetti had her breakfast in front of her, but was still standing in front of her chair.

I set my plate down next to Funfetti and stood, hungry but uncertain.

"We stand until after the morning prayer," Funfetti said in answer to my silent question. The other cabin six girls slowly filled the empty places at the table and stood patiently. I wondered if every single one of them had been coming to camp here for years and how many other unspoken rituals I would have to navigate on that dreaded first day.

A middle-aged man with a receding hairline and cargo shorts approached the stage and picked up a microphone from its stand. "Let's bow our heads."

Each girl held her hands out for the others to grab. The girl next to me put her hand out, palm up, which seemed unnecessary and yet somehow mandatory. That's camp, I guess. I put my hand out and placed it into the girl's palm. She already had her head bowed and eyes closed.

"Father God, we thank you for the meal and for the hands that prepared it. We ask that you bless this day and the minds and hearts of the young women who have come here to know you better and to develop a personal relationship with you. In the name of our Lord and Savior Jesus Christ, Amen."

The man said all this in almost one breath. When he finished, I crossed myself automatically, as I had been doing in Sunday mass ever since I could remember. I became aware, as my fingertips moved from my forehead to my chest to my left shoulder to my right, that no one else had made this gesture. Hayley, who was settling herself into a seat across the table from me, gave me a look.

"So…you're Catholic?" she asked.

I shrugged. "That's how I was raised," I answered diplomatically. I wasn't exactly about to admit to a table full of girls at a Christian camp that I was an atheist or at the very least agnostic.

"You know this isn't a Catholic camp though, right?" Hayley continued.

I watched Funfetti give Hayley a small frown as I shoveled berries into my mouth. I was too hungry to care about either of their reactions.

"Guess what we get to do today, ladies," she said, a somewhat cloying quality in her voice. "We get to go *tubing at the lake* after Bible study."

My heart sank. A water activity. I resigned myself to the fact that this was how it was probably going to be, given that it was summer in East Texas. Every day was bound to include water and religion. Two things I really preferred to not get dressed up for.

I wondered what the agenda would be today at Launchpad and I felt a surge of resentment flare in my chest. I would already be battling multiple obstacles to secure a place at MIT, and wasting a summer that I could have been sharpening my skills and gaining valuable experiences was not going to help. My mom would just blame my rejection on my SAT score and say that it was for the best since we couldn't afford MIT anyway. It always came down to money, after all.

I tried to avert my eyes from the girls around me, most of whom chose to be here, despite possibly missing academic opportunities that would make them more competitive in terms of scholarship eligibility or financial aid assistance. I was certain most of these girls had zero awareness of their own families' financial situations. I suddenly lost my appetite.

After breakfast, cabin six trailed out of the dining hall and into an open grassy area where Funfetti laid a faded floral blanket on the grass and plunked down a well-worn Bible. The other five girls all pulled little travel-size Bibles out of their bags and backpacks and sat reverently in a circle. I feigned rummaging in my backpack, panicking slightly.

"You can share with me," said a redheaded girl sitting next to me. I smiled gratefully and the girl smiled back. My angst dissipated at her generosity.

"I'm Rebekah," she said.

Rebekah's Bible had a pattern of pretty turquoise flowers stitched on the dark brown cover and lots of tiny neon sticky notes jutting out of it at chaotic angles. When Funfetti told them to open to Philippians, Rebekah did so confidently, finding it before anyone else and placing her finger over the chapter Funfetti had told them to find. It was underlined with a tiny heart doodled beside it.

Funfetti read aloud, "Finally, brothers and sisters, whatever things are true, whatever things are honorable, whatever things are just, whatever things are pure, whatever things are lovely, whatever things are of good report: if there is any virtue and if there is anything worthy of praise, think about these things."

Funfetti looked up with shining eyes. "What does this passage mean to you?"

This seemed a strange question and I tried to conjure an answer that might satisfy everyone as to my devoutness, but I could think of nothing. I pulled up a blade of grass from the edge of the blanket and rubbed it between my fingers while Rebekah and another girl began to talk. My eyes moved from the blade of grass across the field to the dock that protruded out from beneath the dining hall. I saw a figure there, scribbling in a notebook. I squinted my eyes, trying to determine if it was Lacey. Who else would be allowed to sit on the dock alone during Bible study time?

I tuned back into the Bible study just in time to see the girls bowing their heads with their eyes closed again. Rebekah was praying aloud, her palms turned up and a smile playing across the corners of her mouth. I glanced across the circle to see Hayley shaking her head at me. I stared back at her, trying to communicate with my eyes that Hayley had absolutely no right to judge me for not closing my eyes when she was disobeying the very same rule.

Apparently the big lake, the one the camp used for boating, was a short bus ride away. Girls from cabins one, four, and six were piling in, waving around brightly colored beach towels, and chattering excitedly. I sat on one of the cracked leather seats next to a window. I could already feel sweat prickling the back of my neck. Without being able to get in the lake, it was going to be a long day of being bored and overheated and possibly seasick.

I felt a presence drop suddenly into the seat beside me.

"How was Bible study?"

Lacey was wearing a baggy green tank top and had piled her hair into a bun on the top of her head. I noticed that she had a dimple on the right side of her mouth when she grinned, which she was doing now.

"What the hell are you doing here?" I asked, trying not to sound too relieved by her presence.

"Heck."

"What?"

"What the *heck* am I doing here," Lacey corrected me. "You're gonna have to break the cussing habit for the next six weeks if you don't want to get in trouble."

"*Cussing?*" I couldn't stop myself from laughing. Lacey straightened up a little, looking indignant.

"What do you call it?"

"Cursing. Or swearing. Or really just talking. Is it really that big a deal to say curse words around here?"

"Yeah," Lacey said, nodding. "My dad tells the counselors that if someone cusses more than three times, he wants to have a personal sit-down conversation with them."

My eyes widened.

"For real?" I was suddenly embarrassed.

"Just be careful," Lacey said. "Unless you want to go on a long, weird walk with my dad and hear a lecture about taking the Lord's name in vain."

"Good to know. Anyway, what the *heck* are you doing here?"

"Um, it's lake day," Lacey said, gesturing broadly.

"I thought you didn't really show up at camp activities. I mean, where were you during Bible study?" I caught myself hoping that Lacey was joining camp today solely to hang out with me. *Have I made a friend?*

"I don't do Bible study with the cabins. My parents let me do it on my own." I watched as she tucked a loose curl behind her ears.

"Is that what you were doing this morning when you were writing on the dock?"

Lacey's head turned sharply as the bus started to grind against the gravel underneath them. "Maybe."

I grinned. "You aren't the only one who pays attention. Being an observer comes with being a scientist! So come on, what were you writing? All about our exciting adventure last night?"

Lacey eyed me warily. I couldn't tell if she was going to tell me about her writing or if she wanted to punch me.

"It's poetry," was all she said.

"What are the poems about?"

"Well, they used to be mostly hymns—like Isaac Watts and John Newton wrote—and that kind of thing."

I nodded, wanting Lacey to keep talking and hoping that the rest of the conversation would not reveal my lack of knowledge about who those people were.

"But lately they've just been…I don't know. About feelings and thoughts and stuff. And sometimes nature, because that's what all poets seem to write about."

I thought about the emo kids at my school, constantly writing sad poems about their feelings in the margins of their notebooks during class and reading them to each other at lunch and after school. I wondered if Lacey knew that such a subculture existed or if she was part of one of those religious families that didn't even watch TV.

"What do you do with your poems?"

For reasons unknown, I found myself absolutely dying to read one of these poems.

"Well, I write them in my notebook," Lacey said. Her tentative tone told me that there were more words on the tip of her tongue and that if I just stayed quiet, they would eventually tumble out. The silence wafted between us with the heavy air of the bus. Someone started a loud cheer and everyone else on the bus joined in.

"Have you heard of this website called Slant?" Lacey asked at last.

"You know about Slant?" I couldn't keep the surprise out of my voice.

"How do *you* know about Slant?" Lacey fired back.

"I mean, it's really popular with all the artsy kids at my school. You can post lyrics and then people can *layer* or something with a beat or a melody?"

"Yep," Lacey said. "Sometimes I post my poems on there, but only a few people look at them and no one has ever layered with them."

"That's still really cool. Your parents are fine with you using it?"

I did not look at Lacey when I asked this, but in my peripheral vision I saw Lacey shift in her seat.

"Well, they don't know I have an account."

"Ahh."

"Don't judge me."

"I would never. Scout's honor." I held up three fingers. "Thanks for telling me."

"Well, you asked."

I had about twelve more questions I wanted to ask, including *how and when do you access the account, what is your handle,* and *when can I read it,* but the bus was already pulling up at the dock of a lake much larger than the one I had blobbed into yesterday.

"So why are you coming with us?" was all I asked.

"I quite literally have nothing better to do today," Lacey said. "Besides, you're gonna be so bored stuck on the boat since you can't get your injury wet. And trust me, you do *not* want that lake water anywhere in your bloodstream."

The girls were piling out, still chanting and laughing and waving their brightly colored beach towels around. Hayley, who had been sitting at the back of the bus, stopped next to the seat where we sat and glanced down at me.

"I see you're wearing your T-shirt again, like a *very* righteous young lady," she said with an edge to her voice like a five-blade razor.

"I actually can't get in the water," I began, but Hayley had already moved past our seat and toward the door of the bus.

"What was that about?" Lacey asked.

"I honestly have no idea," I said. "She got in trouble yesterday for wearing a two-piece, but I'm not sure what that has to do with me."

Lacey rolled her eyes and I immediately knew she'd encountered her before.

"Hayley Hathaway comes here every year. She definitely knows better, but I think she'd rather get in trouble than be caught voluntarily in a hideous one-piece. My dad has to call her dad at least once every summer. It's a whole thing."

The bus rolled to a stop. Lacey stood up to exit the bus and I followed, taking note of what she was wearing. Her green tank top was paired with Bermuda shorts that looked like they might have once been blue jeans and sandals that looked like they could transition easily from the woods to the water. I wondered if she was planning to go tubing herself and, if so, what kind of swimsuit her parents had deemed appropriate for her to wear.

Two motorboats idled at the dock, waiting for their first sets of campers. A guy in a red and white striped tank top with a bright blue bandana tied around his head waved a tanned arm from one and a guy with no shirt on at all waved from the other as the girls scampered toward the dock.

"We'll go cabin by cabin!" shouted a counselor. "Cabins one and three, you'll be playing sand volleyball. Cabins two and four, you'll be playing cornhole and tetherball. Cabins five and six, you'll head to the boats!"

"So which cabin are you?" I asked.

"Honorary cabin six, obviously," Lacey responded, shaking her head as if that were a silly question.

Funfetti led the girls to the edge of the dock and helped them climb into the boat with the striped tank top guy.

"Good afternoon, ladies!" he bellowed over the sound of the engine and the campers. "My name is Crowbar and I'll be making sure you all fall into the lake today!"

The campers screamed in protest.

"You better not," Hayley said. "I will *not* be getting my hair wet."

Lacey and I exchanged glances. The corners of Lacey's mouth twitched just perceptibly.

"How do we get out to the tube?" Rebekah asked. "Do we go one at a time? Are you going to come get us if we fall off?"

"Whoa, Red, slow down," Crowbar said, guiding the boat away from the dock. "I'm gonna explain all the rules to you once we're out on the water. We're all gonna be safe and have fun today, don't worry."

Rebekah smiled broadly at her unsolicited nickname. I resisted the urge to roll my eyes. I would never understand the way that girls her age blushed and giggled at the first sign of *any* attention from a guy—especially an older guy like Crowbar.

"Scoot over, Einstein," Lacey said and sat down on the tan vinyl seat next to me. I felt a grin start to tug at the corners of my own mouth.

## Chapter Five

### *Lacey*

It felt like that afternoon was glowing. The June sun bounced off the waves and sank into my skin as the motorboat made its way toward the middle of the lake. Sweat gleamed off everyone's skin and I could see the faint undertones of brown and pink begin to bloom. Jo was dipping her hand into the water, despite Crowbar's warning to keep all limbs inside the boat. Her fingers were curious, like they just had to know the texture and temperature of everything around her. I watched as she brought her hand to her mouth and tasted it.

"That's going to make you sick," I warned her.

"I'm not going to *drink* it, I just want to know what it tastes like."

"Why?"

Jo shrugged. "It looks so blue. I was wondering if it tasted blue."

I couldn't help but laugh.

Jo chuckled sheepishly. I could tell she was embarrassed.

The boat slowed and Crowbar asked who wanted to tube first. Jo's hand shot up and then back down as she glanced at her wound.

A redheaded girl stood up tentatively. I asked Jo what her name was and she muttered, "Rebekah."

"I'll go."

Crowbar tossed the tube into the water and Rebekah swam out after it, struggling up onto her belly and gripping the handles with whitened knuckles.

"Not too fast!" we heard her squeal faintly over the sound of the motorboat's engine revving. Crowbar's smile was gleaming white against his suntanned skin.

Then we were flying. Crowbar sped up to make huge white wakes and then turned the boat to an angle where it would cut straight across them. We braced ourselves as the boat hit the huge bumps and crashed back down again. The tube was flung wildly and Rebekah's blue-swimsuited body shot up chaotically, and back down as she hung on to the handles with determination. Finally, though, she hit a wake at an angle that caused her to lurch violently and lose her grip on the tube. She fell into the water laughing and screaming, and Crowbar slowed the boat down to turn around and pick her up.

She struggled back onto the boat as she gasped and asked if anyone had sunscreen.

"That was so fun," she said breathlessly to Crowbar. "I held on for a long time, didn't I?"

"I didn't think you had it in ya, Red!" he said with a wink. I watched Rebekah swoon as she dodged the jealous glances of nearly all the girls.

"Okay, me next," Hayley declared and stood up in the middle of the boat. With a swift motion, she pulled her coverup over her head to reveal a dark pink two-piece swimsuit. I knew perfectly well that Crowbar would be too uncomfortable to pull her aside and give her a talk about the dress code. Instead, all the girls gaped a little as Hayley swaggered to the rear of the boat, her tanned back and long legs in full view.

I felt something hot rise inside my chest—a feeling that I could not fully identify. There was just something so show-offy about Hayley's determined subversion of the rules. She didn't just want the attention that came from an immodest swimsuit, she wanted the attention that came from breaking the rules and getting away with it. I wondered if Crowbar would later report her to another counselor, at the very least, but when I looked his way his expression was impassive. He seemed completely unfazed.

Hayley bobbed out to the tube, careful to keep her head and hair above the water. I wondered if she was wearing makeup, too. I knew that my mom didn't wear makeup because she believed that it was an unnecessary vanity, and I had never cared to ask whether I was or would be allowed to. Once Hayley was situated on the tube, Crowbar cranked the engine and set off again. He started off at a smooth pace, and I felt annoyed that he was going easier on Hayley than he had on Rebekah.

I started scooting toward the back of the boat. I motioned with my hand for Jo to come with me. Jo drew her eyebrows together in a silent question, but I waved a hand to indicate that I would explain later. Jo scooted with me until we were both at the far back of the boat, near the little step that the girls used to jump in.

The motor was loud and I had to lean in close to Jo's ear to whisper over it. "I need you to tell me when everyone is looking straight ahead," I said. Crowbar would look back to see how Hayley was doing every thirty seconds or so, but he had to look ahead enough to steer the boat in the right direction. The rest of the girls took turns watching Hayley, talking to each other, and taking in the view.

"Why?" Jo whispered back nervously.

"Just do it. It's a surprise."

Jo kept her eyes fixed on Crowbar. He glanced back again and again, but when the boat was close enough to the shoreline that he was going to have to turn, his whole body turned straight ahead. Jo glanced around. At that moment, all the other girls were looking away from us. She looked at me and gave a nod.

"Don't let me fall," I said, then I leaned over the back of the boat and unhooked the taut rope that was connecting the tube to the boat. Immediately, the tube flew backward, sending Hayley flying. At the same time, Crowbar pulled a sharp left and the whole boat tilted wildly, causing all the girls on the port side to slide out of their seats and causing me to crash into Jo, landing practically on top of her lap. I felt my face burning red with adrenaline.

The next few moments were a chaos of yelling and scrambling. Jo and I were all arms and legs, both trying to regain our balance and our distance from one another. By the time we looked behind us, the tube was several yards back and Hayley was not on it. I squinted into the sun until I saw Hayley's blond head bobbing above the water. She was screeching. I held my breath, telling myself that there was no way that Hayley could have seen me unhook the tube above the splashing of the wakes. I didn't dare look at Jo yet.

Crowbar circled slowly back to Hayley, who was staying very still with only her head above the water. As the boat pulled close to her, I could see that there was a trail of mascara under her eyes and that her arms were crossed tightly over her chest. Crowbar waved for her to get in.

"I don't know what happened!" he said casually. "The knot must have come untied, but I'll knot it again before the next camper. Sorry about that!"

"I can't get in," Hayley hissed.

Crowbar looked confused.

"My bikini top came off when I fell in," she said under her breath. Crowbar's eyebrows shot up.

"Oh…um…you know what, I'm just gonna…go that way and let y'all figure this one out real quick, okay?"

He made an abrupt turn and walked back to the front of the boat. The girls looked around at each other. Hayley's distress and anger increased with every passing moment.

"Do you want your coverup?" Rebekah offered tentatively.

"It's like completely see-through and the arm holes are huge—a whole boob could pop out."

*Isn't that what you wanted?* I thought spitefully, refusing to feel sorry for her.

Jo stood up and with an awkward motion pulled her T-shirt over her head. "Everyone turn around," she said. And they did. "Try to scoot up onto the back of the boat," Jo said quietly to Hayley, "and I'll hand you the T-shirt."

"*Don't* look," Hayley said.

"I won't," Jo promised.

As instructed, we all turned our gazes away. When Hayley was finally back in the boat, she was wearing Jo's dark gray T-shirt. She kept her arms crossed for the rest of the ride.

Jo had a dark blue one-piece swimsuit under her T-shirt, but she still seemed almost as uncomfortable as Hayley with just her shoulders and a glimpse of her collarbones exposed. I shifted in my seat uncomfortably, unsure of whether I should look at Jo. I had meant for Hayley to fall into the water and get soaked, but how could I have known that half her swimsuit would fall off?

Jo did not even glance in my direction until we were back on the bus headed back to the main camp. She sat down next to a window and I dropped into the empty space beside her. I stole a glance at Jo's profile. Her high cheekbones were dappled with freckles that seemed to have multiplied since that morning. Her dark eyebrows were drawn together in a pensive frown. I felt a surge of annoyance. What exactly had I done wrong here? It was a simple prank that had gone slightly wrong.

"Are you good?" I finally asked. It came out sounding more calloused than I had intended. Jo turned and looked at me sharply.

"I very much wish I had a shirt on," she said.

"Well, that's not my fault."

Jo rolled her eyes. "Why do you like to *fuck* with people like that?"

I felt myself shudder at the hard word. I had heard it only a few times in my life and it had shocked me every time. The harsh edge in Jo's voice cut me with a sharp surprise, like the feeling I'd had when I was cutting strawberries and cut into my own finger. I felt shocked, and then a rush of hurt.

"I just thought it would be funny to see her get her hair wet—"

"Well, I'm sure it wasn't funny to her when the top of her swimsuit fell off and she got a big mouthful of lake water. And by the way, it scared the *shit* out of me when you pushed me off the zipline platform."

"I'm sorry," I said. I could feel my heart in my stomach.

"Are you?"

I felt myself getting smaller. I just nodded. Jo sighed and the tension in her shoulders relaxed. A bumpy half mile went by before I worked up the courage to ask, "Did you at least think it was a little funny?"

"Don't," Jo said, but I saw the corner of her mouth twitch and I hoped that she was laughing at the image of Hayley being flung into midair.

"Well, I think you owe me," Jo said.

"Oh really? What do I owe you?"

"First of all, you owe me a shirt," Jo said.

"Done. And second?"

"A poem."

"What!?"

"I want you to read me one of your poems."

"How is that fair at all?"

Jo opened her eyes wide and crossed her arms. "You made *me* feel exposed, now it's time for *you* to feel exposed."

"Okay, well, being exposed emotionally is like—way more intense."

"Not for you to say," Jo said with mock stiffness. Now it was my turn to roll my eyes.

"Okay, fine," I said with a sigh. "but no one else can be around."

The bus was grinding to a stop and the sunburnt, lake-soaked girls were surging from their seats. Jo and I stood and waited our turn to exit the bus.

"Time for showers!" Funfetti declared loudly. It was time for me to go home, but I shuffled my feet slowly, waiting for something I wasn't sure of. Jo turned to me before moving to follow the rest of the group.

"See you at cabin six at midnight, then," she said, and I could have sworn I saw her wink before she turned around.


Dr. Dan looked startled when I burst through the door.

"And where have you been, young lady?" he said with a faux stern voice.

"Oh, just galivanting about, getting into my usual trouble."

"And neglecting your English essay, I take it?"

I glanced up quickly. "Why do you say that?"

"Your mother called me to confirm that you were here doing your work on my computer, since you were not at home doing your program work on the family computer."

I held my breath.

"And I told her that of course you were, but now you owe me one."

I let out all my breath at once. I seemed to be racking up debts today. "Thank you, thank you, thank you!" I said in a rush.

"No problem. You weren't out robbing a bank or taking joy rides, were you?"

I couldn't help but laugh. "No, I went to the lake with the campers."

Dr. Dan's head tilted to the side. "I am shocked," was all he said.

I shrugged.

"Does this have anything to do with the new friend you made in here a couple days ago?"

"Not really," I said, unsure whether or why I was lying in answer to this benign question. "It's just my last summer here and I wanted to have some of those experiences one more time."

"Before you never come back?"

"I didn't say that," I said as I looked down at my shoes. Deep down, I knew that despite my impulse never to come back, I would.

Dr. Dan had hinted before that he thought it might be good for me to spend my summers elsewhere. I think he wanted me to break the rules, although I wasn't sure why. All I knew was that I could trust him to have my back.

"Well, you better write some of that essay now. Your mom is going to expect you to have made some progress today."

My sigh came from somewhere deep inside me. I sat down at the computer and logged into Slant without thinking about it.

Twenty-seven notifications and one message.

My heart skipped a beat. I opened the message.

@MoonBoi11 says: *Your poems are incredible. Have you ever thought about performing at a poetry slam?*

My heart started pounding like I had taken shots of espresso. I typed back a message before I had time to second-guess it.

@HellerHighwater says: *Wow, thank you. Idk if they're that good though. Performing makes me nervous and I wouldn't want people looking at me.*

I held my breath. I could see that *@MoonBoi11* was already typing a response. There was a green light by his username. He must have just happened to be online when I sent my message.

@MoonBoi11 says: *They don't have to be perfect. Performing will make you better. Besides...*

The message disappeared. The green light beside his username turned gray. Did he change his mind or just get distracted by something?

"How's the essay?"

I heard Dr. Dan's voice like it was at the other end of a tunnel.

"It's fine," I said. I was surprised by how irritated I sounded. I tried to take a deep breath and slow down my heartbeat. I had logged on to look for a poem that wouldn't be too embarrassing to read to Jo. I went to my profile and started reading them all, and suddenly heard how mundane and immature most of them sounded. Surely Jo would be listening with a critical ear. I was overtaken by a sudden conviction that I *must* write a new poem for an audience of one tonight. There was simply no other way.

# CHAPTER SIX

## *Jo*

I shuffled my feet in the orange dirt next to the payphone outside the recreation room. I prayed that it would be my mom who picked up the phone. Of course, it was Tía Laura.

"It's so nice to hear from you, Josephine!" she said with a saccharine sweetness that always made me gag. "How are things going at Camp Lilac?"

"They're going fine," I said. "Actually, Tía Laura, there's this thing called Lavender Loot that a lot of the girls have—"

"Are they doing Bible study every day?"

I could tell from the distracted quality in Tía Laura's voice that she was multitasking while talking to me.

"Is my mom there?"

"She's picking up Rudy from school right now."

I sighed.

"She'll be back any minute now, though."

"Yeah, they're having Bible study," I said.

"Are the girls there nice?"

"They're all right."

"They're your sisters in Christ, Josephine."

"Okay." I could not keep a sigh of exasperation out of my voice. I switched the phone from one hand to the other, trying to think of what to say. The silence stretched awkwardly between us in that staticky invisible space between telephones.

"Josephine, I know you wanted to go to that science camp to make models—"

"They do valuable experiments there, Tía Laura. Experiments that could get me a good scholarship at a good school."

"I think you've done enough experimenting for now, Josephine."

I covered the mouthpiece of the phone and shook it violently. When I brought the earpiece back to my ear, I could hear my mother's voice in the background talking to Tía Laura. Then Rudy's bright voice came through.

"Joey!" He squealed with excitement.

"How's school, osito? Are you annoying all your teachers?"

"Yes," he declared proudly. "Mr. Williams said he wishes he could put me in permanent detention!"

I felt a sudden pang in my gut. Hearing the excitement in my brother's voice felt almost as good as receiving one of his famous bear hugs. I wished that I could get Rudy a snow cone and show him the blob. I smiled imagining his petite body flying into the air when I jumped onto the blob with all my might.

"How's white Jesus camp?" Rudy asked in a low tone.

"It doesn't suck as much as I thought it would," I said, lowering my voice to match his, even though the rec room and the dock were both empty.

"Are they…being nice to you?" There was an uncharacteristic worry in his voice that tore a little corner off my heart.

"It's not conversion camp, Rudy. I'm fine." I felt tears welling up in the corners of my eyes.

Then my mom was on the phone.

"Are you having fun?" she asked, with the same distracted tone in her voice Tía Laura had used.

"Yeah, kind of, I got hurt on the first day."

"Are you okay, reyna?" she asked. She sounded vague and disconnected.

"Yeah, the camp doctor bandaged my knee. It's not a big deal," I said.

"That's good, that's good…"

In the background, I could hear pots and pans clanging against each other. She was cooking.

"Mom." I was frustrated. I truly thought I'd never held her full attention.

"Yes?"

I opened my mouth and closed it again. I kicked at some dried pine needles. I wasn't exactly sure why I had called or what I had wanted to say—or what I had wanted my mother to say. The moment rose, fell, and faded.

"Are you being good?" my mother asked. I could hear whisking now.

"Yes," I said quietly.

"Don't forget to wear a hat when you're out in the sun all day or your freckles will blotch."

"Okay. I gotta go."

I slammed the phone back onto the receiver and wandered aimlessly into the rec room, trying to calm down. The rec room sported the same worn carpet of the dining hall directly above it. The back wall was lined with lumpy blue couches that were supposed to look like denim. In front of the couches were a foosball table and a ping-pong table. The wall facing the dock was composed completely of windows. I thought that watching the sunset in this room must be beautiful.

The room also had a carpeted stage, exactly like the dining hall above it, but this one was scattered with instruments: two acoustic guitars, a drum set, and a keyboard. I had been learning guitar in school, and I had promised Rudy that when I saved up enough money to buy my own guitar, I would teach him how to play. I glanced over my shoulder and saw that the dock was still completely abandoned. The campers must all be occupied with arts and crafts, naps, praying, or lying by the pool.

I approached one of the acoustic guitars. It had a navy and teal strap and I wanted desperately to put it over my shoulder. I reached a hand out and ran my thumb across the strings. The sound reverberated through the rec room.

"Play something," said a voice behind me.

"Jesus!" I exclaimed in surprise.

I spun around and saw the older man from morning prayer smiling at me. I set the guitar down nervously.

"No, just Mr. Heller," the man said easily.

"I'm sorry," I said, hoping a blanket apology would cover both swearing and touching the instrument.

"Do you play?" Mr. Heller walked toward me and sat on the bench in front of the electronic keyboard.

"Oh, um, yeah, a little," I said. "I do it as an extracurricular at school."

"Well, you know we have a talent show toward the end of camp," Mr. Heller said. "You should play something. Do you sing?"

"A little," I said. I felt my cheeks burning. Mr. Heller radiated a disarming warmth. He looked like the kind of dad everyone wished they had. I could picture him with his slippered feet propped up in front of a fireplace reading a Winston Churchill biography, or taking little Lacey out for an ice cream cone. Something about his presence made me want to impress and please him at the same time. I picked the guitar back up and slung the strap over my shoulder. Tentatively, I strummed a C chord. Mr. Heller smiled encouragingly.

I played the opening refrain of "Big Jet Plane" and began to hum the tune quietly.

"That's very nice, what is that?" he asked.

"It's, um, it's not a Christian song," I confessed.

Mr. Heller cocked his head to the side and raised an eyebrow. "I was a young person once, too, you know," he said. "Believe it or not, I've heard other songs than 'Amazing Grace' and 'How Great Thou Art.'"

"Those are bangers, though."

Mr. Heller responded with a wry smile. "How would you like to play for worship tonight?"

My eyes widened. I wasn't exactly sure why Mr. Heller was asking me this, but I felt simultaneously a rush of excitement and terror. I pictured the room full of swaying girls with upraised arms just like I had seen in the promotional video Tía Laura had shown me to try to get me excited for the camp. I had rolled my eyes and gritted my teeth, picturing myself as the one girl in the back corner with my hands shoved into the pockets of my basketball shorts. Now, imagining myself on the stage with that navy and teal strap slung over my shoulder, strumming the strings of an acoustic guitar, conjured a different feeling altogether.

"Sure, Mr. Heller, I'd be happy to if you need me to."

"Good," he responded with a smile. "Just come back here at six fifteen to tune up with the rest of the worship leaders."

"Will do!"

I checked my watch. I had enough time to take a shower and wash my knee, limp over to the infirmary to get some more bandages from Dr. Dan, and get back to the rec room in time. I set the guitar carefully back on its stand and stepped down from the stage.

"I'll see you tonight!" I said over my shoulder.


My hair was still wet by the time I made it to Dr. Dan's office. He cleaned my wound, put fresh gauze on it, and told me it would just be another day or two before I could risk submerging it in water.

"I'd start with pool water, though," he said. "Best to avoid the lake for a while yet."

I nodded. "Um, Dr. Dan, I have kind of a weird favor to ask you."

"Shoot."

"Well, you know, they take our phones when we get here. And I—"

Dr. Dan narrowed his eyes at me.

"I was just wondering if I could use your computer for like *five* minutes to check some messages."

"You know they have a pay phone if you need to call home, right?"

"I know. It's not that. It's—something I—"

"Someone you can't call?"

"Something like that."

Dr. Dan leaned back in his swiveling doctor chair and crossed his arms. "Did Lacey tell you to ask me?"

"What? No. I just...saw it on your desk."

"*Five* minutes," he emphasized. "Seriously."

I clasped my hands and held them to my forehead in a gesture of gratitude. "Thank you *so much.*"

I pulled up Slant and logged in. I saw an unread message from @NatsRainbow and grimaced. I knew roughly what it was going to say, give or take a swear word. If I opened it, Natalie would know that I had read it, and I had told Natalie that I would be unreachable for six weeks, hoping that she might have cooled off enough by then not to do anything rash. Instead of opening my messages, I navigated to the search bar and typed *Lacey Heller* into it. I stole a glance over my shoulder to gauge the whereabouts of Dr. Dan. He seemed absorbed in a paperback he had picked up from his desk and I tried to hunch over the screen to conceal it from view. I spotted the username *@HellerHighwater* immediately. It was high up in the list—it must be a popular account. I clicked on the latest post.

*Emily wore flowers in her hair*
*She wanted to run, but she didn't dare*
*She wanted to hide, but she didn't know where*
*to put all the words that she couldn't share.*

*Emily wrote down her lines on a page*
*Filled them longing, with love, and with rage*
*And as her solitude grew with age*
*She played her one-woman show on an empty stage.*

Something a little bit like fear and a little bit like hope pulled at me. I searched the name Emily in Lacey's audience list, but found nothing. I exited the window and gave Dr. Dan a quick thanks before checking my watch and realizing that it was almost time to be at the sound check, or whatever it was, before worship night.

# CHAPTER SEVEN

## *Lacey*

No one was home when I entered our cabin. I raced for the family computer and waited impatiently while it turned on. My parents had promised to get me a laptop before I left for college, but seemed in no hurry to do so a moment before they needed to. My fingers shook a little as I logged into Slant and saw that I had an unread message. I clicked on it.

> @MoonBoi11 says: *I'm sure there are people who would like to look at you.*

I felt a wild heat bloom across my face. I scolded myself inwardly, knowing how horrified my parents would be if they knew that I was talking to a stranger on the internet and even more horrified if they knew that he was making me blush. I stared silently at the screen, wondering whether I should respond and what I should say. While I thought, I absently minimized the screen and looked at the folders on the desktop screen. I clicked on one that held this year's camper information. I clicked on the roster document that listed the full names and emergency contact information for each camper. My eyes ran down it and stopped at one name.

I reopened my Slant tab and navigated to the search bar. I typed in *Josephine Delgado* and scanned the list of users and usernames. Most of them had pictures, none of which looked like Jo, and a few, who wished to remain more anonymous, had only icons of flowers or cartoon characters. No one's username or picture seemed remotely related to Jo. My fingers hovered over the keyboard and I typed *Jo Delgado.*

The username was *@DoubleHerlix* and the picture was a silhouette of someone in a dark blue hoodie with just a tuft of dark hair showing beneath the hood. It might be her. It had to be her. I clicked on the profile and saw with disappointment that most of the posts were just melodies that other people had used to layer their own lyrics. I clicked on the user activity and noticed that *@DoubleHerlix* had commented and layered her melodies on a lot of posts made by someone with the username *@NatsRainbow.* I clicked on the profile and felt my heartbeat quicken inexplicably. I chose one of the *@NatsRainbow* posts at random and saw the usual lyric video pop up. The girl had a nice voice and the acoustic guitar melody was simple and folky. I squinted to read the words of the chorus.

*Starry-eyed girl, my planet spins around you*
*I'm the luckiest girl because I found you*
*I'm spinning for you in my finest dress*
*and all the boys are looking*
*but you're the only one*
*the only one*
*I want to impress*
*my starry-eyed girl*

I felt my ears get hot and a new unsteady feeling in the pit of my stomach. I clicked on the comments and saw that *@DoubleHerlix* had commented on the song.

@DoubleHerlix commented: *I'm the luckiest girl in the world.*

I heard the front door of the cabin slam and exited the web page and cleared my search history with the speed of steady practice. I had been training myself to change browsers with lightning speed ever since my parents had invested in a home computer to help organize their camp spreadsheets and to assist with my homeschooling. It hadn't taken me long to realize that a chaotic and uncurated world of answers awaited just behind the obstacle of digital math problems. As I had gotten older, my mom had taken to running household errands while I guided my own learning on the computer. When I heard the car pull out of the driveway, I would open my little green notebook to a page at the back called *Questions* and begin my journey. I had learned a lot during these forays into the wild west of the World Wide Web. I had seen a few things I couldn't unsee. And this was one of them.

"How's the essay coming along?" my mom called through the front hall, looking through a stack of mail.

"It's good," I called vaguely back, remembering with a jolt that I still hadn't written a poem to read to Jo that night. The phrase *starry-eyed girl* echoed in my mind. I shook my head, as if to physically rid it from my memory. It had nothing to do with me, after all. A creeping sense of guilt wound its way around me, tightening at my chest. Guilt for what, I was not sure. My dad wandered into the living room and gave me a quick squeeze on my shoulder.

"There's a new camper at camp this year and I think she needs some guidance to hear the *still small voice*," he said. "I invited her to play in worship tonight."

I waited for him to say more.

"I've been blessed to be in a position to minister to young women like her and call them back into the fold. So many years at Camp Lavender have taught me that worship night is the most significant opportunity of transformation for the campers that are under my care. It's a beautiful reminder that this is a divine call that came to me while I was in seminary."

I had heard this story many times, but Clyde Heller was nothing if not a repetitive raconteur.

"That *still small voice*, and that money your grandmother left me, allowed me to establish this place. Moments like the one this afternoon remind me why I created a physical refuge from the world to make space for souls such as these to find their way back to Him."

I had a nagging feeling that I knew which camper had inspired this speech.

Wednesday night worship was the one camp event that my dad always asked me to attend. Despite his gentle demeanor, my dad knew that a request to his daughter was more like a command from any other father. He prided himself on the fact that he did not need to raise his voice or threaten punishment in order for me to comply with him. He had raised me in the way that I should go and I would no sooner rebel against him than he would rebel against God. There were moments of his youth that I had heard him characterize as *indiscreet*. When he had pursued life as a musician, or a life of hedonism as he now referred to it, he had spent nights in dive bars and missed church on Sunday. He said that he had pursued fortune, fame, and pleasure and had been "in his own will instead of God's."

He was raising me better than that. For seventeen years, he had made sure that the allure of secular hedonism had no place in my world. I had known Jesus from an early age and not a night of my life had passed that my dad did not pray for me to move through the world unscathed by its darkness after I left his care. I overheard him tell my mom that he was worried about my readiness to take on the challenges of a university, with all its philosophy classes, moral relativism, coed parties, and sexual intimacy outside the bounds of marriage.

I was ready on time and smiling when my dad came downstairs to walk with me to the rec room. I had on a dark green T-shirt and black basketball shorts that reached almost to my knees. He often told me how glad he was that I was not the kind of young woman who pushed against the dictates of modesty, pulling at distressed shorts that scarcely covered her backside, or wearing tank tops so tight you could count her ribs. He gave me a pat on the shoulder.

"How's my girl tonight?"

I smiled back at him. "She's good. Ready for some rock and roll." My mom said that I got that tongue-in-cheek humor from him.

"Tonight is late-night capture the flag," he reminded me.

My eyes widened. "I forgot about that," I said reverently. "Can I play?"

My dad's eyes widened. "Of course you can. You haven't played in years!"

The Texas night air was thick and sticky. This was the part of summer where the temperature barely seemed to drop below triple digits. I hoped that my T-shirt would not betray the dampness already forming under my arms and at the back of my neck. Soon the roar of the insects around us was met by the cheerful chatter of the campers gathering on the dock in front of the rec room. They were all dressed for capture the flag in dark colors, some already with black paint under their eyes. I knew from experience that the more seriously you took capture the flag, the more fun it was.

My eyes roved over the group of girls as we walked into the rec room, but I did not see the face I was looking for. And then, with a shock, I did. Jo was on the stage with Crowbar, Lucky Duck, and Trainwreck, apparently part of their worship team. My stomach did an abrupt somersault. Jo looked both out of place among the camp counselors and strangely at ease, apparently looking over chords with Crowbar, who played the other guitar. I thought that every girl in the room must envy Jo, so close to one of the only males they would see all summer. This was Crowbar's third summer and it had not taken long for me to notice that girls tended to swoon over him.

There was always at least one girl who would have an emotional breakdown, and over whom a counselor, or sometimes my dad, would pray, laying hands on her shoulder and murmuring prayers aloud. Many tearful confessions, pleas for forgiveness, and prayers for redemption had been laid out by campers who lingered after the last strains of the guitar faded and the other campers had traipsed upstairs for their nine p.m. snack. Something about this inevitable phenomenon unsettled me, and the unsettling made me feel guilty.

Then the music started and I slipped to the back, where I usually stood near the bathrooms in case I needed a few minutes of escape from the body heat and emotion that filled the room. As always, the music started out loud and upbeat. Campers and counselors jumped up and down and sang along, danced, and swayed. This part was fun. This was the part that I could feel in my bones, a kind of release and joy I could not access at any other time. I felt it surging in me today and I bounced and swayed with everyone else. The members of the worship band were in perfect rhythm with each other.

Jo looked almost like a different person—easy, confident, relaxed. She didn't seem to mind being on a stage in front of a crowded room. There was something about her abandon that lifted both my spirits and the corners of my mouth. Jo tapped her foot along to the beat and I was impressed by the agility of her fingers as she transitioned between chords and strummed the strings with adroit precision. I watched Jo glance up and scan around the room several times, as if she were looking for someone. Then she locked eyes with me. A grin flashed across her face and she gave a mischievous little shrug. She looked back down and her smile spread wider.

As the worship dragged on, the campers got more sweaty and more emotional in direct proportion. Even I felt a surge of intensity that I had not felt in a long time during worship night. Ordinarily, I used this time to daydream about my East Coast future, but tonight I felt a sharp appreciation of the music filling the air, the moon beginning to rise over the lake, and even the sunburnt teenagers swaying and raising their arms in spiritual ecstasy. As the session came to an end and the static fell to a lower vibration, I started making my way toward the side of the stage where Jo was taking off her guitar. I knew that the room would be divided into two teams, and I had already made up my mind which side I wanted to be on.

I glanced back up at the stage and realized that Jo was no longer visible. I slid my hands into my pockets and looked casually around the room, suddenly worrying that Jo might have gone to the other side. I wondered if we would even have the chance to meet at midnight—I had forgotten when I agreed to this that capture the flag was happening tonight. A feeling of annoyance settled over me.

"Do you have any of that face paint?" said a voice at my elbow.

I turned with a start to see Jo with her arms crossed and a feigned look of seriousness on her face.

"I refuse to lose to the other cabins or the other team or however this works."

Hayley appeared out of the crowd as if called for. "I have some."

My annoyance rose and my face flushed hot as I avoided eye contact with the victim of my earlier prank. Hayley pulled a tin of face paint out of her pocket and motioned for Jo to move closer to her. I watched as she opened the tin and dipped some of the black paint onto her index finger. She put the hand that held the tin on the back of Jo's head and tilted her face back ever so slightly, using her finger to smudge the black paint under Jo's eyes.

"Maybe you should let her do that herself," I interjected. I realized only after the fact how rude I sounded. Hayley glanced down at me.

"It's fine," mumbled Jo, who was standing very still.

"Would you like some?" Hayley said sweetly when she had finished with Jo's other eye.

"Sure," I muttered.

Hayley delicately placed the tin in my hand and gave me a saccharine smile. "I'll let you do it yourself."

# CHAPTER EIGHT

## *Jo*

I could feel myself holding my breath while Hayley's hand was on the back of my head and her hands were on my face. I felt nervous and somehow guilty, aware of Lacey's sharp eyes on both of us. Why I had the urge to apologize to Lacey, I did not know. Before I could sort out the tension buzzing through the air, Clueless, the counselor for cabin four, was speaking into a megaphone and my thoughts were drowned out by instructions for capture the flag. This was the first land activity that had actually sounded fun to me—like a hell of a lot of fun, in fact. Ahem, I mean, a heck of a lot of fun.

"I am actually kind of a master of sneaking around," I bragged to Hayley and Lacey as we followed the rest of our team funneling out the doors of the rec room.

"Wanna bet?" Hayley said with a laugh. "You have no *idea* what I get up to back home."

"So are you guys gonna stay in a group?"

All three of us turned to see Rebekah rushing up behind us, dressed in a pale yellow shirt, and looking incredibly nervous.

"I don't have any black clothes," she said, in answer to our obvious concern.

"It's better to spread out," Lacey said firmly, "because you're less likely to get caught."

"But if we go in pairs, one person can serve as a lookout while the other person does reconnaissance," Hayley said confidently.

Lacey looked like she wanted to slap her. "Sure. That too." Her tone was clipped.

The teams had been divided into two groups—the Ruths and the Naomis. The Ruths were traipsing to the other side of camp to plant their flag and to strategize. The Naomis, which included Lacey, me, Hayley, and Rebekah, were gathering on the dock outside the rec room, waiting for our opponents to get out of earshot. Clueless and Funfetti jumped up on the benches that lined the edge of the dock, huddled in discussion. I thought there was something undeniably cool about the way they looked, despite their pale purple camp T-shirts tucked into their khaki shorts. They both had beaded bracelets on their wrists and ankles, probably gifts from former campers, and their windblown hair was tied out of their faces. Clueless had a black bandana tied around her head and wore her hair in long brown braids. Funfetti wore a messy bun and both had tattered backpacks with water bottles swinging from them on carabiners. They just looked so…effortless.

"Eyes up here!" Clueless's voice was bright and twinkly and echoed across the lake.

Once the Naomis had turned to face her, she lowered her voice to prevent being overheard by the other team. "Funfetti and I were talking and we think the flag should be hidden in the dining hall on the moose head. What do y'all think?"

The Naomis let out a hushed chatter of agreement.

"They'll never look there!" Rebekah said giddily.

"Remember," Funfetti said seriously, "it's important for us *not* to guard the flag too closely. So don't hang around here. The best thing to do is to split up into pairs and go look for the Ruths' flag, okay? Just remember, if you get caught, they can put you in prison and then you won't be able to help anyone until the game is over."

We all nodded vigorously. My heart was pounding with excitement.

"Okay, everyone choose a buddy! We're going to give each pair one flashlight because we don't have enough for everyone," Funfetti said. "Once you cross the dock, you're in the Ruths' territory. Everything on the dock and on this side is the Naomis' territory. If you're on their side and they tag you, you'll go to jail and you can only get out if another Naomi tags you back out. Got it?"

Out of the corner of my eye, I saw Rebekah clutching at Lacey's arm. She turned to Rebekah, who was staring at her, wide-eyed.

"Be my buddy," Rebekah pleaded.

"Oh, um—"

Lacey gave me the briefest of glances. I tried not to look disappointed.

"You come with me, chica," Hayley said, elbowing me gently. "We can be sneaky together."

With that, the game began.


"On a scale of one to ten, how seriously are we taking this game?" Hayley asked me as soon as the rest of their team was out of earshot.

"Oh, uh, I don't know like a six?" I lied. I was in more of an eight-ish mood.

"Good answer," Hayley said. She started off confidently toward the woods. "I think we should go toward the pool."

"Do you think their flag will be there?"

"I think it will be fun to hang out at the pool."

I hesitated, debating whether to tell this tall girl with the aggressively blond ponytail that I was nervous to submerge my ripped up knee in water. Surely I could just avoid getting into the pool. Either way, Hayley and the light were quickly disappearing in front of me, so I trotted along to catch up. Hayley was not being particularly quiet, but I did not dare to suggest that she point her flashlight lower or step more carefully over the many pinecones strewn in our path. Being put in jail did not sound fun if it meant standing relatively still on a humid Texas night providing a buffet for the ravenous mosquitos, so I stayed a few steps behind Hayley, outside the ring of light she projected on the path, and walked with a little more precision than my counterpart. We walked like this for several minutes. I had not yet been to the pool, so I had no choice but to trust that Hayley knew where we were going and would guide us there and back.

After what felt like half an hour but was probably no more than six minutes, Hayley veered off the main walkway to a side path and I almost lost sight of her. Then I caught sight of a short black fence looming in front of us. This must be the pool. Hayley paused and shined her flashlight around the base of the fence. The light glinted off an opaque orange metal water bottle lying in the grass near the fence. Hayley approached it and picked it up, making what seemed to me to be a cacophony of noise as she did so.

"Left my water bottle here earlier," Hayley said. She took a long swig. "You thirsty?"

"Yeah, actually," I said, having brought nothing along with me. Hayley came back to the path and handed me the water bottle. I took a big gulp and nearly choked, and spat some of it back out.

"*Jesus Christ* what is that?" I spluttered.

Hayley let out a throaty laugh. "Nate's Grapes," she said.

"What?"

"Rosé, dummy. Wine."

"*What?*" Despite being the known troublemaker in my family, I'd never had a drop of alcohol. Something about letting your guard down. That never appealed to me.

"Come on, let's get to the pool."

I stared at the bottle in my hand as Hayley breezed by me and toward the gate. She lifted the latch and held the gate open for me to pass through. Hayley followed and quietly latched the gate behind us. She gestured for me to follow her to the diving board, where she sat at the base and held out her hand for the water bottle. I was relieved to hand it back to her. Having alcohol discovered on me was the absolute last thing I needed. My mom *and* Tía Laura would never believe it wasn't mine and would have my head.

The thought of Tía Laura made my insides burn, along with the generous splash of warm rosé I had unwittingly consumed. I looked at Hayley, who was taking another long drink from the water bottle, her long tan legs crossed and her shorts rolled at the waist to put her legs on display, after Funfetti had checked to make sure everyone's shorts extended below their fingertips. I had been sent here to be around good Christian girls so that the negative influences of the sinful secular world would cease to have a grip on me. Because of Tía Laura's strict faith, I was being denied an educational experience and sent to a place where the people were no more holy than they were in eleventh grade at public school.

"What are you thinking so hard about?" Hayley asked. Her eyes came to rest on me. "You're not going to rat me out, are you?"

"Why would I do that?"

"I don't know, but you really shouldn't. Something tells me you have a secret or two of your own that you wouldn't want getting out to the rest of the cabin."

I cut a sideways glance at Hayley, but decided neither to confirm nor deny this insinuation. *What could she possibly know?*

I just held out my hand. Hayley put the orange bottle back in it. I took a long drink, trying not to grimace. "This is terrible," I said huskily.

"I know," Hayley said. "It's the cheapest there is. Basically syrup. But it's strong, trust me."

I took another sip to indicate that I did trust her. I handed the bottle back to Hayley. A pleasant heady feeling started to swirl around me. If this was how drinking made you feel, it really wasn't half bad.

"It's a good thing goody two shoes isn't with us," Hayley said. "Little Miss Preacher's Daughter would hand us right over to the authorities."

"I don't think so," I said, maybe a little too quickly.

Hayley smirked. "Why are you so smitten with her? She kind of seems like an asshole."

"Oh she is," I said, dodging the question. If Hayley wanted to be provocative, I could too. "So why do you wear the two-piece?" I asked. "This clearly isn't your first time here. Why break the rules if you know what's going to happen?"

Hayley looked hard at me. "Probably for the same reason you have a boy's haircut," she said airily.

"What's that supposed to mean? Girls can have short hair, ya know. Even if God says they shouldn't."

Hayley threw back her head and let out a laugh far too loud under the current circumstances. "And girls are allowed to show off their stomachs and their cleavage—even if God says they shouldn't. Don't you think?"

This last question made my face burn a little.

"Fair enough," was all I managed to say. I was opening my mouth to ask Hayley what kind of secret she thought I had, when a beam of light hit Hayley square in the face.

"Who's there?" someone bellowed.

"Oh, *shit*," Hayley said, shoving the water bottle at me. "Go, go," she whispered. She turned off her flashlight and sprang off the diving board and onto the concrete, running for the fence. I ran the opposite direction toward the swimming pool bathrooms, orange water bottle in hand.

# CHAPTER NINE

## *Lacey*

"Which cabin are you in?" Rebekah asked me as I switched on my flashlight and held it up to illuminate the asphalt walkway. A handful of frogs leaped in panic and scattered into the bushes on either side.

"Cabin three," I said. I felt a little guilty lying to this girl, but she seemed like the kind of girl who was going to have dozens of questions after I explained that I was the daughter of the camp founders. I used to take pride in this, boasting my status early on and telling all the campers about how I lived here all year and knew everything there was to know. When I was very young, I would beg to participate in camp activities with the older girls, who all seemed so knowledgeable and glamorous. Once I got a little closer to their age, they all seemed to want to be my friend. But once the novelty wore off, I quickly tired of girls using me for my unlimited Lavender Loot, asking me for the real names of the camp counselors, or trying to get me to let them into the pool after curfew.

"Where do you think they hid the flag?"

I looked at Rebekah and resisted rolling my eyes.

"I don't know," I said in a low voice. "But probably in the woods. I think we should head toward the long slides and see what we can find."

Rebekah nodded and followed closely behind me as I set off along the walking path. I hoped that Rebekah would take my silence as an indicator that there was no need for us to continue conversing and for a few minutes I felt relieved that I could complete this mission without having to entertain my companion.

"Is this kind of like the parable of the lost sheep?"

Rebekah's voice came hoarsely over the sound of the cicadas. I instantly started to regret participating in this camp activity.

"What?" I said, a little more sharply than I meant to.

"Like how Jesus sets off to look for the missing sheep—the one that got away from the fold—to bring it back."

This question stopped me dead in my tracks. I pointed my flashlight at Rebekah and saw her questioning face glow in the darkness.

"It's just for fun," I said. "It's a fun camp game."

"Oh."

I was surprised to hear disappointment in her voice. Had she come to camp thinking every single activity was going to relate to the salvation of her soul? What did she think the blob was about? Rather than ask her these questions, I continued walking until we came to the pathway that led to two long parallel metal slides that extended about twenty yards into the woods in a gradual decline. I waited for Rebekah to catch up to me.

"Listen," I said in a low voice. "I think there might be members of the Ruths around here. I'm going to turn off the flashlight and I'm going to move very slowly. Just follow right behind me and I will lead us through. I'll turn on the flashlight right when we get to the slides to see if the flag is there and then we'll go back out the same way we came in. Got it?"

Rebekah nodded, eyes wide.

"Here we go."

The reflection of my flashlight was harsh on the metal slides. I held my breath, praying that we wouldn't get captured. There was, in fact, no sign of anyone, which made me suspect that I was looking in the wrong place. Although the teams were not supposed to guard their flags too closely, there was always someone lurking nearby to try to capture prisoners before they got to the flag. By the time we got to the bottom of the slides, I was certain that the Ruths' flag was nowhere near.

"Let's turn around," I whispered to Rebekah, who was hunching unnecessarily low to the ground. Rebekah nodded and we turned around and began walking back up the way we came, toward the main path. I thought I heard a rustling sound in the woods ahead of us. I dropped to the ground and pulled Rebekah down with me. Rebekah lost her balance and crashed hard to the ground.

"Hey!" she said loudly. I put my finger to my lips and widened my eyes, gesturing for her to stay down. All I could hear now was the sound of our breathing and the lustful protestations of the cicadas. Rebekah was clearly displeased. Then I heard voices from along the main path, descending in husky whispers. Two sets of Ruths must be passing each other.

"Have y'all found anything yet?"

"No, but we're going to check the dock."

"Has anyone gone near the pool?"

"They just captured someone there and they said she didn't have anything on her."

The voices and footsteps ceased and I looked at Rebekah with wide eyes.

"Their flag is at the pool!" I said. But Rebekah was pulling anxiously at her shirt.

"I'm covered in dirt," she whimpered. "This is going to stain. I need to change."

I tried to suppress the competitive rage welling up inside me and speak calmly. "Can't you change after the game?"

"No, I need to go back to the cabin now. It'll be so quick!"

I was certain that it would not be quick. We were nowhere near the cluster of cabins right now, and by the time we got back there, Rebekah changed, and we found our way back across enemy lines, the game would surely be over one way or another.

"Do you think you can find your way back by yourself?"

"Not in the dark," Rebekah said in a small voice. I took a deep breath and cast about for a solution, but if I gave Rebekah the flashlight, it would be challenging to find my way to the pool in the pitch dark, and I was not particularly keen to do so on a moonless night.

That was the magic of playing nighttime capture the flag at Camp Lavender—there were hardly any lights anywhere. It was true, pure, East Texas darkness.

"Okay, okay, but we have to be so quick," I whispered. I started scrambling back up the hill and motioned for Rebekah to follow me.

We made our way swiftly along the main path and once we reached the Naomis' territory, I broke out into a walk-jog with Rebekah running a little to keep up with my stride. I checked my watch as we arrived at cabin six. It was ten p.m. now. I wondered if everyone would be in bed by midnight.

We entered the cabin and Rebekah flipped on a light and rushed to her bunk to look for a fresh shirt. I glanced around the room. I had not been in a camper cabin in quite some time. It still looked much the same. That was something kind of eerie about growing up in a summer camp, I thought, things stayed so identical from summer to summer that it was hard to tell if I was growing up at all. Then I saw a dark blue hoodie lying on one of the lower bunks toward the front of the room. It was the hoodie Jo had been wearing when I picked her up from cabin six on the first night of camp. That must be her bed.

I wandered over to it, glancing at Rebekah, who was in the bathroom with her back turned to me, soaking her dirty shirt in one of the cabin sinks. There was a partly open duffel bag lying on the ground at the foot of the bed. I stood by it and gave it a little poke with my foot, jostling the contents around. There were only dark folds of fabric visible from the unzipped part of the bag. Without thinking, I bent down and unzipped the bag the rest of the way. Everything in the bag smelled like sandalwood and pine. Gingerly, I lifted the stack of clothes to reveal the bottom of the bag. I saw a small bottle of what looked like perfume and a folded piece of paper.

I took both items out of the bag. The bottle had a silver cap and the words *Summer Sky* printed in bold silver letters. I took the cap off and spritzed the tiniest amount on my wrist. I held it up to my nose. Sandalwood and pine filled my lungs. It was warm and woodsy and gave me a hollow feeling in my chest. I quickly put the cap back on and put the bottle back exactly where I found it. I unfolded the piece of paper.

*Dear Mom,*

*Camp has not been quite as terrible as I expected it to be. There are some fun activities and people have been nice to me so far. I miss you and Rudy and I still feel upset that Laura sent me here to try to fix me. I know God is important to you, but if you think that God made me, you must know that he made me this way on purpose. In fact—*

"I think I just want to stay here," Rebekah's voice called from the bathroom. I shoved the piece of paper back into the bag. I turned around, my face hot, but Rebekah was just entering the main room of the cabin. I stared at her blankly.

"I'm just gonna stay here," Rebekah repeated. "So you can go if you want."

"Oh, yeah, okay—are you sure?"

I heard her voice speaking, but my mind was elsewhere. "Yeah, you go ahead. Good luck!"

"Okay, thanks!" I hurried out of the cabin and shut the door behind me. I was not at all sure that I had left the bag exactly like I had found it, but there was no going back now. I set off for the pool.

I made my way through the darkness carefully, but confidently. I knew this route as well as I knew the one from my bedroom to the bathroom. And I knew that the Ruths' flag was at the swimming pool. It had been years since I had participated in a camp-wide game like this and for some reason it felt absolutely vital that I return the victor. I had never been lucky when it came to group games, but luck was finally on my side this time.

The clouds obscuring the moon kept the whole camp in total darkness. I smiled to myself thinking about the girls stumbling around, getting eaten alive by mosquitos and tripping over stray pinecones. I wondered if Hayley and Jo had led each other astray yet. A sudden jolt of suspicion shot through me. Maybe they had completely abandoned the game and gone off to the zipline tower and Jo was showing Hayley everything I had shown her. Annoyance and sweat both prickled the back of my neck. But now the pool was in sight.

The pool always had lights in it, which on a moonless night like this made the water glow in an otherworldly way. I lifted the latch to the gate outside the pool as carefully as I could. I did not see or hear any sign of anyone until I had closed the gate behind me. Then I heard it—a shuffling sound from the pool bathrooms. I stood still, waiting. It could very well be a racoon or an armadillo, but it sounded bigger than that. Was someone waiting here to capture Naomis as they came to find the flag? That was against the rules and I was going to tell them exactly that.

Then I saw the silhouette of a head looking out from behind the wall that blocked the entrance to the bathrooms.

"Who goes there? Friend or foe?" said a familiar voice. I recognized it immediately.

"It's Lacey," I whispered back.

Jo emerged from behind the wall. "What are you doing here? Where's Rebekah?" She walked along the edge of the pool, glancing from side to side as if someone would be waiting with a machine gun trained on her.

"Rebekah got dirt on her shirt and gave up. Where's Hayley?"

"She got captured."

"But not you?"

"We ran in opposite directions. I've just been hiding out for a bit." Jo swayed a little and caught herself.

"You sound weird. What's wrong with you?" I asked.

"Uh, nothing, just chilling in a swimming pool bathroom in the dark like any other day." Jo let out a little laugh through her nose. I was annoyed, but I still had victory on my mind.

"The flag is somewhere around here," I said. "I heard one of the Ruths saying so to another one earlier. Which means if we can find it and bring it back, we win."

"Oh, hell yeah," Jo responded. "I mean *heck* yeah. Hayley was right."

I turned on my flashlight and started scanning around the diving board and the lounge chairs.

"Or she just wanted to come to the pool," I said.

"That actually makes more sense," Jo said slowly.

I turned toward her. "Why?"

"Uh, well, I'll tell you, but you can't hand me over to the authorities."

"What's that supposed to mean?"

Jo held up an orange water bottle. "She hid this."

"Why would she hide her water bottle?

Jo stepped closer to me and lowered her voice. I could now hear that there was a slight slur in it.

"Because it's her *wine* bottle," she said, laughing in a low voice.

I snatched the bottle out of Jo's hand and unscrewed the lid. I smelled the contents of the bottle and winced.

"Have *you* been drinking this?"

Jo gave a small shrug. "Yeah, well, what was I supposed to do?" Jo sounded defiant.

"I don't know—*not* drink alcohol with someone who is already breaking the camp rules every other day? Are you trying to get yourself kicked out or something?" I could hear my own raised voice, but I was too angry to restrain it.

"What do you care?"

I was shocked by the timbre of Jo's voice when she asked this question.

"What?" I said blankly.

Jo stepped closer to me, wobbling ever so slightly, but defiant nonetheless. She spoke clearly, but her volume betrayed the state of her inebriation. "What do you care if I get kicked out of camp?" she asked.

A distant rumbling sound made both of us turn, but the source of the sound was unclear. I turned back to Jo.

"I know you don't want to be here. But I thought you were starting to have fun," I stammered. Jo narrowed her eyes on me.

"I think this is about you," she said.

"How is this about me? *I* didn't drink any alcohol."

"But you snuck out, didn't you? Isn't that breaking a rule?"

"I'm not a camper."

"Oh and your parents don't have a curfew for you, just the campers? That's bullshit."

"What's your point?" I didn't bother correcting Jo's swearing this time.

She continued, "I think *you* were starting to have fun hanging out with someone who isn't a—"

"A *what?*"

"—a good Christian girl."

I opened my mouth to respond, then closed it again. My head was starting to feel foggy and the thick night air felt like it was coating my lungs and making the words I wanted to say slide farther apart from each other. It felt like my brain was dialing up.

"So you, what, know a lot about the world?" I heard myself stammer. I wasn't sure if I was issuing a challenge or asking a genuine question.

"I know things, yeah," Jo said.

"Like what?"

"I know that—that poems don't have to rhyme to be good."

I spun toward her. "What's that supposed to mean?"

"It means your Emily poem sounds more like an old-timey hymn than a modern poem."

"My *what?*"

Jo's eyes widened and she swayed a little, trying to catch her balance. "And anyway, who the hell is Emily?"

My jaw dropped. My mind was spinning. "How did you—"

Without warning, Jo leaned toward me. "Why do you smell like that?" she asked.

"Like what?"

Jo took a deep breath.

"Don't *sniff* me," I said, panicking.

"It smells like—"

Before I had an opportunity to consider whether this was the optimal strategic move, I reached forward and shoved Jo, hard. Jo stumbled backward, letting the water bottle fall to the ground, where it made a loud CLANG on the concrete. Her back smacked the water hard.

"What was that?" I heard a voice shout from the woods. Then I heard footsteps crunching toward the pool. I glanced around, looking for the best place to hide, but there was only one immediate solution.

I jumped into the pool.

# CHAPTER TEN

## *Jo*

I felt like I was falling in slow motion. The shock of the moment, or perhaps my level of intoxication, heightened every single one of my senses. I gasped and the smell of chlorine and pine filled my lungs. It was as if I could feel each individual drop of pool water sting my back as I smacked into the surface of the pool. The splash of the water thundered in my ears like a cannon shot. The sharp familiar taste of pool water rushed into my mouth. As I sank from the force of my fall and the surface of the water closed over my head, I opened my eyes and the lights in the pool made it seem like I was suspended in bright golden blue light.

Time resumed, and I came up for air, gasping and coughing. Before I could reorient myself, Lacey had grabbed my arm and dragged me to the edge of the pool.

"Hey!" I yelled, but she put a cold wet hand over my mouth and held her finger to my lips, shaking her head. I stopped struggling and stared at her, listening hard. I heard the rattle of the pool gate as someone fiddled with the latch. We were floating just beneath the edge, clinging as closely as we could to the wall to stay out of sight.

"Stay still," Lacey said into my ear. I nodded and she released her hand from my mouth, using it to keep herself from bobbing up higher than the edge of the pool. We heard the crunch of feet as someone paced outside the fence, but no one came through the gate. I breathed slowly, trying not to cough from the pool water that had infiltrated every orifice of my face. We treaded water as quietly as we could. I felt Lacey's hand on my shoulder and looked at her. She pointed to the bottom of the pool. There, I could just make out a dark shape.

"Those bastards," I said under my breath.

"They hid their flag *in* the pool," Lacey responded. "Stay here."

Lacey used her feet to push herself off the wall of the swimming pool and I watched the light ripple off her as she made her way down to the deepest part of the pool floor. When she resurfaced, she was clutching a beanbag wrapped in a red bandana.

"I got it," she said, grinning broadly. Pool water glinted on her face and her normally wild hair lay drenched and dark against her head and neck.

"Now all we have to do is make it back to—"

Lacey was interrupted by one of the loudest cracks of thunder I had heard in my life. Instinctively, I reached out to grab Lacey's arm and pull her toward the edge of the pool.

"We have to get out of here," I said.

We scrambled out of the pool, Lacey shoving the Ruths' flag into the waistband of her shorts. It must have been nearly eighty degrees, but she shivered a little. I noticed that the curve of Lacey's waist and hips was visible for the first time as her usually baggy clothes, now soaked from pool water, clung to her skin. I saw Lacey pull her T-shirt away from her torso, as if aware of my gaze, and I turned my eyes to the sky.

"Well, that explains all the clouds," I observed.

As if on cue, raindrops started to fall, fast and frenzied.

"We better get back to the rec room," I said.

"Wait—" Lacey said.

"What?" I turned.

"Shouldn't we go set up the electroscope?"

A wave of shock ran over me, as if I myself had been struck by lightning. I felt almost as surprised that Lacey remembered the name and existence of my experiment as I did that I had completely forgotten about it in the excitement of winning capture the flag.

"Oh my God, yeah," I said. "But what about the game?"

Lacey shrugged. "It's fine. Who knows if and when it will storm again? Come on." She started for the gate, her sneakers making a wet squelching sound with every step she took. The first bolt of lightning cut across the sky.

"Holy shit," I said under my breath. "This is it."

The dash across camp was treacherous. This was a true Texas rainstorm, beginning abruptly and proceeding furiously. There was no way of knowing whether it would storm all night or clear up in five minutes, and Lacey seemed to sense the urgency of the situation, because she broke into a run toward the cabins. She waited outside for me as I ran inside, dripping all over the floor, and grabbed my contraption from my duffel bag. Cabin six was empty except for Rebekah, who was sound asleep on her lower bunk, facing the wall.

We ran to the field that held the zipline tower. I jogged after Lacey, barely aware of the discomfort of my soggy clothes and shoes. When we arrived at the base of the tower, Lacey turned to me with wide eyes.

"Listen," she said, "I don't have my key."

"What does that mean?"

"It means we can't get the harnesses."

My stomach dropped into my soaking shoes.

"We can still go," Lacey said, "We just need to be careful."

I nodded, trying to ignore the giant pit opening in my stomach. Lacey stared at me for a moment, but the rain was only coming harder and faster, and there was no time to hesitate or share feelings about how scary this situation was. Lacey turned and started making her way up the spiral staircase with one hand gripping the railing on the side. Without looking back, she held out her other hand behind her back, and I grasped it. The stairs were slippery, and made only more slippery by the complete lack of traction on our shoes, but we made it to the top. At the top, Lacey let go of my hand and dropped to her knees. I did the same.

"Okay, what needs to happen now?"

I was crawling around, trying to set up the electroscope as quickly as I could. "I just need to find a secure place to—"

The loudest crack of thunder I had heard in my life caused me to lurch. As if it were happening in slow motion, I felt the electroscope fly out of my slippery hand and skitter across the narrow platform of the zipline tower. I didn't even have time to yell before a gust of wind sent the contraption flying off the edge of the tower. We crawled to the edge of the platform and looked down. I could barely make it out, so far below us through the rain, but I knew that it had broken upon impact with the ground.

The rain was coming down in slanted sheets now, and the prospect of making our way down the spiral staircase was more than a little intimidating. I was staring blankly at the ground, devastated. I pulled my knees to my chest and rested my forehead on them, almost unaware now of the thunderstorm quite literally crashing down on us.

Lacey scooted toward me, huddling with me in the middle of the sky. I felt raindrops drip off the ends of my hair and down my neck and face. She put a tentative hand on my shoulder, but I was too embarrassed to look up.

"It didn't even have a chance to fail," I said.

"I'm sorry," Lacey said.

The rain filled the pause.

"Can we make another one?"

I shook my head. "I don't know where to get more parts."

"We're going to have to get down from here," Lacey said. "It's dangerous to be up so high during a storm."

I nodded, but did not move. Lacey grasped my elbow and dragged me to my feet. She guided me toward the stairs and stepped in front of me. I placed one hand on the rail of the staircase and one hand on her shoulder and slowly, slowly, we spiraled down.

We must have looked like two deranged, drenched girls as we made our way across the muddy field and back toward cabin six. The other campers and counselors had made their way inside their cabins by now. On the porch of cabin six, I turned to Lacey and gave a small wave. All I wanted to do was put on dry clothes and curl up in my bunk bed to contemplate my utter defeat. Lacey pulled the bandana-wrapped beanbag from the pocket of her shorts and held it out to me. I took it.

"What do I do with it?"

Lacey shrugged. "Just keep it, I guess. A souvenir of victory. Also, don't forget to have Dr. Dan clean your wound again tomorrow since, um, it got wet. Also, sorry I shoved you into the pool."

I gave a short laugh and gestured toward the storm. "I was gonna get wet anyway." I turned toward the cabin door.

"Also—"

I stopped.

"Yeah?"

"I want to do a poetry slam."

I waited.

"In Austin."

"Oh."

"And I—want you to help me get ready for it."

"Oh?"

"Just—don't be mean."

"Okay." I blinked, unsure of what to say.

"I mean do you—if you—want to."

"Yeah, I do," I said, feeling something like a smile form on my face.

"Okay. Well. Go dry off. I'll come find you tomorrow."

I nodded again. Lacey stepped off the porch, then turned abruptly back. "And also—"

"Yeah?"

I squinted through the rain, barely able to make out Lacey's face as she receded.

"It was about Emily Dickinson."

And she was gone.

# CHAPTER ELEVEN

## *Lacey*

I was relieved that I was able to come home with a valid excuse as to why my clothing was absolutely soaked. I couldn't explain the reality—that I had jumped into a swimming pool fully clothed and then I had climbed to the top of the zipline tower in the pouring rain to try to help a camper complete a potentially dangerous and unauthorized experiment that no one but the two of us knew about.

When my parents asked why it had taken me so long to make it back home, I explained that I had been helping lost campers find their way back to their cabins in the storm. In return, I received approving nods and smiles and only a small knot in my stomach from the guilt of outright lying. My mother instructed me to leave my sopping clothes on the tile in the laundry room and to make my way straight to bed.

In the bathroom, I fished my green notebook out of the pocket of my shorts. I gave it a slight shake, but knew almost immediately that it was a lost cause. I opened it and stared at the rippled pages and the blurry words, then tossed it onto the tile of the bathroom floor, where it made a definitive SPLAT. I turned on the shower and felt the sting of hot tears in my eyes. Only some of those poems had been turned into Slant posts. Most of them had been written down only in my notebook and were now lost forever.

I peeled off the clothes that clung to my skin and stepped into the shower. The warm water poured over me as I leaned against the tiled wall of the shower. Something inside me released, and my tears turned into silent sobs. I told myself that maybe the notebook would have been ruined by the rain anyway, but why had I not just left the notebook in a drawer? Why had I not pulled it out of my pocket before I had plunged into the swimming pool to hide from the Ruths and win capture the flag—which didn't even matter because the whole thing had turned into a big muddy mess?

I put my hands over my eyes and tried to take a deep breath. I did not cry often, and when I did, it was only in private. The shower was one of the only places where I felt isolated from my own judgment and could allow a short release of emotion. I thought of Jo, sitting at the top of the zipline tower in the rain, with her head bent over her knees. I wondered if Jo had been crying too. I wondered if the falling electroscope had felt to Jo like opening the soggy pages of my notebook had felt to me. I sat down on the edge of the shower and put my head in my hands.

*Who the hell is Emily?*

I lifted my face out of my hands and smoothed my hair back, thinking about this question. Jo must have found access to a computer somewhere. She must have logged onto Slant and searched for my name. She must have scrolled through the profiles until she found mine and then read at least one of my posts. Not only that, she had thought about the poem long enough to criticize the traditional rhyme scheme and to question who the poem was about. I burned at the thought of Jo reading my poetry and judging it for its old-fashioned style. Who the hell had she *thought* Emily was? I felt the odd sensation of a laugh forming in my throat. There was something funny to me about the anger behind that question. I thought with satisfaction of how cool I had probably looked walking into the rain after stating that my stupid poem was about Emily Dickinson.

Or maybe that was even more embarrassing than how bad Jo thought the poem was. I turned off the shower and reached for a towel.

## Jo

Everyone in cabin six was chattering about the game and how it had been ruined by the storm and how no one had found either flag as they wrung out their clothes and bustled in and out of the showers. Funfetti was trying to get everyone to hurry because it was way past our normal curfew and we were still going to have to get up at the same time tomorrow for breakfast.

I took one of my classic Jo Delgado two-minute showers and put on a fresh T-shirt and shorts. Hayley found her way next to me while we brushed our teeth and asked me in a low voice about the whereabouts of the orange water bottle.

"I must have left it by the pool," I muttered.

"Shit, okay, well one of us will have to go get it tomorrow at some point. It reeks of Nate's Grapes."

I thought about pointing out that the water bottle ought to be Hayley's sole responsibility, but remembered that I had certainly drained the rest of its contents while hiding in the pool bathroom and thought better of it. I nodded reassuringly and Hayley's shoulders relaxed a little.

"So what ended up happening after I was captured?"

I shrugged. "Not much really. I hid until everyone was gone and then I—then it started pouring rain and I was just trying to make my way back to the cabin at that point."

"What took you so long? Everyone else was back like an hour ago."

"Uh…" I did not bother to ask myself why it seemed impossible to tell Hayley the truth about what had happened in the intervening time, and if I *had* asked myself I would not have known how to answer. Thankfully, Hayley answered for me.

"You finished the bottle, didn't you?"

I paused brushing my teeth and looked guiltily at Hayley. I gave her a mischievous smile. "Well, what else was there to do?"

Hayley let out a laugh. "Fair enough, but you owe me a bottle now."

"How the heck am I supposed to get you a bottle of Nate's Grapes? I don't exactly think they sell it in the Snack Shack."

"I'm sure you'll think of something."

This comment was too vague for me to interpret, so I just gave a nod.

I noticed immediately that someone must have touched my duffel bag. I rummaged through it to check whether any items were missing, but they were all accounted for. Funfetti stood by the light switch and started counting down from ten for lights out. I started to zip up my duffel bag when I noticed that the cap of my cologne bottle was loose in the bag. I snapped it back on and leapt into my bunk just as the room went dark.

I stared at the frame of the top bunk, only dimly visible as my eyes adjusted to the darkness of the room. The sound of girls fluffing their pillows and rearranging their blankets and settling in provided a pleasant ambient noise for my flurry of thoughts and emotions. I squeezed my eyes shut as the vision of the falling electroscope faded into my brain like the start of a bad movie. I played it through a few times, trying to ignore the fact that tears were starting to form in the corners of my eyes. If my mom knew that I was crying over a failed homemade science experiment, she would click her tongue and say "Ay, reyna, we are strong women. We do not cry." If I just kept my eyes squeezed shut, the tears wouldn't fall, and then they wouldn't count.

I replayed the memory of being pushed into the pool to be saved from the potential captors approaching. Or had Lacey pushed me for another reason—like the reason she had pushed me off the zipline tower? I thought about what had happened in the moments before. They were hazy. Lacey was annoyed that I had criticized her poetry. I had asked her a question…I took in a deep breath through my nose, my head still swirling a little from the cheap wine. I smelled the sandalwood and pine and my eyes popped open. Lacey had smelled like this. I sat up in bed, staring hard at my duffel bag, trying to make my eyes adjust to the darkness. Had Lacey been in cabin six? Been near my bunk? Touched my things? How? When? Why? I lay back down and pulled the covers up to my chin, my mind whirling in progressively slower concentric circles until I finally fell asleep.

# CHAPTER TWELVE

## *Lacey*

I found Jo the next day during arts and crafts. The smell of the arts and crafts shack was strangely pleasing—a mixture of mod podge, puff paint, and cedar. Jo was stringing a beaded bracelet with light green, dark green, and black beads. I selected a small box and some paint colors at random and sat down at the long table across from her.

"How's it going today, Einstein?"

Jo's head shot up. She had been utterly absorbed in the tiny beads and had not noticed when I entered the room.

"Can't really call me that anymore," she said. "I'm not a scientist now, just a camper."

"And not a happy one, I take it?"

Jo let out a deep sigh. "Honestly, and don't judge me, I think I have a mild hangover."

"Ooh," I said in a sweet voice, "I have no idea what that's like since I'm a good Christian girl."

Jo rolled her eyes. "Well, it's rather unpleasant. I didn't see you on the dock this morning during Bible study. Did my criticism yesterday put you off of working on your poetry?"

I ducked my head and started squeezing out light blue paint onto the long piece of paper that served as an arts and crafts tablecloth. "Please," I said with affected nonchalance. "My notebook just got ruined in the rain."

"Oh, shit, for real?"

I was surprised when I looked up to see an expression of genuine concern on Jo's face.

"Did you have them written down anywhere else?"

"Well, as you apparently know, a few of them are on Slant. But no. A lot of them are gone."

"I'm so sorry," Jo said.

"I'm sorry too," I said. "About your experiment. And your hangover."

We worked on our art projects in silence for a few minutes. I tried to focus on painting, but the visual arts never seemed to come naturally to me. I frowned at the little box, then watched Jo stringing beads. She seemed utterly engrossed in her project, delicately selecting the tiny beads and holding the wire steady as she strung them on.

"How do you pick the colors?" I asked without a preamble.

Jo blinked like someone who had been suddenly interrupted while reading. "What?"

"How do you, uh, pick the colors you want to use?"

Jo pursed her lips. "I actually associate colors with feelings," she said. "And people and sounds and stuff."

"Seriously?"

"Yes," Jo said.

I grinned. "Cool. So, uh, what color am I? If I have one." I looked down at my paintbrush, embarrassed by my curiosity. Maybe it was presumptuous to assume that I was important enough to even have a color. But Jo answered without hesitation.

"Dark green," she said. "Like a pine tree."

I wasn't sure why I tried not to smile. I put down my paintbrush. "I think I know something that will make you feel better," I said.

"What?"

"A slush baby and a cold chocolate bar from the Snack Shack."

Jo's face lit up. "That *does* sound good," she said. "But I don't have any Lavender Loot, remember?"

I gave her a wave. "I got you."

I stood up and put my box on a shelf designated for unfinished crafts; Jo followed suit. She followed me toward the middle of the camp grounds where the Snack Shack was located. It occurred to me that she had probably never even set foot in there, not wanting to be tempted by cold drinks and sugary treats, which cost Lavender Loot or cash, which I was guessing she didn't have either.

"Why is Camp Lavender the hottest place in the United States of America?" Jo asked, panting. "Like hotter than Houston."

"Gladwall produces a special kind of heat only manufactured in East Texas," I answered.

"To remind us of how unpleasant hell will be so we're more tempted to repent and be saved?" Jo joked. She glanced sideways at me, trying to gauge whether I was amused or offended. My mouth twisted to the side while I tried not to laugh.

"Hush, you sacrilegious Catholic," was all I said.

The door to the Snack Shack made a *Ding!* sound like we were in an old movie. A cool blast of air hit us, chilling the droplets of sweat that had formed on our foreheads during the short walk.

"What's your favorite thing to get from here?" Jo asked.

"Okay," I said, turning toward her with excitement. "I have tried every single combination of slush baby and candy in this place and I am going to tell you what to get. Do you trust me?"

Jo nodded.

I punched the air with excitement. Jo raised her eyebrows at the gesture, but I was too energized to be self-conscious. I hurried over to a shelf that contained an array of candies and chocolates and picked up a bar in bright gold packaging.

"Have you ever had these?" I asked Jo.

"No, what are they?"

"They're called caramel crisps, and if I told you that God made them, you would believe me." I snatched two packets off the shelf and took them to the refrigerated section of the shack. I laid them carefully in between two bottles of soda and turned back to Jo with a solemn face.

"The key is to have them cold," I said. "So we'll get our slush babies, then we'll come back and get them right before we go."

I approached the counter, where a counselor named Mudslide was doing a book of crossword puzzles.

"Can I get two blue raspberry slushies and put two caramel crisps on my tab?" I asked.

Mudslide nodded and I watched Jo watch with wide eyes as a whirling silver machine deposited masses of thick, icy, blue substance into bright red and white striped cups. It was pure summer magic. I picked the drinks up off the counter and motioned with my head for Jo to retrieve the packets of chocolate.

"Where to?" Jo asked.

"To work on my poetry," I said, following it up quickly and self-consciously with, "if you still want to, if you have time."

The beauty of entering the second week of camp was that all of the campers were given three hours of free time in the afternoons in which they could nap, swim, eat, play, and generally get up to various forms of mischief. Those with Lavender Loot were the luckiest because the Snack Shack ran on this particular form of camp currency. If Jo stayed on my good side long enough, she would have access to a generous supply of snacks for the summer.

"I've got nothing but time." Jo laughed.

"Okay, well, I want to make sure we go somewhere where we're not going to run into anyone else, but that involves some rowing."

Jo looked skeptical as I led her toward the dock.

"There's an empty chapel across the lake. We *could* walk to it, but we'd have to go all the way around the lake on the horse trail and it will take forever and the heat makes the horse droppings absolutely reek."

Jo grimaced. "Rowing it is. Take me to the canoes, Heller!"

I grinned and walked faster, taking a sip of my icy drink. "Try it!"

Jo took a long sip. I watched her face as the sour taste filled her mouth. Slush babies somehow tasted just like the electric blue color they were.

"Holy—" she started, but must have remembered not to swear and ended, "slushie, Batman."

I laughed. "It's *so good,* right?"

Jo peeled open her packet of caramel crisps while we walked and popped one of the small chocolate squares into her mouth. They were sweet and crunchy, as the name suggested, and I watched Jo's eyes close in enjoyment. I let a square melt on my tongue. For a moment, the burst of cool sweetness made me forget about the vicious heat pounding down on us. Jo made that *mmm* sound people make when the deliciousness of a treat completely overtakes their senses.

"I told you," I said in response.

"I never doubted you."

We arrived at the dock and I gestured at a corner where a set of oars were stacked together vertically and six red and green canoes floated alongside each other, hooked to the dock, waiting for someone to take them out on the lake.

"Hold this." I handed Jo my slush baby and caramel crisps and pulled two oars out of the stack.

"Which color?" I gestured at the canoes.

"Does it matter?" Jo asked. She squinted at the canoes, which were all more or less the same, take or give some wear and tear.

"I thought it might to you," I said.

"Oh, um, green," Jo said, a smile flickering across her face.

I nodded and jumped into the back of one of the two green canoes. Jo glanced at the row of life jackets hanging from a metal rod near the oars.

"Are we supposed to take these?" she asked tentatively.

"I mean, we're *supposed* to, but we aren't going to need them. We know how to swim, so I doubt either of us is going to drown today."

I set the oars down in the bottom of the canoe and held my hand out for the snacks. Jo handed them to me and put one foot into the canoe, which wobbled violently under her. A guttural sound escaped her throat. I held out a hand for her and Jo grasped it hard.

"Sorry," she said. "First time."

"Really?" I asked with genuine surprise.

"Um, yeah," Jo said as she settled down onto the front seat of the canoe. "I don't live at a summer camp."

"But you've never *been* to—?"

"Look, my family is poor," Jo said. "Poor people don't get to go to summer camp every year. We get summer jobs delivering pizzas and we play in the neighbor's sprinklers and *maybe* get to go swimming if we have a rich white friend with a pool."

I said nothing. I reached back to unhook the canoe and used my oar to push us away from the dock and out toward the middle of the lake. The droplets dripping down my forehead did nothing to cool down the sudden heat that was rising in my face.

# CHAPTER THIRTEEN

## *Jo*

"Sorry, that was—"

"No, I'm sorry, I shouldn't have—"

The awkwardness rippled between Lacey and me as we began to row across the lake. I berated myself for coming on so strong. There was no way to explain the hundreds of little ways I had been reminded that I didn't belong here since arriving—that I was an outsider, unfamiliar with the customs and unwelcome in the territory. Lacey had surely been raised on a steady diet of color-blindness and financial stability that had produced the blithe unawareness so many people seemed to have. All of this crossed my mind, but the words to express it died on my tongue before I could get them out.

Lacey's back was to me. I felt like I could see the tension in her shoulders, but maybe I was imagining things.

So we rowed.

It was the kind of still Texas day that made the chirp of every bird and even the shudder of the grass under a slight breeze stand out, like the moments of stillness in a horror movie that put the audience on edge before a big jump scare. When the canoe finally reached the opposite side of the lake, Lacey jumped out and secured the rope around a tree, loosely double knotting it and letting the clasp dangle. I followed awkwardly. The chapel was at the crest of a small slope, almost hidden from view by scattered pine trees. If you didn't know it was here, you would never find it. I thought it looked like something out of a fairy tale—small and white with brown trim and a wooden cross above the double doors.

Lacey held the door for me and I walked in, feeling an unexpected tingle at the back of my neck. There was a small part of me that expected to burst into flames once I set foot on the wooden floor. It smelled like warm cedar, and the honey-colored afternoon light poured through the small arched windows that lined the sides. There were just five rows of wooden pews with a break in the middle that formed an aisle. At the front of the aisle was a white podium on a small wooden stage, and another wooden cross hung on the wall behind it above another window. There was something eerie about a place that looked so holy and so abandoned. I felt a shiver down my spine.

"You okay?" Lacey asked softly behind me.

"Yeah, just afraid of being smited or something."

Lacey smiled softly. "For being Catholic?"

"Ha. For being"—I stopped abruptly—"an atheist."

The word sounded prosaic and harsh in the light-soaked room, but it was safer than the alternative. I smiled at the look of shock on Lacey's face.

"Are *you* gonna smite me?" I asked.

Lacey bit her lip. "I don't think I have that power," she said.

"Oh, I think you do." I grinned. "Or you could at least shove me again—you could push me into the lake on the way back if it makes you feel better."

Lacey let out a laugh. "I'll try to resist."

Lacey walked up the aisle and stood behind the podium. The light from the window behind her made the frizzy hair that stood out from her bun glow like a halo. I dropped into a pew and stared up at her. She was wearing a white T-shirt today and grasping the sides of the podium so tightly that her knuckles had turned white. She gave me the impression of an untamed and wingless angel.

"Preach!" I called out.

Lacey bent her head down and laughed. "I can't," she said quietly.

"I thought you were going to give me a poem—you owe me one, remember?"

Lacey crossed the back of her hand over her forehead to wipe away the sweat. "Sorry," she said. "I just…nothing feels…good enough."

I shifted in the pew. "Look, I'm sorry for—"

"No, please don't—I'm sorry for being such a…such a…"

I waited for Lacey to find the right word.

"A jackass."

I gasped in mock horror. "I can't believe you're *cussing* in *church*," I said, clutching at invisible pearls. Lacey smiled, but did not look up.

"You know," Lacey said slowly as she wandered around in front of the pulpit, "I actually haven't read a ton of modern poetry."

Something told me that this was the start of a longer train of thought, so I nodded and gave Lacey an encouraging, "Oh?"

"Yeah," Lacey said. "My dad just has books of old hymns and my mom has this old book of poetry that my grandmother gave her when she was little, y'know, Wordsworth and Robert Frost and that kind of stuff."

I nodded again.

"And I actually had to beg my mom to give me a book of Emily Dickinson poetry for my birthday. I don't think my dad wanted her to, but she let me have it because I was so annoying and stubborn about it."

"I can't picture that," I said drily.

"But yeah, I guess I learned about poetry from Emily Dickinson and I just always liked her because she was this...this..."

I found myself holding my breath.

"Recluse, I guess. She didn't get to experience much of the world, and yet she wrote all this incredible poetry..." Lacey trailed off.

"That makes sense," I said quietly.

"I guess I just thought if I could copy her formula somehow that maybe I could become a famous poet too, or something, but like while I'm still alive."

"Totally," I said.

"But I guess I'm realizing that maybe the only thing I have in common with Emily Dickinson is, like, no life experience."

Lacey dropped her eyes and put her hand to the back of her head, smoothing some curls that had escaped captivity.

"I see you more like Rapunzel," I said without thinking.

"Oh, great." Lacey rolled her head back and groaned at the vaulted ceiling.

"I mean, Camp Lavender is like your tower and you just have to stay here and you're never allowed to leave."

"I'm allowed to leave," Lacey cut in defensively.

"You are?"

Lacey blinked several times.

"Well, no," she said finally. She stared out the window, seeming to forget that I was there at all. I watched her, wondering what thoughts were passing through her mind, wondering if I had said too much and crossed an invisible line and was about to lose the only friend I had made in this place. Then, suddenly, Lacey seemed to snap back into the present moment and looked directly at me.

"So you think this is all there is?" she said. Her voice had an accusing edge.

"What?"

"You said you're an atheist," Lacey prompted.

"Oh, well, yeah—most scientists are."

"But why?"

I heaved a sigh. "Well, because religion and science don't always mix well...and like, there's no proof? And it's kind of arrogant to assume that this giant man in the sky knows everything and made everything and that *you*, this tiny human speck whose existence is like nothing in the grand scheme of the universe, know all his rules for how to live and are going to enforce them on everyone."

All of this tumbled out of my mouth and I paused, bracing myself for a response. Lacey pursed her lips and frowned.

"Have you memorized some of Emily Dickinson's poems?" I asked, breaking a silence that had pooled around us like afternoon light.

"Yeah," Lacey said, looking down at her sneakers.

"Can you recite one for me?"

"Why?" Lacey asked, suspicion in her tone.

I shrugged.

"I just wanna hear one."

Lacey hesitated, but she walked backward toward the podium until she was standing behind it. She put her hands on either side, like a preacher about to deliver a sermon, I couldn't help thinking. She began with a voice more loud and clear than I had ever heard her use before, perhaps granted some sense of authority by her surroundings.

"I'm nobody! Who are you?
Are you nobody, too?
Then there's a pair of us—don't tell!
They'd—banish us, you know.

How dreary to be somebody!
How public, like a frog
To tell your name the livelong day
To an admiring bog!"

She finished with a broad, dramatic gesture and bowed deeply. I clapped fervently. There was something in Lacey's face that I recognized—a shine that I could feel come over me when I talked about scientific discoveries. Lacey must love English class. Or, well…

"How did you learn that?" I asked. "Does your mom teach you those?"

"Ha! No, my mom hates poetry," Lacey said. "I guess a lot of people do, actually."

"Oh, so your dad?"

"No," Lacey admitted. "I just…I just like it."

My curiosity got the better of me before I could help it. "Do they have you memorize Bible verses?"

"Yes," Lacey said. "They do."

Another uncomfortable pause sat between us.

"Do you think religious people are—unintelligent?" she asked. Lacey plopped down in the pew next to me. Her question held no hostility, only a stiffness that made me feel guilty for what I had said earlier.

"Not necessarily," I said quickly. "I just think that they can be, um, closed-minded."

Lacey nodded. When she asked her next question, it was in a low voice, as if she had already answered it for herself. "Do you think that I'm ignorant?"

I could not hide my surprise at this question. I ran a hand through my hair, which was starting to stick to my forehead from the lack of air conditioning in the chapel.

"I think that you're sheltered," I said matter-of-factly.

"Like Rapunzel."

"Right. And like Emily Dickinson."

"Who died without marrying," Lacey added.

"Is that the worst fate?" I laughed.

"Well, no, but she died alone—"

"I think the only really sad thing is to die without experiencing the world—without gaining some kind of perspective on things by going places you've never been and talking to people who aren't like you."

"Sometimes I feel like I was born at the wrong time," Lacey said. "Like maybe I was meant to be born in a different century."

"Not me," I said quickly. "I want to be as far into the future as possible."

"Why?" Lacey asked, genuine curiosity in her voice.

"Because," I said, "women have more rights now than we've had at any time in human history, and it's *still* not very much. I want to be part of making that future where women and other minorities can do whatever we want."

"I like that," Lacey said. I realized that she had probably never heard anyone say anything like this before. The people around her probably idolized Biblical times or the days where *men were men and smelled like horses* or whatever it is people say.

## *Lacey*

I wondered if Jo realized the way she waved her hands wildly when she spoke about anything she believed strongly—which was most things. I felt a pang of discomfort as Jo talked about not wanting to live in the past. I wondered if she thought that I was really narrow-minded. I wondered if I was.

"You know, people from all different walks of life come to Camp Lavender," I said when Jo slowed down. "Especially the counselors— some of them have absolutely wild stories from their lives before they became Christians."

Jo stood up from the pew and started pacing around the perimeter of the chapel. She seemed agitated, but I wasn't sure why.

"What does that mean—'all different walks of life'? Because from where I sit, both the counselors and the campers in this place have a lot in common."

"Like what?" I wanted to prove to her that I knew more about the world than she thought.

Jo enumerated her points on her fingers, still pacing. "Like their race, their gender, their politics probably, their religion, their class, their—their sexual orientation?"

I felt as if one hundred thoughts had swarmed into my head simultaneously. I looked at the person pacing in front of me and replayed what she had just said in my own mind. That the world was full of people unlike me was a thought that had, of course, occurred to me many times before. I was not one of those teenagers who had never used a computer before and thought that everyone milked their own cows or something. When I was younger, I would crouch on the staircase and listen to stories told by counselors at my parents' kitchen table, in hushed tones because they didn't want me to hear. These stories had been full of things like college parties, sexual encounters, substance abuse, and all manner of hedonism. I would creep back to bed during the moment my father would lay a hand on the young person's shoulder and pray with them. I had felt a sense of gratitude that I would not expose myself to such danger, equipped with the gift of knowing better. I was proud of myself for knowing better. Nothing that Jo was talking about had ever been brought up before—not like this.

"Lacey?"

Jo's voice cut through my reminiscence and snapped me back into reality. She had a worried expression on her face. This was the first time Jo had ever said my name.

"I'm sorry," I said. And then I said it again. "I'm sorry."

I shook my head, trying to sort one hundred new thoughts into new containers, but they were rolling around like marbles.

"I didn't mean to get all political on you, I just—"

"No, you didn't," I said. "I'm just…thinking."

Jo sat back down in the pew next to me and bounced her fists together nervously. "Are you thinking I'm kind of a bad influence?"

I smiled and put a palm to my forehead. "No," I said. "I'm thinking that I'm—I'm feeling like I'm kind of an idiot."

"You're not an idiot," Jo said. "You just—haven't been out there yet. And I think when you are, you're gonna be blown away."

"Like in a good way or a bad way?" I laughed, trying to sound light-hearted.

"Both."

❖

When I got back home that night, my head felt heavy with summer air and with a new feeling that I couldn't quite place. The last time I had inquired into the nature of my education, I was twelve years old. I was reading *Emily of New Moon* for the second time, which I had liked better than *Anne of Green Gables*. This second reading had prompted me to ask my mom why I didn't go to a regular school, like Emily did.

I walked up the stairs to my bedroom, trying to remember how my mother had answered me. I could remember only snippets of the conversation. My mom had said something about how they wanted me to be a critical thinker and a lover of learning and to have an individually curated education. This had all made sense to twelve-year-old me and had, in fact, given me a kind of inner glow of superiority to think that my parents didn't send me to some school to be taught by some stranger. They had selectively and personally dedicated themselves to honing my learning material for me specifically. I had thought of myself as exceptional.

I paced around my bedroom, stopping in front of my bookshelf, which was full of spine-broken paperbacks. I would often reread my favorites, like *Emily of New Moon*, *Little Women*, *Heidi*, and of course *The Chronicles of Narnia*. It occurred to me that this collection of literature had been curated for me before I had even been taught the alphabet. I narrowed my eyes at the spines, thinking of the words Jo had used to describe the similarities of the people surrounding me. Most of the protagonists of these books had those things in common, too. Some of them were poor, or had lost a parent, or had some other kind of obstacle to overcome, but they had the same striking similarities Jo had waved her hands about in the chapel, as if they were obvious. Because they *were* obvious. But only from the outside.

My thoughts wandered again to the counselors who sat at the kitchen table with my dad and sometimes my mom, if she wasn't running errands or making sandwiches for everyone. Most of them were only a year or two older than I was now. I had seen many of them break down in tears—I had seen all of them pray. The stories of their sinful lifestyles seemed to me now like confessions of wrongdoing, and my father like an Old Testament God who had the power to change the course of their lives by granting them forgiveness.

As these thoughts swelled and tumbled, I sat down on the edge of my bed. I heard the front door of the cabin open and close and heard the muffled voices of my parents. The tone of their conversation was strained.

"Lacey!"

It was my dad calling my name. I stood up.

"LACEY!"

His voice was louder now. It sounded scarier than normal. I opened my bedroom door and came down the stairs. My parents were at the kitchen table. Sitting between them was an orange water bottle.

## CHAPTER FOURTEEN

### *Lacey*

I stayed in my room until my parents left for breakfast at the dining hall. Rarely had I seen my father as angry as he had been the night before. I generally thought of him as soft-spoken and scholarly: a man who liked to expound on scripture and theology and a dedicated husband, father, and founder. Anytime I had met my father's requests with resistance or an abrasive tone, I had been wracked with guilt for upsetting someone so concerned with the best interests of those around him.

But last night was different.

My brain bursting with new thoughts, expanding at every moment until it felt like it was about to burst, I had come downstairs to see a stern face on my father that I barely recognized. My mother's lips had been tightly pressed together during the whole conversation and I had somehow felt that she might as well have been a hundred miles away. My dad had taken the lid off the orange water bottle and waved it under my nose.

"Do you know what that smell is?" he asked.

I didn't know—or I would not have known if I had not recognized the bottle and understood the context of the question. I had never had a drop of alcohol in my life and did not recognize the rich, sour scent. My parents, as far as I knew, had never consumed a drop of alcohol and certainly did not have it lying around the house. All I could do in the moment was to shake my head.

"This is *alcohol*," my father said, enunciating the word the way a detective might enunciate the word *murder* in a room full of suspects in a whodunnit movie.

"Where did it come from?" I asked.

"Lucky Duck found it by the pool when the counselors were cleaning up after capture the flag," my dad said. "It belongs to one of the campers."

"Wow," I said, feeling more and more as if I were playing out a scene in a play written by someone else. "What are you going to do?"

My dad shook his head. The shadows on his face seemed somehow harsh and angular in a way that I had never noticed before. I wondered if they had always been this way and I simply had not noticed until now. I felt as if something inside me that had once been soft and warm was getting harder and colder as he spoke.

"I am going to have a very serious talk with these young women about this at breakfast tomorrow," my dad said. He gave me a long look. "You are a young woman now, too," he said.

The hard cold thing got a little colder.

"I know that you have been spending more time with the campers this year. I am happy to see that, but I hope you understand that many of the young women who come to us are damaged. Many of them are in the world *and* of it."

I said nothing. My father went on.

"I hope that I have raised you to be able to discern between young women who are going to sharpen your iron with theirs and those who are going to try to pull you into their broken world because they want to break you, too."

He put a hand on my forearm. "I hope you are mature enough and secure enough in your faith to avoid bad influences."

I flinched. My father kept his eyes on me.

"Of course," I said, hoping that there was more of an earnest tone to my voice than a bitter one. My mom pushed back her chair and left the kitchen. My dad gave my arm another squeeze.

"Good girl," he said as he stood up from the kitchen table.

## *Jo*

At breakfast, Mr. Heller stood beneath the moose head to give the morning announcements as usual. He announced that today would include horseback riding, which made my stomach do an unpleasant flip as I raised a forkful of grits to my mouth. To say that I did not have a good relationship with horses was an understatement—I did not, in fact, have a good relationship even with the *idea* of horses. I glanced around the table and saw only glowing excitement. Even Funfetti pumped her fist in the air.

"Before I bless this meal," Mr. Heller said into the microphone, "I would like to ask a question."

I felt my chest and stomach tighten the way they did when anyone announced that they *had a question*. I looked down into my lap and pretended to fiddle with the zipper of my dark blue hoodie. It was cool enough in the dining hall, and our breakfasts were long enough that I had begun to bring it with me.

"Has anyone committed the scripture that we're studying to memory?" Mr. Heller asked.

My insides returned to their normal rhythm. I looked around the table, wondering if I was supposed to know that we were going to be asked to recite Bible verses from memory at breakfast, but before I could assess the facial expressions of the other cabin six girls, Rebekah had jumped to her feet. Mr. Heller gestured for her to approach the microphone.

In a solemn voice, she began, "Finally, brothers and sisters, whatever things are true, whatever things are honorable, whatever things are just, whatever things are pure, whatever things are lovely, whatever things are of good report: if there is any virtue and if there is anything worthy of praise, think about these things."

She took a breath, smiled, and added, "Philippians 4:8."

"Thank you, Rebekah."

Rebekah smiled at Mr. Heller and returned to her seat. I wondered if Camp Lavender might be the only place in Rebekah's life where she was popular and confident. Her pleasure at reciting a Bible verse impromptu was so sincere that even I had no desire to take it away from her. Mr. Heller approached the microphone again.

"Young ladies," he began, and my intestines tied themselves into knots again. "Camp Lavender is a place to connect with Jesus. It is a place to connect with other young women who are believers and Christ-followers."

I noticed that everyone looked a little uncomfortable now. The clink of forks and the morning chatter had ceased and everyone had turned in their seats to look at Mr. Heller while he spoke.

"I know that the temptations of the world can be so alluring," he continued. "but you have the beautiful gift this summer of being able to leave those things behind to focus on what is true and what is pure. So I want you to ask yourselves a question."

Mr. Heller raised something in the air. With a queasy feeling, I recognized it as Hayley's orange water bottle. I did not dare look at Hayley, but I could see out of the corner of my eye that Hayley stiffened in her seat.

"Ask yourselves," Mr. Heller said, "if you believe that drinking alcohol is pure. Is drinking alcohol honorable? Is drinking alcohol right? Is drinking alcohol lovely or excellent or praiseworthy?"

The silence after these questions lingered so long that I began to wonder if he was actually waiting for an answer.

"I am not going to ask who this belongs to," Mr. Heller went on. "But I am going to ask that you all reflect today on whether you believe that the things you are thinking about are pure, lovely, honorable, and praiseworthy. I can promise you that your answer will be no. Today is a good day to get right with yourself and with Jesus. If anyone wants to come talk to me about any of these things, I'll be on the dock today."

A pall hung over the dining hall as Mr. Heller exited the stage. I kept my eyes on my lap, where I zipped and unzipped the bottom of my hoodie. My hands shook a little. When at last I lifted my eyes, Hayley was looking directly at me. All she did was mouth the word *wow* and open her eyes wide. I grimaced at her, still fearful that Funfetti or Rebekah or anyone in the room would suspect me as the trespasser. There were at least two people who knew that I had been in possession of the orange water bottle, and one of them had probably been interrogated when it was found.

I pulled my hoodie up over my head and a piece of folded paper dropped out of it. I unfolded it and read:

*Are we just writing fiction*
*and reading it back to ourselves?*
*looking through microscopes*
*at tiny cells.*
*Are the constellations really*

*just kidding themselves?*
*And even if we are*
*does it matter at all*
*is it all just chaos*
*does it all just fall*
*around us*
*as we spin*
*endlessly*
*into the void?*

I looked around, wondering when this piece of paper had been dropped into my hoodie. Where was she? I was seized with fear that the water bottle incident might have caused Mr. Heller to send Lacey away or to lock her in her room like the real Rapunzel. I told myself that I was being paranoid and there was no reason for them to connect it to Lacey. I imagined throwing stones at her window, and the image of a long mop of unruly dirty blond curls cascading toward me made me smile. As the campers finished breakfast and cleared their tables, the chatter was subdued to subtle murmurs. I knew logically that the other campers were not talking about me—that they did not know that I had been one of the sinners to drink contraband wine from a water bottle by the pool. And yet, I felt something unpleasant and familiar twisting around inside me.

Hayley grabbed my elbow on the way to Bible study.

"You didn't tell anyone else about the—water bottle—did you?" she asked under her breath.

"No," I lied, telling myself that it was a half-truth. I hadn't *told* anyone, but I had been *seen* by someone. But Hayley would be horrified and jump to all kinds of panicky conclusions if she knew that.

"Good," Hayley said. "Well, now you owe me a bottle of Nate's Grapes *and* a new water bottle since I can't go claim that one."

"Fair enough, but how am I supposed to get those things?"

"I drove myself here," Hayley said.

My eyes widened.

"You have your own car?"

"Yep, and it's parked in the counselors' lot."

Hayley sounded proud.

"So what do we do?"

"Well," Hayley said, flipping her hair over her shoulder, "I thought maybe you would want to come into town with me during our free time this afternoon. Aren't you itching to get the hell out of here for a little while before they start burning us at the stake?"

I couldn't prevent a laugh. Hayley and I were straggling at the back of the group and Funfetti looked over her shoulder at us with a small frown. I thought about Hayley's proposal. All I had to do was get through Bible study, horseback riding, and lunch, and I would get a break from Camp Lavender.

"What, do you have plans with the preacher's daughter or something?" Hayley jabbed an elbow into my side. "Surely you two can take a break from each other for *one* day."

Sweat prickled at the back of my neck, as it always did while cabin six trudged around looking for a picnic table at which to convene.

"Let's do it," I said resolutely. "Let's get the hell out of here."

"Good girl," Hayley said with a broad smile.

# CHAPTER FIFTEEN

## *Jo*

I strongly preferred riding a bike to riding a horse when it came to ways of getting around. As Funfetti led cabin six to the stables, I cast about for an excuse to go back to the cabin. I was not the kind of girl who was obsessed with horses and parchment paper and princesses or who believed that I had been born in the wrong century. On the contrary, I wished that I had been born even later, when I could have become a meteorologist on Mars. The chances of that happening in my lifetime seemed slim.

Rebekah, on the other hand, and a blond cabin six girl named Isabelle, seemed utterly giddy at the prospect of riding horses.

"Wouldn't it be cool," Isabelle said, "if they'd let us do archery *while* we ride the horses? It would be like *Lord of the Rings* or something."

"*Yes*," Rebekah said, holding a hand to her chest. "We could be like the riders of Rohan."

I raised an eyebrow, but even Hayley seemed pleased by this flight of fancy.

"The only thing from *Lord of the Rings* I want to ride is Aragorn," Hayley said. The other girls gasped, then giggled.

"That is *so* inappropriate," Rebekah chided, even while a smile played at the corners of her mouth.

"Come on, you're telling me you've never lain in bed thinking about Aragorn and gotten a *little* turned on? Even you have to have fantasies sometime."

This was aimed at Rebekah, but I could feel the energy of the group rising. Funfetti was just enough ahead to be out of earshot, deep in discussion with a girl named Lindsay, focused on leading us up the dirt trail to our destination, and probably too worn out from the heat to focus on monitoring the conversation of the rest of the cabin. I knew from experience that wherever teenage girls are gathered, it is only a matter of time before the subject of *boys* arises. I said a silent prayer of gratitude that Lacey was not here for this discussion. I just…didn't want to know.

"Fantasies?" Isabelle said. "You mean, like…*sexual* fantasies?"

This word was said almost in a whisper, like a tacit taboo that might echo through the pine trees and find its way to God's ears more easily at Camp Lavender.

"What about you, Kristen? You look like someone who knows how to have fun," Hayley asked the other girl in the group. Kristen had effortless blond hair and always had a choker on. The religious weight of Camp Lavender, which hung so heavily on me, seemed neither to faze nor to trouble her. She looked like someone whose mom had little inspirational quotes like *Live Laugh Love* strewn around the house every few feet.

"Ha! Thanks a lot," Kristen said breezily. She grinned at the other girls. "I do, actually."

Rebekah clapped a hand over her mouth. Isabelle waited, wide-eyed. Hayley smiled. I held my breath.

"I just don't think Jesus cares if my boyfriend and I get to third base, you know what I mean?" Kristen said. Hayley gave her a high five.

Rebekah folded her arms. "I don't know about y'all, but I want to save everything for my future husband. And I think he'll be really glad I did."

The rest of us exchanged glances, sizing each other up, waiting for someone to respond.

"Last year," Isabelle said, breaking the silence, "Lucky Duck said at a worship night that he had—had been with someone when he was in high school and that now he regrets it because his future wife is going to feel less special when he tells her."

Rebekah gave a firm nod and let out a knowing sigh. "That's why it's important for us to be careful with how we talk—and how we present ourselves." Rebekah gave a meaningful look to Hayley and

Kristen, the hems of whose shorts did not come anywhere near their knees. I looked down at the ground, but a smile flashed across my face knowing that Rebekah would never reproach me for being a temptation to boys.

"We dress like this because we go to *public school*," Hayley said dramatically, "where all the heathens go. We've been *corrupted.*"

I pressed my lips together to keep from laughing as Rebekah pulled Isabelle with her to walk ahead of the group.

"Why do you taunt her like that?" I asked Hayley when they were out of earshot.

"Because it's fun and I'm bored and because if I don't teach her not to be a little prick, no one will."

"She's going to be up all night praying for your soul," Kristen added, and the three of us laughed. Rebekah and Isabelle had caught up with Funfetti and Lindsay; Rebekah was pulling at Funfetti's arm, speaking close to her ear. Funfetti looked over her shoulder at us and Hayley let out a groan.

"Oh no, now I'm in for another *talking-to*," she said.

"I wonder if she would freak out if she knew that you haven't even slept with anyone," Kristen said casually to Hayley, who elbowed Kristen and looked at me.

"That's not the point," she said. "Everyone at my school is just ugly."

The barn was in view and my stomach knotted itself again. A counselor in the barn showed us to our horses, most of whom looked old and tired and overheated. There was just something unnerving about standing next to a creature who could seriously injure you and who didn't know you at all.

"Please be cool," I muttered to the horse that had been assigned to me, digging my foot into one of the stirrups and swinging my other leg over the saddle. "I don't want to be here any more than you do."

Once we were all on our horses, we were lined up with one counselor at the front and one at the back. I had ended up behind Lindsay and in front of Rebekah. I felt claustrophobic and sorry for the horses who had to trudge around with campers on their backs all summer long when they would probably rather just be playing in a field or whatever it is horses do. I worried that my horse could sense my discomfort and resented me, so I gave its neck a small pat with my hand.

❖

The first mile was calm enough. But then I was flying before I knew it, holding on for dear life, and one hundred percent clueless about how to get the horse to stop. Maybe it had been just the rustle of a leaf or a twig snapping at the wrong time, or maybe I unwittingly gave the horse some kind of command that made it believe that I *wanted* it to break away from the line and tear across the field at breakneck speed. It wasn't until Rebekah and her horse caught up with me that things finally started to slow down.

Rebekah called to the horse and did something that made the horse want to calm down. I had somehow managed not to fall off when the horse had taken off, but now I slid out of the saddle and into the grass and collapsed, my knees wobbling.

"Are you okay?"

Rebekah was dismounting her horse.

I held up a shaky thumbs-up from the grass. "I think so. I just… don't like horses."

Rebekah gave me an amused smile. "They don't seem to like you either."

I stood up and brushed myself off, and looked over my arms and legs to make sure I hadn't somehow been injured.

"I'm okay," I said, "except for, like, psychologically."

"We can just walk the rest of the trail. I'll lead the horses."

This was a kind offer, and I was in no position to refuse it. Rebekah gathered the bridle of her horse in one hand and of mine in the other.

"Thank you," I breathed. "I will respectfully stay six feet away so I don't offend him anymore than I already have."

Rebekah laughed.

We set off in silence, accompanied by the two horses, and a merciful breeze started to play around us, sending the grass into a frenzy and cooling the backs of our necks. The horses flicked their tails, keeping the flies away, and I thought that if I could just go on walks *with* horses, it might actually be pretty pleasant. It was the whole riding business that felt so unnecessary.

"What's Jo short for?" Rebekah asked. I was surprised by this question, but assumed that Rebekah was making awkward small talk.

"Josephine," I answered.

"Why do you go by Jo?"

"Um," I furrowed my brow, "I just like it, I guess. People at school have been calling me Jo forever."

"What about at church?"

I looked ahead of us to see how far behind we were. I could not see the rest of the group, and I began to wish that one of the counselors had come to get me.

"Yeah, there too."

"What kind of church do you go to?"

"Um, it's a Catholic church."

Rebekah's silence told me that this was somehow not the answer she was looking for. I braced myself for an impending discussion of theology in which I was going to have to feign interest and investment.

"It's a boyish name."

"What?"

"Jo."

"Oh, yeah, I guess so."

Rebekah looked at me out of the corner of her eye.

"Do you wish you were a boy?"

I wished that if there were a God, she would kindly open up the ground and let me sink into it so that I did not have to finish this conversation. I considered the possibility of remounting my horse and setting off galloping into the trees to start a new life. The question Rebekah had asked, so invasive and sinister, hung in the air and seemed somehow to kill the breeze that had been providing us with a little relief from the oppressive heat.

"Sometimes," I answered, maintaining a neutral tone. "Don't you?"

"No," Rebekah said firmly. "I'm very happy to be a woman."

"You don't ever wish, I don't know, that you didn't have to wear a bra or shave your legs?"

Rebekah seemed aghast even to have the question put to her.

"Those things are inconvenient, of course," she answered, "but the joy of being a woman of the Lord is so much greater."

"Sure," I said, hoping I sounded agreeable.

"Josephine," Rebekah said, coming to a stop with a horse on either side of her. "The Lord has laid it on my heart to ask you something."

I looked around her for any sign of escape, then at Rebekah, waiting.

"Are you a homosexual?"


By the time cabin six had been guided back to the stables, and then to the cabin for showers, and then released for free time, I felt like I hadn't taken a breath in hours. Hayley wandered casually to my bunk and asked if I still felt like going into town.

"Yes, God, please," was all I could say.

Hayley gave me a nod and gestured for me to follow her, saying audibly enough for the other girls in the cabin to hear, "Let's go to the Snack Shack and then down to the dock to go fishing." I was grateful that I did not have to work up some clever lie or maneuver because Hayley already had a plan in place.

The sunshine felt almost unbearable as I followed Hayley to the parking lot, where a small white Mazda responded to the pressing of a button in Hayley's hand. Despite the sunshade Hayley had put up, getting into the car felt like closing ourselves into an oven. I recoiled as I touched the metal on my seat belt and drew my breath in sharply. Hayley turned the key in the ignition and blasted the air conditioning. I leaned forward and put my face in front of one of the air vents, willing the sharpness of the cold air to calm me down. I finally took a deep breath as Hayley backed the car out of her parking spot.

"Are they going to realize that we're gone?" I asked.

"Not unless we don't make it back by dinner," Hayley said. She turned on the speakers in her car, and a song that I recognized wafted through the speakers.

"Is this the Lyrical Ballads?"

Hayley nodded and I saw a smile steal across her face.

"Of course you have good taste in music," she said.

"Don't sound so impressed."

Hayley laughed.

I ran a hand through my hair, bending my head to let the air conditioning run over my scalp. The relief of being in an enclosed space, moving steadily away from Camp Lavender, brought a guttural groan out of me.

"So," Haley said tentatively, "what the hell happened back there?"

I groaned again.

"Not ready?" Hayley asked.

"Not ready."

Hayley simply nodded and turned up the music. For all her show of brazen bravado, I was beginning to realize that Hayley was an incredibly intuitive person. Whether she used this power for good or for evil, I was not yet sure. In my ordinary life, I kept an internal vow to get to know the contours of someone's wants and motivations before revealing any of my own. I had learned the lesson too many times to let my guard down without some emotional collateral. But in this particular case, I was desperate for an ally, and for now at least, I seemed to have one.

"Rebekah asked me if I was a homosexual."

Hayley's jaw dropped. "No. Fucking. Way."

"Yep."

I continued to hold my head to the air conditioning, not looking up.

"She did not say *homosexual.*"

"She did."

"Wow. Wow, wow," Hayley repeated, shaking her head, as if to herself. "No wonder you looked so pale and shaky. I thought it was because you fell off your horse."

"Only metaphorically speaking."

I braced myself for the inevitable next questions. *What did you say? Are you?*

"Dude, did you freak out?" was all Hayley said.

"Um," I leaned back in the passenger seat and put my hands over my eyes, "I definitely panicked."

"You said no, right?"

The careful phrasing of this question did not escape me.

"I said, 'What makes you think that?'"

"Okay," Hayley sighed. "And she said?"

"She said that God had *laid it on her heart* that I *struggled with same-sex attraction* and that she wanted to pray over me."

Hayley let out a noise somewhere between a scream and a groan.

"And then she did."

I saw Hayley's knuckles tighten around the steering wheel.

"Are you...like...okay?"

I considered this question. It seemed simple enough, and yet I felt at an utter loss to answer it. But my body answered for me. I gave a small shrug and then a slight shake of my head.

"I want to go home," I said quietly.

Hayley's face wore a knowing grimace.

## CHAPTER SIXTEEN

### *Lacey*

I could not wait to get to Dr. Dan's office that day. All I wanted was to be away from everyone—and to check Slant. I didn't want to be home when my dad got home from breakfast and I didn't want to go horseback riding with cabin six. I just wanted to think.

The steadying presence of Dr. Dan immediately made me feel more at ease and less like the ground was shifting rapidly under me. At the sight of me, Dr. Dan leaned back in his chair and put his arms behind his head.

"Well, well, look who finally decided to show her face again."

"Sorry, I guess I've just been so busy developing social intelligence I haven't had time to stop by." I flashed Dr. Dan a smile and sank into the chair opposite his desk.

"Speaking of which, your clumsy little friend was in here the other day asking to use my computer—she must have gotten that idea from you."

My head spun toward Dr. Dan, but I tried to keep my tone casual. "Oh?"

"Yeah, I guess she needed to check her email or something. Crazy how your folks expect teenage girls not to talk on the phone for six weeks."

"I don't even have a phone," I replied.

"That doesn't surprise me."

It occurred to me then that Dr. Dan was a completely separate person from my parents, with his own thoughts and opinions about them, about me, and about Camp Lavender. As one of the only adults beside my parents whom I had known for the majority of my pubescent years, I had always seen Dr. Dan as somehow an extension of my parents, aligned with them on every thought and feeling.

"They'll have to get me one before I go to college in the fall." I said this as a statement, but I eyed Dr. Dan for his reaction to it.

He raised his eyebrows. "Not if they send you to community college," he said.

"What? Why would they do that?" I did not keep a casual tone this time.

Dr. Dan steepled his fingers together, taking longer to respond than I had anticipated. After a moment, he simply said, "They just seem to prioritize keeping you close."

I nodded slowly. "You don't think I'll get into NYU or—"

"That's not what I'm saying," Dr. Dan cut in. "I just think that Clyde and Marsha might—*encourage* you to stay closer to home."

I leaned back in my chair and crossed my arms. I stared at my sneakers. My mother had bought me these sneakers on a trip into town. I had liked them because they were made of light blue canvas and had white laces. Now, they were stained with the inevitable orange dirt of Camp Lavender that invaded everything with which it came into contact. Now, I wondered if there was something about these shoes that would tell a knowing observer that I didn't have a cell phone or a driver's license or a locker with my name on it.

"Can I use the computer?"

"Be my guest."

Dr. Dan gestured to his desk chair and leaned against the wall to consult a crossword puzzle. I logged into Slant and typed up the poem I had slipped into Jo's hoodie and posted it. Then I opened up a new tab and searched *Austin poetry slam July*. The results popped up immediately. The poetry slam was at the Ballroom at Spider House, whatever that was, on July ninth. Signing up was easier than I had expected—all they needed was a name and an email address, both of which I had. I checked my email and saw the confirmation. Something like fireworks went off in my stomach. As of yet, I had no idea how I was going to get there, what I was going to tell my parents, or what I was going to perform. But none of that mattered right now.

I returned to my Slant page and opened up my chat with *@MoonBoi11*.

@HellerHighwater says: *I'll be at the Austin poetry slam. Gonna try some new stuff out. Maybe I'll see you there.*

I logged out of Slant and closed the window. I turned to Dr. Dan, who was looking at his crossword puzzle with a furrowed brow. I decided that I was going to try something.

"Do you think you could take me into town?"

## *Jo*

I looked out the window and saw that we were pulling into a small town—the kind of quaint, timeless place that presents itself between stretches of fields full of cows in small-town Texas. Hayley was pulling into an angled parking spot in front of what I presumed to be the only coffee shop the small town had to offer.

"You drink coffee?" Hayley asked.

"Actually, yeah, but I don't have—"

"I'll buy you one."

Hayley unfolded her sunshade over the windshield and turned off the car. I noticed, as I got out of the car, that I felt a little lighter—a little more at ease. I attributed this to the distance between myself and Camp Lavender, but my mind wandered to Lacey. Lacey would notice that I was gone. Would she be troubled by my absence? I thought about Lacey's poem, folded into the front pocket of my hoodie, which was now tied around my waist.

"Is there a bookstore here?"

"Yeah, but it probably doesn't have a lot of books you'd want to read."

"Can we go there after coffee?"

Hayley flashed me a perfect smile—the kind of smile that orthodontists brag about in brochures. The door chimed as we entered the coffee shop. It had the antique charm of an old-fashioned soda shop, with a big window in the front, ice cream chilling behind a glass counter, and red barstools lining the counter. There was even a jukebox in the corner, and a tinny Frank Sinatra song mingled with the smell of espresso and transported me entirely away from the events of the morning.

Hayley ordered two iced vanilla lattes and paid with a heavy silver credit card that had the name *Sean Hathaway* embossed on it. She led me to the high counter in the front window, where the stools had metal bars at the bottom for the patrons' feet to rest on if they couldn't reach the floor, which mine couldn't.

"So," I said, feeling the sudden pressure of spending time with someone one-on-one outside the confines of the camp structure. "Have you been coming to camp for a long time?"

"Oh, yeah," Hayley said, bending down to take a sip of her latte. I took a long sip and let the flavor of the iced latte flood the contours of my mouth. It tasted like the color lavender, gentle and sweet and soft around the edges.

"My parents have been sending me here every summer to get me out of the way so they can go on their real vacations."

"What kind of vacations?"

"Italy, Greece, cruises in the Caribbean…"

This confirmed my suspicions.

"Why don't you go with them?"

"Because—" Hayley started the sentence like she was at the top of a hill on a bike and about to ride down very quickly, but halted and cut her eyes toward me. I neither asked for her to continue nor led the conversation in another direction. I just took another sip of my latte. Hayley rolled her head all the way around her neck, as if giving into some inevitable reality. "They say it's because I need to be around other Christian girls, but honestly I think it's because I'm an inconvenience to have around."

She shrugged and returned to her latte, but I could feel the heaviness of these words. I knew it all too well. "You've never been here before." Hayley stated it as a fact, but it had the hue of a question.

"I usually spend summers working, but my aunt paid for me to come here this summer."

"Did you do something bad?"

"Depends on who you ask."

Hayley flashed her perfect smile again. "It's always the quiet ones who get into the most trouble."

She tucked a strand of blond hair behind her ear, and when her hand came back down, it rested on my forearm with all the casual intimacy of two people who had been close for a long time. I took a sip of my coffee, trying to move as naturally as I could. And I wondered if my heartbeat was loud enough for Hayley to hear.

## *Lacey*

I had only ridden in Dr. Dan's red convertible once before. It was the kind of car you would see in old films, in which the romantic male lead with the chiseled jawline would show up for a heist or a party or a meeting with an important businessman. I felt like I should be wearing vintage sunglasses and driving gloves as I slid into the passenger seat. Dr. Dan had not asked whether he should check with my parents before bringing me into town—had allowed me the small mercy of unchecked freedom and simply pulled up a list of movie times and titles that would be showing at the only movie theater in downtown Gladwall. I had chosen *Polite Society* and Dr. Dan had purchased our tickets. It was the kind of movie I had first seen with my dad—full of witty banter, flowing champagne, and stunning costumes. My parents had raised me on the Hays Code Hollywood era, brimming with highbrow characters in black and white, who would do no more than hint at the indiscretions of the lower class in which married couples slept in side-by-side twin beds.

It would still be many years before I would come to understand the impact of this carefully curated film library on the way that I carried myself through the world. When we arrived at the theater, Dr. Dan showed our tickets and purchased a large soda for each of us and a large popcorn with extra butter. The theater was old, but well air-conditioned, and I sank into the cushioned seat of the theater with a sense of relief.

My favorite feeling was the one that settled over me when the lights in the theater went down and the only source of input was a giant glowing screen, larger than life and all-consuming. No longer was I aware of my hair, my face, my body, my age, my location—I was Katharine Hepburn in an elegant dressing gown in 1940: wealthy, educated, unconventionally attractive.

When the lights came up at the end of two hours, I found myself unwilling to return to normal life. I wasn't ready to go back to the sweaty, prosaic world of Camp Lavender, to the nuanced problems of the modern world. Perhaps Dr. Dan could sense this, because the next thing he said was, "Ice cream?"

For a moment, I basked in the warmth of the sun as we stepped out of the cool, dark theater. Moments later, my familiar resentment for it swept in.

"Maybe I was born in the wrong place," I said. "And at the wrong time."

"Where and when do you wish you were?" asked Dr. Dan, bemused.

"New York City—1940. Or Paris in the 1920s."

Dr. Dan put his hands in the pockets of his shorts. "You want to go to dinner parties and fall in love with Spencer Tracy?"

I laughed. "Everything just seemed so new then. People were sharp and sophisticated and full of ideas. But if I lived back then…I would want to be a man."

Dr. Dan paused. "Why? You're not full of ideas now?"

"What ideas can you have when you spend your whole life living in the same place doing the same thing?"

"Fair enough," Dr. Dan said.

"And if I lived back then, no one would listen to my ideas unless I were a man."

"But you'd get to be an elegant socialite," Dr. Dan countered.

I grimaced at him.

"Anyway, this summer has been better, hasn't it?" Dr. Dan asked. "You made a friend this year…what's-her-name."

"Well, yeah…" I said.

"What *is* her name?" Dr. Dan asked again.

I felt an unfamiliar sensation as I answered the question, the name sticking in my throat like it was a secret that I wanted to keep to myself.

"It's Jo."

And there she was. I stopped on the sidewalk and stood utterly still, like a deer by the side of the road waiting for someone to pass. We had arrived at the front of the coffee shop and I saw the unmistakable form of Jo through the large front window, sitting next to Hayley Hathaway. And Hayley's hand was resting on Jo's arm. She was laughing at something Jo was saying and Jo was smiling, taking a sip of the coffee in her other hand.

I backed up a step and almost ran into Dr. Dan, who looked up and saw the tableau in front of us.

"Wait, isn't that—"

"Yeah, actually, let's go," I heard myself say, as if I were listening to myself from the other side of a wall. "I can't—I don't—want to talk to them."

"Why?"

But I was already walking quickly the other way on the sidewalk.

"I hate that girl," I spat out.

"Who? Jo?"

"No, the other one."

"What did she—"

"She's just—she's—"

My sentence tapered into an angry noise.

"Okay," Dr. Dan said. "We can go."

## CHAPTER SEVENTEEN

### *Jo*

Hayley was right about the bookstore. It was full of porcelain figurines, Bible verse bookmarks, and Christian self-help books with shiny-haired women on the covers. I scanned around for the section that might contain empty notebooks. I wandered the bookstore slowly, taking in deep breaths. The bookstore smelled like a rich shade of mahogany. It was comforting to know that, regardless of the ideology of their contents, bookstores almost all had this familiar smell.

Hayley departed for the fantasy section, which contained thick books with rich jewel-tone covers and dark-haired protagonists. I noticed a section at the back of the store with the word *Journals* printed on a card above one of the shelves. I meandered toward it, my pulse quickening inexplicably. Many of the journals had kitschy gimmicks to them—inspirational quotes printed at the top, journaling prompts, sections set aside on each page for gratitude. I scanned them carefully, remembering the green notebook I had seen briefly with Lacey and wondering where it had come from. She seemed exactly like the kind of person who was very particular about the notebooks she wrote in. I smiled to myself, hearing Lacey's voice in my head giving some impassioned rant about the spacing of the lines or the ability of the notebook to lie flat while she wrote in it or the bendy-ness of the cover.

Then my eyes came to rest on a journal. It looked like a hardcover book, and were it not for the lack of title and author on the cover, I might have mistaken it for a novel. For a moment, I thought it might even be a mislaid Bible. Then I saw that there was a quill embossed on the black cover. The edges of the pages were gilded with gold. I picked it up and let it fall open in my hand. The pages were smooth and matte, cream colored with widely spaced faint lines. This was the one. I checked the price tag, knowing that it wouldn't make a difference either way, but wincing at the $14.99. I looked for Hayley, who would probably be willing to lend me the money for it, but I would have no way of paying it back.

I decided not to overthink this. I tucked the journal into the waistband of my shorts and fluffed my baggy T-shirt over it. I reasoned that the moral weight of this theft was nothing compared with my other supposed sins. If I was more than worm food, I was already destined to burn. So why not have a little fun on the way down?

"I'm ready to go."

I tried to sound nonchalant and Hayley did not seem to have any desire to linger.

"We just have one more stop," she said, pushing out the door of the bookstore. I breathed a sigh of relief when there was no one chasing after us. I followed Hayley to the convenience store, where no one checked her ID when she purchased two bottles of Nate's Grapes and a bag of salt and vinegar potato chips. We carried our contraband to the car and reveled in our stolen freedom as we drove back to Camp Lavender with the windows rolled down.

## Lacey

My parents were out of the house when I arrived home, a small mercy for which I was grateful. I needed time to think. I had been home alone occasionally growing up, but my mother was usually in the house somewhere, folding laundry, paying bills, or preparing a meal. I liked the feeling of being at home with her, but in separate rooms, each aware of the other's presence, but focused on our own tasks. I found it simultaneously comforting and intimidating to observe my mother's dedicated and flawless homemaking abilities. I admired them, as I had been taught to, but found myself resistant to the training that I would need to emulate my mother.

I paced around downstairs, reveling in the freedom of moving around my living space unobserved. I replayed the image of Jo and Hayley in the coffee shop, trying over and over again to analyze the crack that seemed to split open in my chest at that exact moment. No matter how many times I rewound it, I couldn't make sense of it.

Now I found myself wandering into my parents' bedroom. Over the years, I had retained very little curiosity about them. I had heard their stories, the edges worn smooth from the erosion of retelling, and had long ago run out of questions that they were willing to answer. Occasionally, but rarely, my father would surprise me with a new story from his past—something from his hedonistic musician days, the edges still sharp from lack of use. I would listen with rapture, picturing a world more saturated with sound and color than the one we inhabited now.

I found myself in front of my mother's bedside table, stacked with nonfiction books about Biblical womanhood, with her reading glasses perched on top. This stack lay generally undisturbed either by me or my mother, more aspirational than habitual. But now, as I gazed at it, I noticed something beside the didactic titles—an envelope, the edge barely showing from beneath the pile. Whether it was intuition, suspicion, or simply idle curiosity that drew me to it, I found myself gently moving aside the stack of books, careful not to disturb them, and drawing out the envelope. When I saw that it was addressed to Lacey Heller, it felt like my heart stopped and then started again at double the pace.

Abandoning my former caution, I opened the flap of the envelope, the seal of which had already been broken. Inside I found a typed letter, sent from New York University. It began "Dear Ms. Heller, We are pleased to inform you—"

I dropped it to the floor, my hand shaking. I dropped down beside it and picked it up again, one shaking hand over my mouth and one clutching the letter, trying to steady it until the words became legible. After letting my eyes race over the official-looking words over and over, my eyes wandered to the date at the top left hand corner of the letter. It was dated March fourteenth.

❖

## *Jo*

I had forgotten that it was Wednesday and worship night again. I sat through dinner impatiently, anxious to run back to the cabin, where I had stashed the notebook in my duffel bag. I glanced around the dining hall while I pushed my mashed potatoes around my plate. I knew logically that I would definitely be able to find Lacey the next day if I didn't see her tonight. I would be able to find her at breakfast, or spot her during Bible study, or at the very least find her during their afternoon free time. But patience had never been my strong suit, and now that I had possession of the notebook, it felt like I would explode if I couldn't get it to Lacey as soon as possible. I tried to convince myself that there was plenty of time, but the urgency vibrated through my body as I waited for dinner to end.

Worship night dragged on even from the stage, where I found myself for the second time, feeling the heat and energy of the room swell with the chord changes of each song. But Lacey wasn't there. I remembered what she had said about staying away from camp. Maybe she had grown bored or irritated and she would spend the rest of the summer lurking like a shadow, weaving in and out of whatever camp spots were not occupied by rowdy campers.

I thought and overthought about Lacey as the evening wound down and cabin six made its way back to home base and went through the mechanics of evening hygiene. When Funfetti turned the lights out at ten p.m., I lay in my bunk bed with my eyes wide open, willing them to adjust to the darkness faster. My thoughts whirled around in circles like dancers on a shiny ballroom floor. I blamed the iced latte for setting them in motion. I listened to the breathing of the other five girls, trying to detect the exact moment when it became rhythmic in the way that waking breathing never is.

I felt as if I had been lying still for hours, although my watch told me it had been about forty-five minutes, when I dragged my duffel bag out from under my bed and pulled out the notebook, pen, and a small flashlight. I grabbed my hoodie from the foot of the bed and my sneakers from the floor and rose as slowly and noiselessly as I possibly could. I paused, listening to the rhythm of the room. As far as I could tell, it had not changed.

Opening the cabin door was the hard part. I had plenty of practice with this process—the twist of the knob and the aching slowness of its release once you had stepped to the other side. I was almost an expert in passing in and out of rooms undetected. But I also knew from experience that one wrong move could cost you more than whatever you were sneaking around for was worth. The look in Natalie's mom's eyes when I had gotten to the last creaky step at the bottom of the stairs had made me wish that I had never been born. Even now, as the memory loomed before me in the dark, I shut my eyes, trying to block out the image and the cold nausea that had washed over me then and now.

But I had already decided that, if worse came to worse, I would just tell Funfetti that I was going outside to get some air and pray. I knew that if there were some kind of higher power, they probably did not appreciate being used as an alibi for illicit activity, but hopefully it would not come to that anyway. I had reached the cabin door, and once again, I paused, holding my own breath so that I could hear the breathing of the room. Slowly, I twisted the handle of the cabin door. It opened without a sound. With a single motion, I stepped to the other side, turned, and slid the door back into place. I inhaled silently as I slowly released the handle, not fully letting it go until it had silently clicked into place.

When I turned, I was struck by the stunning beauty of the night as if it were an arrow to my chest. The sky was the kind of deep blue that somehow seemed richer and darker than black. The stars pinned it in place and the full moon lit the night in a way that a cityscape would never allow. I lowered my gaze slowly, savoring the decadence of the scene before me and my aloneness with it. The pine trees cut a silhouette across the sky and the other cabins dotted the surrounding area with a kind of arbitrary spacing as if someone had shaken them and rolled them like dice.

I zipped up my dark blue hoodie, but kept my shoes in my hands as I descended the porch steps. The pine needles were both soft and sharp under my feet and gave way easily to the earth beneath them. Were it not for my compulsory exile here, I thought, this would have been a place I delighted to find myself. I sat down at a picnic table outside of the ring of cabins and slid on my shoes. No one had come out of cabin six, or any cabin. I stood and turned, looking at everything around me and reassuring myself that I knew where I was going. Technically, I had not been there before, but I felt sure that I could find my way.

## *Lacey*

I said a polite good night to my parents when they came into my bedroom to check on me after they got home. I had told them that I was very tired and ready to go to sleep and had shut my door and turned off my bedroom light before collapsing onto my bed. I lay there, adrenaline coursing through my body, until I heard my parents' bedroom door shut. Unable to lie still anymore, I stood up and paced around the confines of my bedroom like a caged tiger.

I had felt angry before. When I was young, my frustration would boil over like a pot on a stove and I would feel the uncontrolled anger spill over and run everywhere. My mother had told me that my manner was unladylike and my father had told me that my tone was disrespectful. Their cold shoulders had chilled the burning edges of my emotions until I learned to keep them contained to the four walls of my own room. There, I would write them down. There, I would pull the covers over my face and hold my breath until it felt like my heart was going to explode. Now it felt as if nothing could possibly deflate the rage swelling inside me.

For the first time, I thought of running away.

A *crack* against my bedroom window jolted me out of my rumination. It sounded like an insect hitting my window, but with much more force than I had ever heard. I jumped up from the bed and opened the curtain. At first, I could not make anything out in the darkness below. Then I saw her. She was just a faint shadow, moving around the ground below in a way that I almost could have mistaken for a raccoon or an armadillo. But I could see the outline of a dark blue hoodie with the hood drawn over her head.

Nothing like this had ever happened to me before.

I knew that I wouldn't wake my parents and I hardly cared about anything else. I slipped on my sneakers and glanced down at my outfit—blue and green plaid pajama pants and a faded yellow Slush Baby T-shirt. I didn't bother to change. I crept down the stairs and out of the cabin as smoothly and silently as a piece of paper slipped under a door. When I rounded the corner of the cabin, Jo was waiting for me, holding out her arms in a dramatic gesture. In a rasping whisper, she said, "Good evening, Rapunzel."

"What the heck are you doing here?"

"That is hardly a polite greeting," Jo said with mock formality.

"I'm sorry," I said, echoing her tone by bowing from the waist. "Good evening, sire. What the heck are you doing here?"

"Follow me," Jo said as she started off toward the lake.

I took a deep breath of the night air once we were out of sight of the cabin. A breeze that could almost be described as cool caressed my cheek like a courtly lover, cooling the heat of my rage until it was just an ember glowing in the dark.

"You were nowhere to be seen today," Jo said, not looking behind her. I was amused that Jo was taking the lead so confidently, leading me through the stomping grounds of my childhood as if she had something new to show me.

"Did you miss me?" I teased.

"Well, people were saying maybe you had been locked up in your tower for good after the *great water bottle incident.*"

I felt Jo smile in the darkness.

"Well, tell *people* that I still have the keys to the castle. I was just…doing my own thing today."

I remembered the movie. The coffee shop. The hand on the arm. The laughing.

"And what about you?" I asked, unwilling to divulge the extent of my knowledge.

"I too was on my own journey today," Jo said, and I found myself wincing at the excitement in her voice. Then Jo was stopping, not at the dock, but amidst a cluster of trees that lined the pathway around the lake. I knew this spot well—the picnic table that had a perfect view of the lake. The one where Silly Putty had led me through that lifesaving prayer when I was seven years old.

"Please, sit," Jo said, gesturing politely as if this were her personal dining table and I was a guest at her dinner party.

"Why thank you," I said, lifting the pant legs of my pajama pants in a feigned curtsy. I sat and folded my hands, expectant. My body still buzzed with adrenaline, now with a new element mixed in, both sickening and sweet. Jo sat opposite me and, with great ceremony, unzipped the front of her hoodie. She drew something out and laid it on the table before me.

With a start, I realized that it was a journal.

"For me?"

"For you."

"Why?"

"Because you need one."

I lifted the notebook off the table and felt, almost reluctantly, my irritation and anger shed off of me like a winter coat. The notebook was beautiful—black, hardcover, etched with a quill pen. I opened it to the middle and ran my palm down the smooth pages. It had the kind of lines I preferred—spaced wide apart and faint enough to let only the letters show once filled.

"Where did this come from?"

"I got it in town," Jo admitted. She didn't mention Hayley. "If you don't like it—that's okay," she said.

"I love it," I said quickly.

"I know it can't replace the old poems, but—"

"I love it," I repeated, laying a palm over my chest to emphasize the words. "Thank you, Jo."

This was the first time I had said her name to her. I didn't know why, but it felt alarming.

"You're welcome, Lacey."

My eyes moved from the journal to Jo's face.

"Your eyes are like that color between green and brown that looks like the woods just at the beginning of fall," she said.

"They call it hazel," I said, lowering my gaze.

"Did you want me to get to work right now?" I asked, breaking the silence. "I don't have a pen."

Jo laughed, the throaty sound echoing over the steady buzz of the insects. "No, I brought you out here because it's a full moon tonight and I thought—you might want to see it."

I saw Jo wince at her own words, but I nodded encouragingly. Jo stood from the seat of the picnic bench and sat on the picnic table itself. Then she lay longways across the top of the picnic table, pulling her hoodie up over her head and lacing her fingers behind her head. I set my new notebook on the bench beside me and joined Jo. The tabletop was just wide enough to fit both of us side by side with my ankles dangling off the edge. I felt acutely aware of the slight pressure of our hips brushing as I lay down backward, holding opposite arms like a cross over my chest.

"Do you see it?" Jo asked. I tilted my head upward. It was hard to miss—a full orb glowing in the sky, throwing the tops of the pine trees into sharp relief against the deepening blue.

"My mom says there's a rabbit in the moon," Jo said offhandedly. I squinted up at the sky, trying to see it. "Some people think the full moon makes you crazy."

"That's where the term *lunacy* comes from," I added. "People used to get lighter sentences for murder if they did it under a full moon."

"Beautiful," Jo joked.

The silence that settled over us as we lay side by side on the picnic table in the bright stillness of night was not the awkward silence of strangers or the beat of a lapse in conversation between friends. It was the silence of the night itself, woven through with the rustling of the trees, the calling of the cicadas, and thoughts that could not or would not be spoken aloud. It was Jo who broke the silence, propping herself up on an elbow and turning toward me, our faces both lit pale by the moon.

"Do you want to try something?"

My heart skipped a beat.

"Sure," I said, not quite in a whisper.

"I want you to try writing a poem—or actually, just saying a poem. But don't worry about what you're going to say—the meter or the rhyme. Don't even worry about remembering it. Just say what comes into your head."

It took me a moment to soak in the meaning of Jo's words.

"Isn't that just—thinking out loud? Like a stream of consciousness?"

"Basically."

"So what makes it a poem?"

"Don't worry about what makes it a poem." Jo laughed. "In fact, don't even think of it as a poem. Just think of it as letting your thoughts spill out in their natural shape."

"And you're going to listen?"

"Yep."

I uncrossed my arms and put them over my eyes.

"Fine," I said. "But *don't* look at me."

"Fine," Jo agreed.

"And don't make fun of me."

"Of course not."

"And don't judge—"

"Lacey."

The name slipped off her tongue—a reassurance, a command. I sighed and put my arms down by my side, staring up at the night sky and letting the edges of my vision blur. As I looked, I felt as if something in my chest that had been wound very tightly was slowly beginning to unravel. I began to speak, haltingly at first, and then more quickly, the words skipping like stones across the midnight air.

> *"Is everyone disingenuous or am I just cynical? When people*
> *are poised and graceful,*
> *I think* that isn't real. They're putting on a show. *But when*
> *people are easy and casual,*
> *it's even worse. Like—a studied performance of everything*
> sincere, genuine, real,
> *so what is this nagging sensation I feel? Like I'm in a play,*
> *and no one gave me the*
> *script. And everyone else speaks in the same cadence*: casual,
> natural, humble, *but the*
> *imposters are indiscernible from* the real thing, *whatever that*
> *is. So I think that I should*
> *play too, and I do. And who can say that I'm not* lovely,
> noble, true. *No one does. So*
> *everybody look alive, is anyone else dead inside? But I am*
> *not poised,* nor graceful, nor
> casual, nor offhandedly cool, *nor more intelligent, nor more*
> *sincere, than any of my*
> *Godly peers. Just torn, constantly, between the head and the*
> *heart, and whether it's*
> *worth making art about it, or it's just a waste of time. But*
> *either way, I just want you to*
> *know,* I mean it."

I did not turn to look at Jo, but instead kept my gaze on the sky. When I finally stole a glance at my companion, Jo too was looking straight up at the sky. She turned her head to look at me and a smile spread slowly across her face.

"How do you feel?"

"Embarrassed. Awkward. Exhilarated."

Jo nodded and turned her head back toward the sky. She kept her right hand behind her head, but her left hand came down to rest at her side, palm down, next to mine. I couldn't tell which one of us shifted our hand ever so slightly, but I found the edge of my hand resting against Jo's, the brush of bare skin sending a spark down the center of my chest. I turned my hand over so that the back of it rested against the grainy texture of the picnic table. Jo's fingertips lifted ever so slightly and my hand slid underneath them. We lay there, fingertips intertwined, in the easy silence of the summer night, until the full moon began to fade into the morning light.

# CHAPTER EIGHTEEN

## *Jo*

I awoke to the clatter of the other cabin six campers getting dressed and the bright light streaming through the window. I might have thought last night to be a dream, except for the fact that I had fallen asleep still dressed, with my shoes still on, on top of the covers. I rubbed my eyes and there was no doubt that I had stayed awake most of the night. I blinked my eyes slowly, willing myself to rise for breakfast. I trudged to the bathroom and splashed my face with cold water in one of the sinks.

Funfetti was hurrying all of us out the door. I could feel Rebekah's eyes on me and I wondered if she was going to approach me again—maybe she was going to ask if her prayer had worked. I hung back, putting Lindsay and Kristen between Rebekah and me. Hayley skipped up next to me and leaned on my shoulder conspiratorially.

"Long night?"

I started. "Um, yeah, I—I couldn't sleep."

"Uh-huh," Hayley said. "And that's why you did a walk of shame back into the cabin at four a.m.?"

I looked at her sharply. "Yeah, I—I fell asleep at a picnic table."

"Right."

I met Hayley's eyes. "Are you—" I started.

"Going to tell anyone? Of course not. I thought you knew me better than that by now."

"I do. Sorry. Just a weird day."

"We're partners in crime," Hayley said, looping her arm through mine. Rebekah glanced over her shoulder at us and I looked at my feet, but Hayley gave her a wave.

"Maybe we should give her something real to talk about."

My stomach lurched.

"Next time you sneak out, you should take me with you. You know, *I* have the bottle of Nate's Grapes, and whatever you're up to, that will make it more fun, I promise."

## *Lacey*

I ran my fingers over the feather quill etched into the cover of my new notebook. It felt heavy and solid in my hands—something permanent that would still be here long after the summer was over. I opened the cover and saw something I hadn't noticed before—a few words, written in a slanting hand, covering the very first page of the notebook. *For all your brilliant thoughts.*

I stared down at the words, written out in a careful hand, and felt the glowing embers of last night's languid fire in my chest. I felt my face flush at the thought of the poem—or whatever that was—I had made up as I went along last night. I turned the page of the notebook and wrote down what I could remember. I thought about seeing Jo in town, wondered if she had been honest about what she was doing there, why she hadn't mentioned Hayley. I thought about the envelope under my mother's stack of books. I thought about the poetry slam and the fact that I had signed up with no idea or plan for how I would actually get there.

I came downstairs with my notebook tucked under my arm.

"Good morning!" my mom said brightly. I feigned a smile, not stopping as I passed the kitchen.

"Are you going to breakfast with the campers?" my mother called after me.

"Yep!" I called over my shoulder, as I let the front door slam a little too hard behind me.

Dr. Dan was just unlocking the infirmary when I arrived.

"Let me guess," he said, "you're here for my computer."

"Yes, sir!" I said.

"You need to do research first thing in the morning?"

"English essays wait for no man," I replied.

I used the email address for the NYU admissions office from the signature on the letter and started a new email. My fingers hovered over the subject line as realization began to wash over me. I wasn't really sure how any of this worked. Filling out the application had been easy enough, finding the acceptance letter had been shocking, but what was next? I blinked at the computer screen, hearing the echoes of my parents' voices to my questions about college, about moving away from home, about a life without them. *We'll figure that out. Don't worry about that yet. We'll talk about it when the time comes. We'll see.* My fingers shook as I composed the email.

> *Good afternoon,*
> *I recently received an acceptance letter from your school. It was lost in the mail and I wanted to inquire whether the date to confirm my attendance had passed. If not, I would like to confirm and ask what I need to do next. I apologize for my late response, but I am looking forward to the possibility of attending NYU in the fall. Thank you for your time.*
> *Sincerely,*
> *Lacey Heller*

I drew in a shaky breath and pressed *send*. I opened a new tab and logged into Slant. I had not one but two direct messages waiting for me.

> @MoonBoi11 says: *I can't wait to see you there. If you are even half as beautiful as your poetry, I'll have to buy you a drink.*

My face burned when I read the message, a feeling both intoxicating and sickening washing over me. My heart lurched when I saw the handle next to the other unread message.

> @NatsRainbow says: *I hope you burn in hell.*

# CHAPTER NINETEEN

## *Jo*

I glanced around the empty dock while I listened to the ringing on the payphone receiver.

"How are you doing, mija?"

My mother's voice on the other end of the line was heavy with concern.

"I'm actually doing pretty good, Mom," I said, shifting from one foot to the other as sweat slid down my back. "I fell off a horse, though."

"Ay, please be careful!" my mom exclaimed. "Those things will trample you and kick you!"

"I *know*, that's why I didn't want to go." I laughed.

"And you are staying out of trouble?"

"Yes, ma'am," I said.

"I don't know what your tía was thinking sending you to an all-girls camp," my mom said with an edge of laughter to her voice.

"Mom!"

"What?"

"I didn't—I didn't think you wanted to talk to me about—I thought you wanted me here."

"I did, mija. But I got your letter last week."

"Oh." I ran the back of my hand over my forehead to wipe away the sweat, feeling somehow even hotter than I had a few seconds ago.

"I think maybe you are right. If you think that God made you this way, maybe we should not try to change you."

I took a deep breath, a swirl of gratitude and confusion blooming in my chest. "What about Tía Laura?"

"Tía Laura is very angry. She believes that things ought to be a certain way and that any other way of thinking is very dangerous."

An awkward pause.

"Do you want to come home, morrita?"

I caught my breath. It was at once the last thing I wanted, and the last thing I had ever expected my mother to offer.

"Oh no, Mom. I don't want to make Tía Laura angry after she spent all this money. Besides, I've made some friends here and—it's really not so bad."

Another pause.

"Natalie called me."

I felt as if all the air had evaporated from my lungs, suddenly dizzy. I put my hand on the top of the phone booth to steady myself.

"What—did she say?"

"She said that we should not have sent you away," my mother said, a catch in her voice. I willed her not to cry. I hated it when my mother cried. "She said that I was wrong to let Laura send you away and that she was sorry for how she handled things. She wants another chance with you, mija. She said that she told you she loves you."

*Damn you, Natalie.*

"Okay, well, that's not really something she needs to be talking to my mother about," I said. I heard the icy edge in my own voice. "I mean—I'm glad if—if that conversation helped *you*, but she shouldn't—she doesn't—"

I couldn't find the words. So many things had happened in the nine months that Natalie and I were together. So many firsts and fights and insecurities and then—the betrayal. The big fight. The tears. The begging. The ending. My mother had not been there for any of it. And now here she was, volunteering to play middleman when it was far too late.

"I need to go," I said through gritted teeth.

"But mija—"

"I love you, Mom. I love Rudy. Tell him that, okay? I'll see you in a few weeks."

I put the phone on the receiver much harder than I intended. I slammed my palm against the pay phone box and then recoiled at the sting of the hot metal.

❖

Wednesday night worship that week was different than usual. I had become accustomed to the songs, so different from the ones I had heard and sung at Sunday evening mass. They were like a strange cross between hymns and pop songs.

"You could write better songs than these," I said offhandedly to Lacey as we filed through the doors. I was both glad and surprised to see her there. She moved away from me, but I found my glance drifting to her as the throng of sweaty girls swayed, danced, jumped, and held their hands toward the sky, as if their fingertips could brush something holy if they held them aloft. Lacey kept her hands in her pockets most of the time, I noticed, but there were moments I would catch her with her eyes closed, swaying with the rhythm of the music, and I wondered what she was thinking. What she was feeling. What she was visualizing in her head.

Mr. Heller sent the musicians to sit on the rec room floor with everyone else and invited Crowbar to take a seat alone on a stool in the middle of the stage. Crowbar took off his baseball cap and held it in his hands. Something about his presence sent a ripple of energy through the room. Out of the corner of my eye, I saw Hayley nudge Kristen in the ribs with her elbow and Kristen give Hayley a small shove. I saw two campers from another cabin whispering to each other and giggling.

I had witnessed this phenomenon before—the way a group of girls would tense and titter at the sudden and unexpected presence of a male, especially one who was only a few years older than them. The masculine figure would become their singular focus, the object of much more attention than was warranted, in my opinion. As usual, I found myself vaguely irked by the hold that this guy's presence had over the room. What exactly was it that made him such a valued commodity, such an easy and acute object of feminine attention?

Crowbar held a microphone just below his chin, speaking into it softly, evoking an immediate and reverent hush over the rec room.

"Good evening, ladies," he said in a low voice. It was met with a rising murmur of the same.

"Mr. Heller asked me to talk to y'all tonight about love."

"*Yes*, please," I heard Kristen mutter under her breath.

"Y'all are at an age now when you're starting to think about your future husbands," he said, as if it were a matter of fact. "And your future husbands are out there right now, fighting the good fight, keeping themselves pure, and building themselves into the kind of men who will be able to lead you. But out there"—he gestured broadly, indicating the outside world—"you're going to face a lot of pressure from a lot of different people, especially young men who aren't walking in the faith, to give away parts of yourself—to compromise your purity—to get love in return. I know because I used to be one of those young men."

The room tensed with the anticipation of disclosure.

I scanned the room for Lacey. I saw her standing near the door, arms crossed over her chest, with her father's arm wrapped around her shoulder. Crowbar looked up and Mr. Heller gave him an encouraging nod.

"When I was your age," Crowbar continued, "I hadn't found Jesus yet. I was dating a young woman who was not walking with the Lord, and we fell into temptation together."

I felt like I could hear everyone's pulses, so all-consuming was the silence.

"I gave away something that I could have saved for my future wife. That I wish I had saved for her. And I took something that wasn't mine—something that belonged to her future husband."

Crowbar's voice cracked. I felt an unsettling silence settle over the room like a rust-red mist. I wished desperately that I were anywhere other than watching a twenty-something man have an emotional breakdown on a stage in front of a crowd of sweaty pubescent girls. I noticed that Funfetti had a hand over her heart, nodding and smiling encouragingly, and that Rebekah was wiping a tear from her eye.

"I want y'all to learn from my mistakes," he finally continued, "and remember that—*none* of us are worthy of love. It's only by the *blood of Christ* that we are washed clean of our sins. That we can start new again."

I pulled my knees up to my chest and wrapped my arms around them. Then Crowbar picked up one of the guitars and strummed gently, accompanying the sound of his own voice.

"I want to recite for y'all my favorite Bible passage of all time. First Corinthians 13. You know it—it's the one about love."

He continued to strum the same three chords while he recited, "Love doesn't envy. Love doesn't brag, is not proud, doesn't behave itself inappropriately, doesn't seek its own way, is not provoked, takes no account of evil; doesn't rejoice in unrighteousness, but rejoices with the truth; bears all things, believes all things, hopes all things, and endures all things. When I was a child, I spoke as a child, I felt as a child, I thought as a child. Now that I have become a man, I have put away childish things. But now faith, hope, and love remain—these three. The greatest of these is love."

The mood of the room was solemn as we all stood to file out. Mr. Heller was up on the stage with a hand on Crowbar's shoulder, speaking to him earnestly, Crowbar's tan face bent toward him, listening. Hayley grabbed my elbow as I stood up, almost pulling me back to the ground.

"You look kinda queasy," she said.

"Uh, yeah, it's just—ya know—all the love talk."

"And slut shaming?"

"Yeah, the shame and the fried chicken dinner are not sitting well together," I said.

"I think tonight's the night," Hayley said.

"For…?"

"For opening up another bottle," Hayley said.

"When?"

"After lights out," Hayley said. "What—you have plans?"

"No, no," I said. My eyes wandered involuntarily to where Lacey was standing. Hayley glanced over her shoulder, following my gaze. She turned back with a sigh and rolled her eyes.

"If you *promise* she won't narc on us, you can bring your girl-friend."

Before I could protest the word, Hayley trotted off to find Kristen, looping her arm through Kristen's arm the same way she had done with mine and whispering in her ear conspiratorially. I made my way toward the door, where Lacey still lingered, leaning against the door frame and making small talk with Clueless. I paced my steps so that I would be one of the last people to leave, hoping to catch Lacey by herself before she went home. *If you're sure*, Hayley had said—and I wasn't sure. I wasn't at all sure if Lacey would be angry, if she would refuse to come, or worse—tell one of her parents and get everyone in trouble.

But I couldn't resist.

"Um, hey, I have a question about some of the fish in the lake," I said casually as I approached Lacey.

"Well, you're in luck, since I am the Fish Expert at this camp," Lacey replied without missing a beat. She gestured for me to follow her out to the dock.

"So what's up?" she said. "Just pressing curiosity about large-mouth bass?"

"*What* did you call me?"

Lacey laughed. I noticed that when she laughed, her eyes crinkled up until just a glimmer showed and she tilted her chin up as if the laugh knocked her a little off balance.

"So, um," I began carefully, "Got any plans for the evening?"

"I'll have to check my schedule," Lacey joked.

I looked down at my shoes and back up.

"It's not, uh, it's actually not *my* invitation per se, so ya know, no pressure, and actually you probably won't want to, so let me just—"

Lacey clapped a hand onto my shoulder. "You're freaking out, Einstein."

I ran a hand over the back of my hair. It was starting to get the shaggy look my mother hated. *If you're going to have a boy's haircut, keep it clean, mija.*

"Okay," I said in a rush, "I'll tell you, but I'm not telling you as the camp founder's daughter, okay, I'm telling you as…my friend, so—"

Lacey put both her hands on my shoulders now and shook me. "Just *tell* me, for the love of the blob," she said.

I took a big gulp of air. The words spilled out fast. "Hayley is sneaking out of the cabin tonight with a couple other girls to drink some cheap wine that we got in town and I know you don't like Hayley but I'm kind of obligated to do this with her for some reason and I know that's probably not something you want to do but—"

"I'll be there."

My eyes widened. "Really?"

"Yeah," Lacey said, shrugging. "I want to come."

"Okay, uh, just meet us outside cabin six at like eleven?"

Lacey turned and began to walk away from the dock and toward her family's cabin. "See you there," she said over her shoulder, with a smile that I couldn't interpret.

## CHAPTER TWENTY

### *Lacey*

In all of my seventeen years and something days of being alive, I had never once set out to do something that I already knew to be a bad idea. But tonight was different. Tonight, I was full of a reckless momentum that had only seemed to build as June wore to an end. Maybe, I thought, I was experiencing some kind of heat-induced mania. Maybe whatever higher power I had prayed to on the first day of camp had seen fit to answer me in the form of mischief, the way the ancient gods often did in Greek mythology. Maybe, somewhere deep inside me, I knew that this would be the last summer I would spend at Camp Lavender.

Although I did not yet have the words for all my thoughts, or for my feelings, there was something rising up in me that would not be easily put down. And so I sat, hands folded as if in prayer, at the mercy of the night. Still, I jumped when the door of cabin six opened and I saw three figures making their way slowly out. There were clouds weaving their way through the stars tonight and I could not tell at first who was who. Hayley was the tallest, and she carried herself with a self-assured air that irked me for a reason I could not identify. Jo had her dark blue hoodie pulled up over her head. The other girl I had seen with the cabin six campers, but never spoken to. The girls were halfway to where I sat before the door opened and the three of them froze in their tracks and turned.

But it was not Funfetti. It was another camper. She ran down the steps after them, demanding in a harsh whisper, "*Where* are y'all going?"

Hayley turned around and held a finger to her lips, motioning for the other camper to follow them with a jerk of her head. She scampered down the path and caught up with the other three.

"We're just going to have some non-camp-sanctioned fun, Lindsay," Hayley whispered. "So you can either come with us or go back to bed, but you can't tell Funfetti."

Lindsay gasped in offense at the idea that she would betray her fellow campers. "I'm coming with you," she announced, although her eyes were still wide with shock.

"Fine," Hayley said, and set off toward the lake.

## *Jo*

I stole a sideways glance at Lacey as we all trailed after Hayley. Tonight Lacey was wearing frayed denim shorts, a little shorter than her usual knee-length attire, that revealed a sharp tan line across both her thighs. She wore a forest green flannel with just a glimpse of a tank top underneath. Her burnt sugar curls hung loosely around her shoulders. She looked different tonight, some kind of poise and confidence rising to the surface in the small group of young women.

"You nervous, Rapunzel?" I asked as I hung back and slowed my steps to align with Lacey's.

"No," Lacey said, the claim belied by the edge in her voice. "I'm totally comfortable with breaking curfew to do group underage drinking."

"Hey," I said gently. "You don't have to do this, you know. I'm sorry if I—"

Lacey turned her head toward me for the first time that evening, her eyes shining with a feverish brightness I had never seen before.

"I want to be here," she said firmly.

"Okay," I responded, putting my hands up in surrender.

"You invited me," Lacey added. "Why?"

"Because," I said, fumbling for a good answer and finding only the truth. "I wanted you to be here."

❖

## *Lacey*

Hayley led the group onto the trail that wound around the lake. I wondered if we were going to walk all the way around until we reached the chapel and I bristled at the thought. Something about the building was sacred, although I wasn't exactly sure what it was. But Hayley only led us along the lake trail for a few minutes before making an abrupt departure into the woods. I was surprised when Hayley stopped in front of a fire pit. I realized then that, although I knew Camp Lavender better than anyone, I wasn't the only one who had spent summers wandering off the beaten path.

I couldn't help but be a little impressed that Hayley was able to start an actual fire in the fire pit, expertly arranging the kindling and striking a match with the confidence of someone who had done it many times before.

"All right, Girl Scout!" Kristen proclaimed. She pulled two thick logs close to the fire for seating. Kristen sat down on one log and unzipped Hayley's backpack. Lindsay sat beside her, and Jo and I took the other side. Once the fire showed no more signs of going out, Hayley tossed in the rest of the kindling and brushed the dirt off her hands. She dropped into the empty spot next to Lindsay, catty-corner from Jo. I observed that she wore a black spaghetti-strap tank top—an item of clothing that was forbidden by camp modesty rules. She stretched out her long legs as she pulled two bottles out of her backpack.

"Nate's Grapes Wine Blend," she announced. "It's what's for dinner!"

Kristen laughed and took one of the bottles out of Hayley's hand, and unscrewed the top.

"Did anyone bring cups?" asked Lindsay. Kristen and Hayley laughed and I was glad that I had not asked the same question. Hayley leaned her head back and took a long swig from the neck of the bottle, then handed it to Lindsay.

"Only the cups God gave us," she said. Lindsay giggled, took a small sip, and made a wry face. For all my determination not to give into my rule-following instincts, I found myself clutching at Jo's arm, grasping a handful of the dark blue fabric. Jo looked at me with a concerned face and leaned toward me, away from Hayley and the others, her face a question.

"Just," I said under my breath, "just don't let me get *drunk*, okay?"

Jo gave a quick but decisive nod and I let go of her arm. The truth was that I had never had a drop of alcohol in my life—even the church I attended with my parents substituted tiny plastic cups of grape juice during communion. I had a feeling that Jo could read this on my face, and when Jo took the bottle and took a sip from it, she made an exaggerated face and shouted, "Blech! *So* gross."

"Wimp," Hayley laughed, but Jo continued making a show of her disgust until I had finished my first sip of wine, unnoticed by the others. I was grateful for the privacy as I felt myself gag when the sour liquid touched my tongue. I felt my chest and stomach warm as I followed the path of the wine in my mind. I forced myself to take another sip before I could lose my nerve and winced only slightly as Jo's charade came to an end.

"Slow down," Hayley said. "Leave some for the game."

"What game?" Lindsay and I asked in unison.

Hayley's grin was all mischief.

"Never have I ever, obviously." She smirked.

My stomach twisted. I didn't know the game, but context told me that the odds of winning were not in my favor.

"Remind me how to play," Jo said casually, and I thanked her in my head.

"It's very simple," Hayley said. "You say something you've never done, and anyone who *has* done it has to take a drink."

"You're in deep trouble," Kristen said, bumping Hayley with her shoulder.

"Oh, shut up!" Hayley groaned in mock horror. Then she turned to Jo. "Why don't you start?"

Hayley unscrewed the cap on the second bottle of wine while Jo thought.

"Never have I ever…eaten red meat."

I gasped involuntarily. "*Never?*"

The other three girls passed the bottle around and then passed it to me. Jo grinned, obviously pleased with herself.

"Boring!" declared Hayley. "Okay, we'll go counterclockwise, so me next. Never have I ever been naked with a boy."

She looked around, daring the other girls to reveal themselves. Kristen slowly took the bottle out of Hayley's hand and took a long swig. No one else moved. Hayley's jaw dropped in scandalized delight. Kristen shrugged.

"I was dating Ian for two years," she explained. "You can't date a boy in high school for *two* years and never get naked."

I felt a shockwave of nerves rush through me. I had known that I was getting in over my head before the evening began, but there was no turning back now. Lindsay took the bottle from Kristen.

"Never have I ever pooped my pants," she said, turning the game in a direction that was at least a little less overwhelming. Jo raised the bottle to her lips and the other girls all screamed in horror.

"I had food poisoning in fourth grade," she said, wiping the wine from her mouth. "My mom picked me up from school, but…not in time."

I gave Jo an exaggerated pat on the back. "Happens to the best of us," I teased.

"Clearly," Jo said. She gestured to herself with a self-deprecating laugh.

It went on like that for a few minutes. *Never have I ever been skiing. Never have I ever broken a bone. Never have I ever puked in public. Never have I ever dyed my hair. Never have I ever been out of the country. Never have I ever been outside of Texas. Never have I ever played a team sport.*

I felt my face starting to sting as the bottles were passed around. Of course, I thought, no one would know if I was lying if I just took a drink, pretending that I'd had at least *one* of these experiences so that I could shield myself from the undeniable fact of my boring and sheltered existence, the depth and breadth of which was being revealed to me in a way that I had never seen it before. Jo must have sensed my growing discomfort, or perhaps she just wanted to see me get tipsy, because when her turn came again, she said, "Never have I ever driven a golf cart."

I felt a sense of pride flutter in me when I was the only one who picked up the bottle. Hayley gave a short laugh.

"Thank the Lord," she said in an exaggerated Southern accent. "I thought you were gonna end the night stone cold sober, bless your heart."

Instantly, the pride I had felt dissolved and I was thankful that the only break in the darkness was the small campfire, because I felt my eyes start to sting. The few sips of Nate's Grapes, swirling inside me with almost nothing to absorb them, were starting to take effect. When it came to be my turn again, I decided to change my strategy.

"Never have I ever been to school," I announced. I folded my arms across my chest and watched all of the other girls take sips from the bottles.

Hayley put a hand to her chest and asked, "You've really never been to school, Lacey?"

"Nope," I said, taking a strange, vicious pleasure in my own humiliation. Now that any hope of assimilation was gone, I relished my ability to manipulate the outcome of the game with my own inexperience. Now I could simply use my turns to learn things about the rest of them without having to worry that they could reverse the tactic on me.

"Never have I ever smoked marijuana," I said when my next turn came around. Hayley and Jo were the only ones who drank. Hayley put a hand on Jo's arm, just like she had in the coffee shop in town.

"Looks like we're the bad girls." She giggled. Jo laughed softly, stealing a glance at me in the glow of the fire.

## Jo

The whole thing was starting to feel like a mistake. I shouldn't have invited Lacey—I had set both of us up for humiliation. I tried to assess the look in Lacey's eyes when my swig from the wine bottle indicated that I had smoked weed. Was she horrified? Was she judging me? Was she thinking that maybe I really *was* a bad influence—a Godless, pot-smoking, curfew-breaking hoodlum? I had taken enough sips of Nate's Grapes at this point that my head was starting to feel fuzzy, as if the campfire smoke were inside my brain. I was surprised when Lacey started to test the boundaries of the game, to reveal more about herself than she had in the two and a half weeks that I had known her. Was she already tipsy, or was she just feeling reckless?

We had started playing out of order, each tipsy girl piping up with her never-have-I-ever as soon as it popped into her mind. Lindsay was starting to mumble a little bit, despite having taken only a few more drinks than Lacey.

"Never have I ever kissed a boy," she said. Hayley and Kristen each picked up one of the wine bottles. They clinked them together and giggled, taking simultaneous sips. Kristen, still clutching the bottle, leaned forward conspiratorially.

"Never have I ever kissed a *girl*."

My stomach dropped like an elevator with a broken cable. Maybe it was in my head, or maybe everyone's eyes really did turn toward me. Maybe it was just Hayley. Maybe Lacey wasn't paying attention. Maybe I should just sit still. Maybe no one would be able to tell that my whole body had started to vibrate. Hayley was holding out the bottle to me, a question in her eyes.

I picked it up.

Hayley took the other bottle from Kristen.

Simultaneously, Hayley and I each took a slow sip out of our bottles, like we were drinking in slow motion. I could see that Hayley's eyes were on me, and I could feel that Lacey's were too.

"I knew it," announced Kristen, pointing at me. Lindsay gaped.

"Never have I ever been in a fight," Hayley continued nonchalantly.

Lacey snatched the bottle from my hands and tipped it into her mouth. My eyes widened as I saw her take not a sip, but a long and steady pull.

"Hey!" Hayley said, but Lacey ignored her. She let the rest of the bottle drain, not coming up for air until it was empty, and then tossed it on the ground.

"Holy shit," said Hayley. "I guess you left those goody-two-shoes at home."

"Shut up," snapped Lacey as she stood up. She swayed for a moment and I reached out an arm to catch her, but she jerked her arm back and stumbled off into the woods, muttering something about needing air.

Hayley laughed. "I think we successfully corrupted her."

## CHAPTER TWENTY-ONE

### *Lacey*

I had never felt anything like this before. My head felt like a sponge that had been plunged into warm water—heavy, slow. I sank to my knees once I was outside the campfire light, letting the darkness sweep over me while trees started to spin. Usually my thoughts proceeded in a logical order, like bullet points on a list that I would read over and over. Now they were scattered and messy, like splashes of paint on a canvas. I could not organize them even if I wanted to.

I was snapped out of my reverie by the crunch of leaves behind me.

"Lacey?"

Jo was crouching by my side, a hand hovering over my back, but not quite touching me. I turned to look at her, the question surging out of my mouth before I could stop it.

"So…you're…you're gay then?"

Jo straightened and took a step back. "Yeah," she said in a colder voice than I had ever heard her use. "You gonna tell your dad?"

I looked up at Jo, who was now towering over me, her arms crossed over her chest. "What? Why would you think that?"

Jo ran a shaking hand through her hair. "Because—that's what this camp is for, right? To encourage wayward young women to walk with the Lord? You can't have some *homosexual* walking around converting all these innocent young women, right?"

The sharp edge in her voice cut through my intoxication and I stumbled to my feet. "Well, you're not trying to convert people, are you?" I said.

"Aren't *you*?" Jo asked.

My mouth fell open. "What do you mean?"

Jo took a step backward, putting more distance between us. "That's not why you've been spending so much time with me?" she asked, an angry quaver creeping into her voice. "Because you knew or—or you suspected? Or because my aunt called your dad? And you're trying to—to get me to let my guard down so you can lead me to Jesus or whatever?"

I put a hand to my head, which was starting to ache. "What? Jo, no. I didn't—I don't care about trying to *convert* you. I was hanging out with you because I *like* you. I didn't even know." Whether this statement was entirely true, I wasn't sure.

"And now that you know?"

The question hung in the air between us.

I opened my mouth, looking for the right words. Before I could answer, Lindsay crashed through the trees beside us, retching. Her hair hung around her face as bile and pink wine spewed from her mouth. Jo ran over to her and pulled her hair back from her face. Hayley and Kristen were not far behind.

"I'm hungry!" Hayley declared loudly.

I looked at Jo, but she was occupied with keeping Lindsay's hair out of her vomit. I looked at my watch. The numbers swam before my eyes.

*So this is what drunk feels like.*

"Follow me," I said, and the rest of the girls trailed after me through the woods, Lindsay leaning heavily on Jo's arm.

I knew that Sidewinder arrived at the dining hall to start prepping at four a.m. Once, when I was eight years old, my dad had woken me up at sunrise to go to the lake with him. That summer, he had been determined to teach me how to fish, for a reason I never understood. But first, he had taken me to the dining hall and Sidewinder had whipped up fresh french toast. When I asked, she had explained that people who worked in kitchens, especially bakers, often had to arrive very early in the morning so that everything would be fresh and ready for breakfast at seven sharp. This, Sidewinder had said, was why she never married—there was no time to find a husband when you were asleep by eight p.m. Now I found myself wondering idly if there might be another reason.

The other thing I knew about Sidewinder was that she wasn't like the other people who worked at Camp Lavender. Her forearms were covered in tattoos, mostly of snakes and flowers, and her hair was bright red. I had heard my dad disparage tattoos, piercings, and colored hair many times throughout my life and wondered why Sidewinder was the exception to the rule.

"She's an amazing cook," was all my dad had said.

When I pulled on the dining hall door, I was pleased to find that it was already unlocked. I ushered the other girls in and told them to wait in the dining hall itself. The four of them wandered around like lost puppies, weaving through the round tables without their surrounding chairs. I pushed through the swinging door and found Sidewinder by herself, rolling a thick dough into biscuits, her hands covered in flour.

"Lacey?" Sidewinder raised her eyebrows, but she did not look angry.

"Hi," I said, feeling a sloppy grin spread across my face. "Do you have any leftover snacks from yesterday?"

Sidewinder's mouth quirked to one side. I heard a stray giggle from the dining hall.

"How many of you are there?" she asked.

"Five."

"Go have a seat. I'll grab the pancake batter. Go get a pitcher and bring everyone water."

"Yes ma'am."

"I mean it!" Sidewinder called over her shoulder as she bustled to the walk-in. "I want *all* of you to drink as much water as you possibly can."

I brought a full plastic pitcher of water to the table and a stack of plastic cups and repeated the instructions. Within ten minutes, a giant stack of fluffy pancakes sat in the middle of the table and Sidewinder was passing out plates. I thought that I had never smelled anything so good in my whole life. I ate with the ravenous energy of an explorer who hadn't found food in days.

Once the girls had finished, I gathered up their plates and utensils and carried them back into the kitchen to the dish pit. Sidewinder was back at work, humming quietly to herself, utterly unperturbed and uncurious about what she had just witnessed. I approached her, my steps still swaying.

"Thank you," I said quietly. Sidewinder glanced at her watch.

"You'd better get those young ladies to bed ASAP," was all she said. "I'll see you in a few hours."

## *Jo*

Cabin six was dark when we arrived. Hayley, Kristen, and Lindsay shuffled and shushed their way in, but I hung back with Lacey.

"Are you going to make it back to your cabin okay?"

"Um, yeah," Lacey said in an absent voice. I studied her face. Her eyes were cloudy and unfocused.

"I'm going to walk you home," I said firmly.

Lacey waved a hand at me. "No," she said, "You gotta get to bed."

"Come on."

I began walking toward the Heller cabin and gestured for Lacey to follow me. "I'll walk you there and then I'll come right back. I'm afraid you'll wander off into the woods."

"Because I'm drunk?" Lacey asked in a whisper.

"Yes," I said, laughing in spite of myself. "Because you're drunk, dummy."

A small shock ran through me as Lacey ran to catch up with me and grabbed the sleeve of my sweatshirt to steady herself. Lacey did not speak during the few minutes it took us to get from one cabin to another. She did not let go of my sweatshirt either. When we arrived, Lacey held up a finger to her lips.

"We have to be very quiet," she said, reaching for the door. She swayed and I caught her by the shoulders to steady her. I let her go slowly, making sure that she could stay upright on her own.

"I'm sorry I let you get drunk," I whispered. Lacey waved a dismissive hand at me.

"I did it to myself," she said, the blur of alcohol doing nothing to diminish her acute self-awareness.

I took a step back, but Lacey caught me by the arm and with one word made my heart skip what felt like a hundred beats.

"Stay."

I felt like a burglar as I followed Lacey up the stairs. I told myself that Lacey was safely home, that there was no reason I shouldn't leave right now, that there was no reasonable explanation I could give to Funfetti for why I had been gone the entire night. But now I was at the top of the stairs. Now I was following Lacey into her bedroom.

Lacey collapsed onto the bed, groaning a little. "I don't feel so good," she murmured.

"Are you gonna be sick?" I asked.

"I don't know," she said. "I've never been drunk before."

"Well, you probably have little to no tolerance for alcohol, then," I said, trying to reason out my next course of action. "And you drank kind of a lot of wine at one time."

Lacey put her head into her pillow and groaned. I sat down on the floor beside the bed, wrapping my arms around my knees. Lacey reached one arm over the side of the bed and grabbed the hood of my sweatshirt.

"It's so soft," she said, as if to herself. And then, even more quietly, "Like you."

"What?" I said, a little louder than I meant to. Lacey sat straight up in the bed, suddenly shivering. I stood up and unzipped my sweatshirt, draping it over Lacey's shoulders. Lacey immediately put her arms through the sleeves, zipped it all the way up, and pulled the hood over her curls.

"It smells so good," she said.

"It smells like me," I said.

"Well, you smell good," Lacey said, flopping over again.

"I should go," I said softly. Lacey's eyes were closing. I wandered around the perimeter of the room, looking at Lacey's things. I felt guilty, but I had technically been invited, and my curiosity outweighed my politeness. There were two bookshelves, filled to the brim with paperbacks. There was a neatly organized desk. In the center of it sat the notebook I had stolen for Lacey when Hayley and I were in town. There was also a piece of paper that looked like some kind of official document. I leaned over the desk, telling myself that if it was readable without my touching anything, it was fair game.

My eyes widened as I read the acceptance letter. I looked over my shoulder at Lacey, who was face down on the bed with the hood of my sweatshirt pulled low over her face.

"You got accepted to NYU?" I asked quietly.

"Mm-hmm," Lacey said. "But they didn't tell me."

"What do you mean? Who?"

"My mom. My dad."

"What? Why?"

I tried to keep my voice low. I saw Lacey give a faint shrug.

"They don't want me to go."

I suddenly felt hot with anger.

"Why?" I demanded, but Lacey had turned her head the other way. I approached the bed and pulled the hood slowly off Lacey's head. My hand shook a little as I let my fingers graze Lacey's hair. The sun-bleached curls were soft to the touch and I let my fingers tangle in them for just a moment. Then, in a soft whisper, I asked, "When did you get into a fight?"

A smile curled the corner of Lacey's mouth, but she did not open her eyes.

"When I was five, a camper tried to take my fish. So I punched her in the stomach."

The story made as much sense as it could have in the given moment. "I have to go," I said in a low voice, but Lacey had fallen fast asleep. "Good night, Rapunzel."

I slipped out of Lacey's bedroom door and closed it quietly behind me. I spent what felt like a lifetime creeping down the stairs and out of the front door, my heart hammering as I slowly released the doorknob into its place. Back in my bunk, hoodie-less and exhausted, I lay on my back with my hands folded over my chest, feeling like electricity was racing through my body and into my fingertips.

# CHAPTER TWENTY-TWO

## *Lacey*

When I woke up to the sun streaming through my window, the first telltale sign of the previous night's adventure was the pounding headache behind my eyes. I sat up stiffly and put my head in my hands, moaning softly. Slowly, I became aware that I was still in my clothes—and not just my clothes, but Jo's hoodie. I pulled it up around my face. It smelled good—like Summer Sky. I heard the sound of my mother stomping around the kitchen and put my head back down on my pillow, trying to think. I could just see the outline of the previous night like a grainy VHS tape. The campfire. The bottles of wine. Never have I ever. Pancakes.

I shot back up. My dad would be at the dining hall by now—he would already have spoken to Sidewinder that morning. Would she have said anything? Would she have felt obligated to tell my dad that his daughter had led four other inebriated young women to the doors of the dining hall at an ungodly hour, begging for pancakes? My eyes were watering and I stood and dragged myself to the bathroom where I vomited into the toilet as if it were part of my daily morning routine, after which I felt almost human again.

I made my way downstairs and slipped into the living room while my mother was still distracted in the kitchen. I logged onto the family computer and checked my email.

*Ms. Heller,*

*Thank you for your email. Unfortunately, New York University is unable to hold spots for accepted students after*

*the response deadline detailed in their acceptance letters.
This policy is in place to allow NYU to reach out to wait-listed
students to offer them admission during the second round of
the admission process. You are welcome to apply again for
spring admission, the deadline for which is December 15.
Please let me know if you have any other questions.*

*Best,*

*Diana Stewart, Admissions*

I fell back in my chair, as breathless as if someone had punched
me in the chest. I heard my mother's voice from the kitchen.

"Lacey, are you awake?"

I jumped up from my chair and stormed into the kitchen, unable to
think, or to strategize, or to decide what my best move was.

"Why didn't you tell me I got accepted to NYU?"

My mother took a step back as if I had hit her. Her mouth fell
open and her spatula hung in midair like a conductor's baton. "How
did you—"

"I saw it on your nightstand," I said.

"You shouldn't be going through my nightstand," my mother said
in a scolding voice.

I scoffed. "It was a letter addressed to *me.* That had been opened
by *you.*"

"Your father and I have a right to your mail, Lacey Ellis."

"Are you serious?"

My mother pursed her lips at the sound of my raised voice. I had
never raised my voice to my mother, and the expression on her face
made me feel momentarily cowed. "Your father and I needed to have a
discussion about whether or not you were ready to move two thousand
miles across the country and start an independent life."

"And did you have that *discussion?*"

"We are still in the process of having it, but you know that in the
summer Camp Lavender takes priority, Lacey."

I threw up my hands in a gesture of aggravation. "Well,
congratulations, Mom. It looks like you got your way, because the
acceptance deadline has passed and now that spot has gone to the wait-
listed kids and I won't be able to go until the spring, and I will have to
reapply."

My mother's lips had pressed into a dangerously thin line. "Young lady, you need to watch your tone."

"My *tone*? You jeopardized my whole future and you want me to watch my tone?"

I could feel that my hands had balled up into fists. I looked down at them and the knuckles were white. Without saying another word, I turned on my heel and ran out the front door, not bothering to close it behind me.

Breakfast was already in full swing by the time I burst into the dining hall. My dad was at one of the tables surrounded by other members of the staff. He looked up when I appeared before him, his face full of surprise.

"Dad."

I could hear the urgent quaver in my voice. The other counselors looked at me with concern.

"Can you come talk to me for a minute?"

My father rose from his seat and followed me to the stairs outside the dining hall. I was still wearing Jo's hoodie and I pulled the sleeves over my hands, crushing them in my palms, pacing for a few steps back and forth on the step below where my father stood.

"Dad," I said again. "Did you know that I was accepted to NYU?"

My father stood completely still for a moment, then let out a deep sigh. "Yes," he said simply.

I felt my eyes filling with hot tears. "Well, did you…did you see that in the acceptance letter they listed a deadline for acceptance?"

He crossed his arms. "Yes, I was aware of the deadline."

A wave of cold cut through the heat bearing down from the early July sun. "Why didn't you tell me?"

"Lacey, this is a discussion we should have at a different time, when the camp day is over and when you are calm enough to have a rational discussion."

A strangled, guttural sound escaped my throat. His words were not uncommon in our family. Extreme displays of emotion were seen as a barrier to logic and reason, which were of the utmost importance in all decision-making.

"Dad. *Please.*"

My father's voice was not loud, but it was stern. "Frankly, Lacey, I'm not sure that New York University is an appropriate place for you.

That is a *very* liberal school, and I am not sure you are ready to walk in faith if you are not surrounded by other believers."

The words punctured me like tiny needles. For a moment, I thought I was going to fall backward down the stairs from the force of them.

"That's what you were debating?" I asked. "Whether I would—stay Christian?"

"Whether you would stay *strong* in your faith, yes. You are only seventeen. Most young people need the guidance of their parents until they are at least twenty-one, especially if they are exposing themselves to so much of the secular world. You are still young, still naive, and susceptible to the teachings of professors who do not believe the same things that we believe."

"So when you let me apply, you were just…pretending to trust me?"

"We didn't want to deny you your dream school until we had looked into it more," my father said. "And now we have."

"So you're keeping me here?"

He frowned. "We would certainly like to see you develop a stronger relationship with the Lord," he said in the way of a response. "We would like for you to consider applying to some universities that have a better standing in the faith. Or maybe waiting another year or two."

I could only stare at him. A thousand questions raced through my mind. *Why didn't you tell me? Why did you pretend to support me? Why didn't you lay out the rules and restrictions for my future before I got my hopes up?*

"We will talk about this more at home," my father said before I could verbalize anything. He turned and re-entered the dining hall. I turned and fled down the dining hall steps and out toward the lake.

My parents didn't used to let me walk around the lake by myself. One of them would have to accompany me if I went any farther from their cabin than the dock. It didn't occur to me to ask until I was twelve, and at first they refused. What if a stranger had sneaked onto the camp grounds and kidnapped me? What if I was bitten by a poisonous snake or fell into the lake? Eventually, my pleas had worn them down and they had agreed to let me walk the full circumference of the lake on my own. By the time I was fourteen, I had the full run of the camp grounds as long as I was home by the camp-wide lights out at ten p.m.

When my feet hit the gravel path that stretched the three miles around the lake, I found myself running at full speed. I was not a runner, but the adrenaline pumping through my body made me feel like I could run for miles, the gravel flying up around my feet and orange dirt caking my shoes and ankles. From the first time I had questioned them as a little girl, my parents had told me that they had my best interests at heart. I had always and wholeheartedly believed this as fact—as true as the story of creation, and as reliable as the rise of the sun in the sky every morning. Now, for the first time, the seeds of doubt that had burrowed into my mind that summer were beginning to sprout.

I slowed to a walk when I saw Funfetti coming toward me on the path. She gave me a friendly wave and I could not think of any excuse not to stop and greet her.

"Hi, Funfetti," I panted.

"Hi!" Funfetti said brightly. She had the deeply tanned, spent, somewhat grimy look that all the counselors took on during the second half of the summer. She had endured enough boat rides, mosquito bites, and meltdowns for a lifetime, I thought. But she continued to come back with the same bright smile and the same unyielding certainty that this was the closest place to heaven you could get on earth. She would probably keep coming back until she graduated from college.

I knew all this.

I knew that there was not a single camp counselor at Camp Lavender who did not adore my father and that each and every one of them believed that he held the keys to their spiritual growth. I knew this, and yet in that moment, I faltered.

"Are you okay?"

The genuine concern in Funfetti's voice disarmed me and made me forget for a moment about the homogeneity of thought and feeling that draped over the camp like a heavy blanket.

"I'm…yeah, no, I'm…" I stammered.

Funfetti put a hand on my arm and said, "Walk with me."

I followed her obediently back the way she came.

"Where are you headed?" I asked.

"I just went to grab some Band-Aids for Rebekah. She has blisters. The girls are in an archery lesson right now." Funfetti peered into my face. "Do you want to share your burdens with me?"

I let out a sigh. "I just found out that I won't be going to college in the fall."

Funfetti put a hand over her heart. "I'm so sorry, Lacey."

"And it's because my parents hid my acceptance letter. Because they didn't want me to go."

Funfetti's mouth opened in surprise. I felt shocked at myself for so openly blaming my parents out loud. It was the last thing either of us expected. "Did they say why?"

"I guess they don't think I'm ready," I blurted out. "Like…they don't think I'm ready for the outside world or something."

"Are you?"

"How the heck would I know?" I felt a stab of guilt for the bitterness in my words. We walked for a few more paces, only the sound of the gravel under our feet and the shriek of insects breaking the silence.

"You know, Lacey," Funfetti said, "college is a really different environment from what you're used to. Here, you're surrounded by people who support your spiritual journey and who believe the same things you do. At college, you'll encounter a lot of people who want to challenge what you believe. Are you ready to answer them?"

I had no idea how to answer such a question. "I know what I believe," I said. I knew it to be a lie before I even finished saying it.

"I know that sometimes our parents do things that seem confusing and frustrating to us," Funfetti continued, "but your parents know you better than anyone and they want what's best for you."

"Right," I said flatly. I felt as if my heart were in my shoes.

"The heart is deceitful above all things and desperately wicked—who can understand it?"

I looked longways at Funfetti. "The Bible?"

"Yes."

"If the heart is deceitful—"

"Some translations say *incurably sick*," Funfetti added.

"Right. If the heart is deceitful, or wicked, or incurably sick—how are we ever supposed to know—anything?"

Funfetti wiggled her index finger in a now-you're-catching-on motion.

"Exactly," she said. "That's why you need people around you to guide you spiritually—people who have been practicing turning over their deceitful hearts to the Lord for much longer than you have. That's why I love to come back here. It's like…everything finally makes sense again. Out there, it's just chaos."

Funfetti gestured at the trees and I followed her motion, as if I could see the East Coast if I just looked hard enough.

At the archery station, the girls in cabin six were lining up in two rows to shoot arrows at the targets that were set up across the field. Jo looked over her shoulder as Funfetti and I approached and her smile held a question. I felt overheated and confused, unsure of where to go or what to do. I walked up to the back of the line, and Jo gave up her place at the front to get in line behind me.

"You were craving some archery practice?" Jo teased.

"Yeah, I really feel like shooting something," I said grimly. Jo's cheeky grin faded as she looked at my face.

"What's wrong?" she asked quietly.

"I'm having a bad day," I said simply. Jo nodded as if no further explanation were needed. We watched Lindsay shoot an arrow so weakly that it hit the ground halfway to the target.

"These bows will be useless during the actual zombie apocalypse," Jo commented to no one in particular.

"Don't joke about that," Rebekah scolded from the front of the other line.

"Watch this," Jo whispered into my ear. She then turned to Rebekah. "Why not? The Bible definitely confirms that people can be raised from the dead."

Rebekah scowled and started to answer, but the other girls gave her a nudge and told her that it was her turn. Jo suppressed a laugh. Lindsay returned from retrieving her arrow and handed the bow and arrow to me as Rebekah released a nearly perfect shot that landed in the bull's-eye of the other target. She shrieked with delight.

"You've only made her stronger," I muttered to Jo. "Why'd you antagonize her like that?"

I lifted my bow and arrow and closed one eye as Rebekah trotted across the field to retrieve her arrow. I pulled my arrow back until the string was taut and took aim.

"Because," Jo said, "she cornered me and asked me if I was a homosexual."

"*What?*" Shocked, I turned to look over my shoulder at Jo.

"Watch out!" Jo shouted.

Rebekah screamed as the head of the arrow struck her in the fleshy part of her buttocks.

I vehemently denied that I had done it on purpose. In fact, I was almost completely sure that I had not done it on purpose. I had been surprised, distracted, and had accidentally released my arrow at the wrong angle as Rebekah made her way back across the field. It was definitely an accident. Almost definitely.

# CHAPTER TWENTY-THREE

## *Lacey*

Jo had been right. The bows and arrows used at Camp Lavender were not strong enough to do lasting damage to any living creature. Nevertheless, the paperwork had to be done. After profuse and awkward apologies, I slipped out of the chaos at the infirmary to the relative safety and isolation of the dock. There I sat, unshielded from the violent heat of the Texas sun, letting the bright reflection of the lake make spots dance before my eyes.

"Contemplating your next victim?"

I didn't have to turn my head to know that it was Jo slipping into the seat next to me.

"I appreciate your valiant protection, but you didn't actually have to try to *kill* her," Jo said. I couldn't work up a smile.

"I have a feeling this is going to be the last straw for my parents," I said flatly.

"Last straw? What else have you done?"

"Well, I got into something with both my parents this morning that was as close as we come to fighting in the Heller family."

"What happened?" Jo asked, her tone softening. I explained. I started with the story of finding the NYU acceptance letter and emailing the admissions office, then stumbled into a clumsy explanation of the questions that had been crowding my mind for the past few days. The words came out haltingly at first, then started to crash out uncontrollably like they had been behind a dam that was now broken.

"I've never really questioned things this way," I concluded. "Until now, everything has just—made sense."

Jo sat staring out at the lake. I wondered what she was thinking, immediately filled with doubt and regret about sharing so much with someone I had only known for a few weeks—someone I wasn't altogether sure I could trust. But she was the only person I knew who didn't feel and believe exactly like everyone else.

"Do you still want to go to the poetry slam?" Jo said at last.

"Yes," I said quickly, "but I don't know if I can."

"Why not?"

"I need—I need someone to drive me."

Jo turned toward me and put her head to one side. "You don't know how to drive," she said, a statement rather than a question.

"Right."

"Are you asking me to drive you?"

I looked down at my arms, which were folded over the back of the built-in bench that ran around the length of the dock.

"Yeah," I said. "I'm asking you."

"Well, I've got good news and bad news," Jo said. "The good news is—I know how to drive. I learned last summer. The bad news is—I don't have a car. Do you have a solution for that?"

"I will," I said. Jo looked at me skeptically. "I'll take care of that part," I repeated.

"Okay," Jo said simply. "Then we've got a deal."

Jo reached out a slender hand. I noticed that the brown in her skin had deepened over the weeks since her arrival. I took Jo's hand and shook it firmly. I couldn't be sure if I imagined it or if Jo held my fingers in her grasp for a moment longer than necessary.

When my parents arrived home for the evening, I was not surprised to hear my name called and to find them sitting expectantly at their kitchen table as if they were waiting to give a job interview or a prison sentence. I was not surprised that they asked me to sit down, nor was I surprised that they asked me whether I thought that my behavior had aligned with what the Bible said about children and their parents. I was not surprised when they told me that I would not be spending any more of the summer interacting with campers. What surprised me was the calm, measured tone of my response.

As they talked, I became conscious of feeling something familiar, like a flashback. It felt like I was not seeing directly through my own eyes, but rather watching everything in black and white, as if it were all a scene in a movie that had happened in the past. On the black and white screen, I saw myself talking and acting as though everything had been preplanned for me by someone else and there was no way to change it. I apologized to my parents, accepted their sentencing, bent my head so that they could pray for me, rose from my seat, and ascended the stairs to my bedroom.

I continued to watch myself in black and white that whole week as I stayed curled up on the bed in my room, watching the sunrise as I reread *Emily of New Moon*, and watching it set as I made my way through my Emily Dickinson anthology. I haunted the dining hall like a ghost, showing up no sooner than half an hour after the campers were scheduled to finish their meals, and getting out one folding chair to eat in solitary silence at one of the empty round tables. I felt as if each moment were happening in slow motion, one dragging into the next as the timeline of reality slowed.

But I knew it would be worth it.

I knew that if I could just live with this flashback feeling for a few more days, and appease the ever-watchful eyes of my parents, I could escape my sentencing for a night without them ever suspecting a thing. My confidence grew every time I crept down to the living room to use the family computer, pausing at the top of the stairs by my parents' bedroom door to listen for the rhythmic sounds of their breathing. I spent at least two hours on Slant every night—writing, reading, commenting, studying. Sometimes *@MoonBoi11* would log on at the same time and we would message back and forth in the closest thing to a normal conversation I had had in days. I confided in him about my parents' betrayal and subsequent punishment. I felt a tingle at the back of my neck as I read his response.

@MoonBoi11 says: *Honestly, fuck them. You are an adult and they shouldn't be telling you what you can and can't do.*
@HellerHighwater says: *Well, I'm not quite an adult…yet.*
@MoonBoi11: *Well how old are you then?*

My fingers hovered over the keyboard. I glanced over my shoulder as if the honesty police were going to break down the door as soon as I began typing. A mixture of wariness, guilt, and excitement threaded through me. The hours I spent on Slant were the only ones in which

I felt truly transported from the reality in which I currently felt so trapped. I was surrounded by the same walls, floors, and furniture that had sat unchanged by trend or style since I had been born. But here, in the liminal glowing space of the screen, with the familiar stasis of the living room shrouded by darkness, anything felt possible.

@HellerHighwater says: *You first.*
@MoonBoi11 says: *Fine. I'm 20.*
@HellerHighwater says: *18.*

The honesty police were nowhere to be found. No alarm or siren gave away the lie, ever so slight, that I had let slip from beneath my fingertips and out into the void.

@MoonBoi11 says: *You might not feel like an adult, but technically you are one! Going to college will really help you mature. Trust me. ;)*

At that moment, I heard the creak of my mother's feet upstairs and I quickly stabbed at the button that would turn off the monitor and snap me into darkness. I heard the light step that could only be my mother descending the staircase. I held my breath, wondering if my mother had looked into my bedroom and come downstairs in search of me. But she crossed directly into the kitchen, not even glancing at the living room, where I sat frozen, now unable to return to my room without being noticed. I heard the sound of the refrigerator opening and saw the faint glow of the refrigerator light around the corner that divided the two rooms. My mother sighed and closed the refrigerator without extracting anything. I heard the scrape of one of the kitchen chairs and the slight thud of my mother's body dropping into it.

At first, I didn't know what to make of the silence that followed. Then I heard it—a gasp, ever so slight, and what could only be a sob. I realized that my mother must have pressed her face into her arms, muffling the sound so that I had to strain to make out what it was. For a moment, the black and white of my world faded into muted colors and I saw myself getting out of my chair, gliding into the kitchen, embracing my mother, and holding her until whatever surge of pain she was feeling had ceased.

But the vision dissolved again into grainy grayscale. There were too many variables at play for me to make such a gesture. My mother would know that I had been up and out of bed, downstairs, on the computer. Whatever was troubling her might be laid somehow at my feet, rightfully or not, and make everything about my situation worse. I put my own head into my hands, feeling my breath against the skin of my forearm. After what felt like an eternity, I heard the scrape of the kitchen chair again, then the sound of the kitchen sink running, and then the sound of my mother's feet climbing the stairs back to the main bedroom.

After a few minutes, I made my way gingerly up the stairs and back into my bedroom, where I slept fitfully for the rest of the night.

## CHAPTER TWENTY-FOUR

### *Jo*

I knew, or at least suspected, that something was wrong when Lacey stopped appearing on the dock during Bible study, stopped appearing at the dining hall during mealtimes, and disappeared altogether, as if she had been a figment of my imagination. But I knew that this was not the case when Hayley elbowed me after lunch one day and said, "Stop moping just because your girlfriend got grounded."

"I'm not moping," I defended myself, ignoring the other part of the sentence. "I'm trying to figure something out."

Hayley had a car at camp. This I knew. But Lacey had told me that she would provide a vehicle and surely that was still the case, even though the plan had only been briefly agreed upon. Besides, I thought, if I told Hayley that I was going to sneak out of camp with Lacey at night to go to Austin for a poetry slam, she would either invite herself to come along, mock Lacey, me, and the whole idea, or worse, let it slip accidentally-on-purpose and blow the whole thing.

I reasoned with myself that I did not want Hayley to come because Lacey didn't like her and it would probably make her feel ill at ease performing in front of Hayley. I knew there was another reason for me to avoid telling or inviting Hayley or anyone else, but I did not discuss it with myself. I also knew that Lacey could not be a figment of my imagination because she still had my dark blue sweatshirt. An abrupt and vivid image of Lacey in her bedroom in my sweatshirt flashed through my mind. I shook my head, as if I could physically clear away both the image and the rapid beating of my heart that accompanied it.

When July ninth arrived, I awoke even before Funfetti turned on the lights and I stared at the bottom of the bunk bed above me. I felt almost as excited as I had when I had gone to the zipline tower to check my electroscope.

But this was a different kind of experiment.

I went through the motions of camp that day in a haze, my mind utterly preoccupied by anticipation. Anticipation was my favorite part of anything—a trip, a meal, a date. There was something about the giddy flutter and the intoxicating anxiety that gave me a high that the actual event never seemed to. The first time I recognized the heady pleasure of anticipation was when I was very young and Tía Laura took me out for ice cream. First, there was the rush of *finding out* that something exciting was going to happen. Then, for the minutes, hours, or days until *it* happened, there was the suspense of *imagining* what it would be like—would the ice cream store be bright pink or teal or yellow like in the movies? What flavors and toppings would they have? Would I get a cone or a bowl? Then, there was the feeling of being *on the way*—driving to the ice cream shop. *It's all about to happen.* Then, finally, the thing happened. And the concrete, sensory experience never quite lived up to the anticipation of the experience. The anticipation was effervescent, intangible, weightless.

The reality was always just a little disappointing. That was how my first kiss with Natalie had been. The ice cream dripped and made everything sticky. I wasn't as naturally talented at guitar as I thought I would be. My mother didn't come to the school play. Always, I told myself, there would be something or someone to disappoint you or ruin the experience. But the anticipation was yours alone. My mom always used to tease me that I wanted everything to be *like it was in the movies*. She would sigh and say, "Life isn't like that, reyna. You have to learn to be *realistic*."

I wondered if anyone had told my favorite scientists that—to be more realistic. Would Tiera Guinn be a literal rocket scientist for NASA if her mother had told her to be more realistic? Marie Curie's husband didn't tell her that radioactivity research was unrealistic—he helped her win the Nobel Prize. In truth, someone probably told Elizabeth Blackwell that being the first woman to graduate from medical school was unrealistic, but she did it anyway. That was what I loved about science—it proved, despite the clamoring doubts of an unbelieving public, that *anything* is possible.

I wasn't sure whether it was a curse or a stroke of luck when Mr. Heller announced at lunch that tonight was the night of Camp Lavender's late-night pool party. All of the campers would arrive at the pool at eight p.m. for a showing of *Finding Nemo* that would start promptly at nine. I figured that Lacey and I could use this to our advantage—an all-camp activity, a later curfew, and distracted campers and counselors were all going to be helpful for our mission. By the end of dinner, I was starting to get nervous. As the campers crowded down the stairs to head back to the cabin cluster for their *flush and brush* (I never understood why everything and everyone had to have a cutesy name in this place), I saw a familiar head of wild curls ascending the steps, working against the tide of the crowd.

Lacey and I never came face to face, but Lacey got close enough to me to say in a low voice, "Be outside my place at eight o'clock."

Briefly, she met my eyes. I gave her a nod.

The anticipation increased.

## *Lacey*

I stood in front of the dresser in my bedroom feeling like I was going to throw up and faint at the same time. In all the time I had spent scribbling poems in my notebook, editing and re-editing my poems for Slant, reading comments from other poets, and pacing around my room reciting them aloud to myself, I had never for one moment thought about what I was going to wear.

Now, the question stared me in the face, daring me to try to make some cool or edgy ensemble from the worn T-shirts and basketball shorts strewn around my room. This was the first time I had felt properly panicked about the whole thing. After I had discovered the acceptance letter, my resolve to carry out this quest had hardened into something unbreakable. Now my self-doubt was swirling around me like some invisible, heavy cloak.

Right now, I was wearing light blue jeans that were clearly a little too short for me and a maroon Camp Lavender Staff T-shirt from two years ago. I must have been standing completely frozen in place for longer than I realized, because I jumped when I heard a *crack* on my window. At first, I thought it might just be an aggressive and idiotic bug hitting my window at full speed. But then it happened again. I went to the window and looked out. In the faint glow the porch light lent to the side of the cabin, I saw Jo standing with her hand behind her head as if she were about to throw something. Jo paused when she saw me come to the window and gave a sheepish wave. I raised the window halfway and leaned out, only about ten feet above where Jo was standing.

"What are you doing?"

Jo stretched her arms to her sides in a dramatic gesture.

"Rapunzel, Rapunzel, let down your hair," she said in a stage whisper.

I laughed even as I rolled my eyes. I leaned partway out the window and shook my head around, letting my mop of hair fly wildly. Jo mimed reaching up to grab it. I motioned for Jo to wait where she was and closed the window. I grabbed Jo's sweatshirt and the notebook she had given me and raced down the stairs, not making any effort to be quiet since both my parents were busy setting up and supervising the late-night pool party.

Jo was standing on the porch when I opened the front door.

"I have a problem," I said breathlessly, letting the door swing shut behind me.

"What is it?" asked Jo, an apprehensive tone in her voice.

"I don't have anything to wear."

I swept my hand over my current outfit to bring Jo's attention to it. Jo put her head to one side and pressed her lips together. I had half-expected her to rush in with some kind of no-your-outfit-is-fine reassurance, but she did no such thing. She walked around me, making a show out of assessing my outfit and finally saying in an exaggerated pretentious voice, "Your pieces do have a certain—how do you say— *homeschool-esque* quality about them."

My jaw dropped. "How dare you!"

Jo laughed. "Too far?"

I put both her hands over my face. "No," I said, my voice muffled by my hands. "Help me."

Jo stroked her chin with her hand. "What time is the slam?" she asked.

"Ten o'clock."

Jo glanced at her watch. "I think we've got time," she said.

"For what?"

"To get you an outfit!" Jo declared.

"You're kidding. Where?"

"In Austin. We'll stop by a thrift store and get you something to wear to the poetry slam. Something that will make you feel confident and cool."

"And edgy," I added, "like I go to public school."

Jo let out a throaty laugh. "Did you bring any money?"

"I have exactly fifty dollars in cash. Birthday money from the past two years."

"Excellent." Jo rubbed her hands together. "So," she said. "How exactly are we getting there, Ms. Heller?"

I grimaced and gestured for Jo to follow me toward the dining hall. We saw no sign of other campers, and whenever we came within earshot of a counselor, I said loudly, "I'm so excited for *Finding Nemo!*"

Behind the dining hall was a parking lot. In the parking lot, there were only three vehicles: a battered SUV and two windowless white vans that looked like their main purpose was to transport food and cooking supplies from town.

"Whose car is that?" Jo asked, pointing to the SUV. But I shook my head and pointed. Jo followed my gaze and immediately started shaking her head. "What? No. No way."

"Why not?"

"You want me to drive a giant van? All the way to Austin? I just got my driver's license *last* year, Lacey. This thing is huge!"

"It's not that big!" I said defensively. "And it has all the same controls as a regular car. I think. And also, it's the only option."

Jo groaned.

"We're just a little over an hour from Austin," I said. "It's just like…one highway. You can do it. I believe in you."

Jo turned and narrowed her eyes at me. She snatched the keys from my hand and pointed a finger in my face.

"No, *I* believe in *you*," was all she said before she turned on her heel and headed for the van.

# CHAPTER TWENTY-FIVE

## *Jo*

Lacey was right—it was a straight shot to Austin from Camp Lavender. Navigating the van out of the camp grounds had been the scariest part. I had learned to drive in my mom's ancient Subaru Outback, and that was all I had driven since. But technically, driving this van required only the same set of skills that I had confidently boasted to have mastered last summer. Thankfully, Lacey knew the ins and outs of the camp roads and guided me to the main road with ease. I felt like I was holding my breath until I got on the highway. I switched on the radio, and classic rock filled the van.

"Who's normally driving this?" I asked, surprised. "I thought the radio would be on Christian music for sure."

"Sidewinder," Lacey said. "The cook."

"The one who gave us pancakes?"

"The very same."

"She seems cool," I observed. Pine trees were flying by us, and I took deep breaths to calm the nervous thrill causing my hands to shake a little as I gripped the steering wheel. I couldn't believe that I was doing this—that *we* were doing this—but I wanted to seem nonchalant to Lacey, lest I spook her and change her mind about the whole thing.

"By cool, do you mean…non-Christian?"

"No," I said slowly, "I assumed everyone who works at Camp Lavender is a pretty strong Christian."

Lacey shrugged. "Maybe," she said, "but I've never seen Sidewinder voluntarily do anything except cook the meals, and that in and of itself is not a religious activity."

"Those pancakes were," I joked.

Lacey gave me a sidelong glance.

To distract her, I flipped through radio stations until I heard something familiar playing. At last, strains of indie folk music wafted through the speakers. It was the same band that I had listened to with Hayley on the way to downtown Gladwall.

"Do you know this band?" I asked. Lacey gave a small sigh.

"No," she said, a little shortly.

"Sorry, was that a dumb question?"

"No, it's just—" Lacey moved around in the passenger seat impatiently.

"What?"

"I just—I don't know a lot of bands. Not ones like this."

"That's okay," I said. "I'm not like…judging you for not knowing bands."

"Aren't you?"

"No, why? Are you judging me?"

"What would I judge you for?"

I cut my eyes toward Lacey, then focused on the road again. "Come on," I said quietly. "There's quite a lot to judge me for."

"Like what?"

"That's a bold question," I said. I forced a laugh.

Lacey crossed her arms and raised her eyebrows at me—a challenge. "I just want to know exactly what it is you are assuming I would judge you for."

"Well, first of all, for being…not a Christian."

"And second of all?"

I sighed and tapped my thumb on the top of the steering wheel. Somehow the stakes of this conversation felt higher than they ever had. "For all the things that would make your parents call me a bad influence," I said, keeping my eyes steadily on the road.

## *Lacey*

I watched the side of Jo's face as she drove, trying to read her expression. It felt like my insides were just a series of knots, all tangled up in each other. I folded my hands together in my lap so tightly that my knuckles turned white.

"I guess I'm not really sure what I think about all that stuff yet," I admitted quietly. "I've been alive for seventeen years, and I thought that I was some kind of, like, well-read critical thinker before you came along—"

"And destroyed all your self-confidence?" Jo asked.

I smiled faintly. "And made me realize that there are a lot of different kinds of people outside of Camp Lavender."

"You knew that, though."

"Yeah, I…" I trailed off as I tried to find the words to express the flurry of new thoughts and feelings I had experienced in the past five weeks.

"I guess I knew," I started again slowly, "that there were a lot of different kinds of people. But up until recently, I'd never really thought about the fact that I've only been told one kind of story about how the world is—about how people are—about what right and wrong really mean."

"Like, capital R, capital W," Jo said.

"Exactly."

"Well, you've spent seventeen years having pretty limited access to different, y'know, ways of being."

"But I never really questioned it."

"Why would you?"

"Because—" I waved my hands around, as if I could grab the words I needed from the air and form them into explanations.

"It's a luxury in some ways," Jo said, "to be so…protected."

This was a word that I had heard many times from my parents. They had told me that it is a parent's job to protect their child from evil influences until they are old enough to operate with discernment. I thought with bitterness of the fact that they obviously hadn't done a good enough job to believe that I was ready to go to college—something every normal kid was supposed to be ready to do by my age. I looked at Jo, whose eyes were fixed on the road, her slender fingers casually gripping the bottom of the steering wheel. I wondered what the concept of protection meant to her. I'd heard the envy in her voice as her mouth formed the word.

"You've been to Austin before?" I asked, as if I were changing the subject.

"Yeah," Jo said hesitantly, "once before."

"What for?"

Jo looked at me and a half smile formed on her face. I met her eyes and saw something there that I hadn't seen before, although I couldn't quite identify what it was.

"For the pride parade," Jo said in an even voice.

An odd feeling of warmth flushed over me, some strange mixture of emotion that created an unfamiliar reaction. "By yourself?" For some reason, this felt like the most important question.

"With my…well, with my then-girlfriend."

"Oh yeah?"

"Yeah, um…yeah. Her mom drove us in."

"That must've been cool."

"It was cool."

It sounded like Jo had much more to say, but I didn't press the matter. "I've never been to Austin," was all I said.

"Well, I'll have to show you around," Jo laughed. "Clearly, I'm an expert." Jo turned up the knob on the radio. "This is one of my favorite songs from the Lyrical Ballads," she said. "It's called 'Whoever Forever.'"

I closed my eyes and let the strains of the song wash over me. The song was full of bittersweet longing—I never understood how just musical notes could make someone feel that way. But when I paid attention to the lyrics, they were like poetry woven into melody.

"They got started on Slant," Jo commented.

My jaw dropped. "No way."

"Yes, way. Can you kind of tell?"

"*Yes*," I said. "That is amazing."

"Yeah," Jo said, "it was actually the bass guitar player who wrote all the lyrics and then this girl—now the lead singer—set the words to all these amazing melodies and eventually they formed a real band and made an album and now here they are on the *radio*."

"That's incredible," I breathed.

"Could be you next," Jo said, leaning over from the driver's seat to elbow me gently in the ribs.

"Ha."

"Hey, you never know."

"No one's ever layered one of my poems before," I said flatly.

"Yet," Jo said. "That could all change after you win the slam tonight."

"Stop! You're gonna jinx me!"

"Nah," Jo said. "I don't believe in that."

The conversation had circled back around to a dangerous word.

"So, what *do* you believe in?" I asked, making an effort to keep my voice light.

"Science," Jo said firmly.

She looked over in time to see me roll my eyes.

"Seriously?" I asked. "Isn't being an atheist scientist kind of cliché?"

Jo snorted. "Cliché is just a derogatory term for common sense."

"Touché," was all I said.

Jo drummed on the steering wheel. I wondered if she was nervous that I was going to become offended or angry at her anti-Jesus convictions.

"So," I said slowly, "you believe that the teachings of religion and the teachings of science are mutually exclusive."

"More or less," Jo said. "I mean, creationism versus evolution, right? It can't be both."

"Okay," I said, "So it's Christianity specifically?"

"Yeah and, like, for me, Catholicism specifically."

"So, is your family very Catholic?"

"Very."

"So…" I said. I faltered for words that didn't make my curiosity sound too invasive.

"So…no, they're not okay with me being gay," Jo said bluntly. "And yes, that's why I'm here. Not sure why my aunt thought an all-girls camp would be the cure to lesbianism, but I think she just went blind with rage after—"

She cut herself short.

"After what?" I asked gently.

"After she caught me and my ex-girlfriend kissing in my mom's car."

The truth filled the van like smoke.

"Was that Natalie?"

The name seemed to strike Jo like a blow.

"How—how could you *possibly* know that?" she asked.

"Well," I said quietly, "I may have snooped around your Slant account a little bit."

Jo's eyes met mine for a moment, then returned to the road.

"You stalked me?" she said. I could hear the smile in her voice.

"A *little*," I emphasized. "And also—she sent me a message."

I thought Jo was going to swerve off the road.

"*What?*"

"Yeah," I said. "I wasn't really sure—I mean I don't know—I mean—"

"I guess you're not the only stalker," she said through gritted teeth. "Shit. I'm so sorry. What…"

"Um, it just said *burn in hell.*"

"Are you kidding me? How did she even find you?"

I felt my face turning red. "My guess is that she was looking through the list of who had viewed, um, her profile, and she read my bio…it mentions camp. Maybe she looked up the camp online. I don't know."

Jo had the steering wheel in a death grip now.

"Why would she…" I started, then stopped.

"We broke up in the spring," Jo said, non-sequitur-ing her way out of the tension. "She kind of—well, she kind of bailed on me. It's a long story. And then my aunt decided to send me to this camp, and I guess she decided she wanted me back or something for whatever reason, and—I don't know—maybe she just made herself crazy. Anyway. I'm so sorry. You—*obviously* didn't deserve to get a message like that."

*Obviously,* as in I was a good person who didn't deserve to burn in hell—or obviously, as in there was nothing to be jealous of—or—

I fell silent, going over every word of what Jo had just said and parsing it for meaning and subtext. The air in the van started feeling suddenly thick and I rolled down the window a little to let in some of the outside air, which I realized with disappointment was also very thick. I was finally getting answers to so many of my questions, and my body felt shaky with a kind of queasy excitement and energy that unnerved me. Why was I so desperate to learn more? One more question rose to the surface and fought its way out despite my better judgment.

"Who broke up with who?"

"I broke up with her," Jo answered firmly. Why this pleased me so much, I wasn't able to answer.

"Well," I said, "that all sounds really stressful and awful and I'm sorry that you got sent here against your will."

"Doesn't everyone?"

"No, actually," I said, wondering if I should be offended. "A lot of people love coming to Camp Lavender. I mean—you met Rebekah, right?"

Jo let out one of her infrequent but rewarding throaty laughs.

"Yes, yes I did," Jo said. "And I also met you."

What was that supposed to mean? "And do I want to be here?" I asked.

I realized with a jolt that I was really asking. I watched Jo take in a deep breath and let it out slowly through her nose. I held my breath, waiting for any kind of response. Camp would be over in another week. What did we really have to lose? I felt myself going cold, like someone had turned off my central heating system in the middle of winter, hardening me up like a stiff limb. But when Jo finally did speak again, her words jolted me out of my frozen stupor.

"I don't know, Lacey," Jo said. "It's not for me to say."

"Not for you to say? But for you to think?" I told myself not to keep pressing, but something inside me was desperate for an answer—and it had to be from her.

"I think," Jo said carefully, "that you have a lot of curiosity about the outside world. I don't think you want to be Rapunzel. Or Emily Dickinson, for that matter."

"Who do I want to be?"

"I don't know," Jo said.

"Neither do I."

## CHAPTER TWENTY-SIX

### *Lacey*

Both of us breathed a sigh of relief when Jo pulled the van safely into a parking lot outside a thrift and consignment store called Uptown Cheapskate.

"We should be able to find you a decent outfit here," Jo said, putting the van into park. We seemed to have reached a tacit agreement to suspend any deep conversation until after the poetry slam was over. I was grateful, because my nerves had started skittering around inside me like so many rats in a basement when the light comes on.

I wasn't sure why I felt nervous entering the shop—like someone was going to see that I was too young, too inexperienced, too uncool to be here. But Jo led me confidently to a row of faded blue jeans.

"I guarantee you," Jo said in a low voice, "that if you pick something with holes in it, you will instantly feel fifty times cooler and more confident."

I couldn't help but laugh. "My mother would kill me."

"My bet is that she would kill you over any one of the things you're doing tonight," Jo said mischievously. "What's one more? You can hide them in your drawer when you get home."

I started touching various pairs of jeans, separating them delicately from the rest of the rack and looking at them with a mixture of excitement and fear. Finally, I pulled out a distressed pair of light-wash Levi's in my size.

"These are pretty cool," I said tentatively.

"They're *awesome*," Jo said with more enthusiasm than was strictly necessary. "Let's go find a shirt."

The shirts were organized by color, and Jo gravitated quickly toward the darker ones.

"I feel like poets always wear black in the movies, right?" she explained. I nodded, suddenly feeling shy at the thought of being the central focus of this event.

"Are you gonna buy anything?" I asked.

Jo looked confused. "We're here for you," she said, shaking her head. I felt my heart racing and sweat prickling my forehead, but Jo shoved five different black shirts into my hands and pointed toward the dressing rooms.

"Go try this stuff on and I'll find you some shoes."

I closed myself into a dressing room and took a deep breath, suddenly feeling like I was a character in a movie I had never seen, surrounded by colors, textures, and smells that were utterly unfamiliar. As I pulled on the jeans, I marveled at how soft and worn-in they felt. I liked the way the frayed edges sat around my knees and ankles and the way that my tan legs peeped through the distressed parts of the jeans. I wondered if my dad would call them immodest or if my mom would call them sloppy. I knew that they would.

My favorite shirt ended up being a loose black tank top, and I stepped out of the dressing room in my socks to ask for Jo's opinion. Jo held out a pair of scuffed Doc Marten boots and commanded me to put them on.

"Aren't these gonna be too hot?" I asked as I struggled to wriggle into them.

"Nah, they're gonna be too *cool*," Jo joked with a roguish raised eyebrow. She stepped back to take a look at her handiwork. "It's missing something," she announced.

"Shirt, pants, shoes…" I said. "What's missing?"

Jo held up a finger, signaling me to wait and disappeared back into the store. When she came back, she was carrying a quilted olive green bomber jacket with black trim and silver buttons. I looked at it skeptically.

"Just try it on," Jo pleaded. "See how you feel in it."

Jo held it up and I slipped an arm into one of the sleeves, allowing Jo to help me into it. As Jo adjusted the collar, the slight brush of the back of her hand against the skin on my neck sent a shiver down my spine. I turned to face her.

# *Jo*

The skin on the back of Lacey's neck was soft against the tips of my fingers, and I pulled my hand back at the shock of it as Lacey turned to face me. I stepped back, putting space between us, ostensibly so that I could appraise the outfit as a whole. I crossed my arms, as if to protect my hands from wandering to any forbidden places. I watched a smile bloom across Lacey's face as she put her hands into the pockets of the jacket and looked down at her new outfit. When she looked up, her eyes were sparkling.

"I don't think I'm cool enough to dress this way," she admitted quietly.

"You're a lot cooler than you think," I responded, wondering if it sounded like a hollow placation exchanged between girls in front of a dressing room mirror. "Does everything fit?"

"It all fits...perfectly," Lacey said, sounding surprised at herself. She turned around to stare at herself in the full-length mirror, looking herself up and down as if she were a stranger on the street.

"Do I look like...cool and edgy, or do I look...like some kind of desperate poser?"

"You look..." I started and stopped myself, trying to catch the words and restrain them before they came tumbling out. I walked up behind Lacey and looked at Lacey's reflection in the mirror. I saw the fearful expectancy in Lacey's eyes when she met mine in the reflection.

"You look like you could be a famous writer, but like not one who's obsessed with being famous, you know? And this is the outfit you're wearing while you take a long train ride and sit by the window and drink black coffee and write down new ideas in your super cool notebook."

I couldn't help myself from returning the bashful grin stealing over Lacey's face, and I couldn't help but feel the heat rising on my face. "What I'm trying to say is that you look like a badass," I concluded.

Lacey jutted her chin up and narrowed her eyes in an over-exaggerated gesture of confidence. "Thanks, kid," she said in a deep voice. I laughed and gave her a light shove.

"All right, don't get too big for your vintage distressed britches," I warned. I glanced at my watch.

"It's probably time to head to Spider House," I said. "If you're ready."

When Lacey approached the counter at Uptown Cheapskate, a girl who looked to be just a few years older than us, but much cooler, with electric blue hair and not one but *two* eyebrow piercings, told Lacey that she could keep the outfit on while she rang everything up.

"Thanks," Lacey said.

I heard tension entering her voice.

"You girls headed somewhere exciting after this?" the cashier asked as she examined the tags on Lacey's clothes and clicked keys on the register.

"Yep!" I announced. "We're going to Spider House for a poetry slam."

"That place is awesome," the girl said with a smile. "Me and my boyfriend go there all the time. Are you both competing?"

"Just me," Lacey said.

"I'm going for moral support," I added. "And so that I can say that I was at American poet Lacey Heller's first ever public performance. She's gonna be famous one day."

"Wow," said the blue-haired girl. "Well, I'm honored to be selling you your outfit for such a momentous occasion."

The girl glanced out the window and saw the white van sitting in the parking lot.

"Is that your ride?"

I nodded, but Lacey, apparently emboldened by her new attire, added, "We're on the lam."

"Is that so?" the girl asked cautiously.

"We, no, we—we drove it in from Camp Lavender."

The girl's jaw dropped and she looked at Lacey and me with an unreadable expression in her eyes.

"That's that Christian girl's camp in Gladwall, right?"

"Yeah," I said, feeling suddenly fearful.

The girl crossed her arms, looking impressed. "I didn't think they let anybody leave that place on their own," she said. "Or like, at all, really. How did you pull that off?"

Lacey and I exchanged nervous glances. Surely there was no way that this cashier would care enough to call Mr. Heller and turn us in.

"We, um—" I started, praying that I would think of a believable lie before I got to the end of the sentence.

"We ran away," Lacey cut in. I stared at her, utterly shocked, and saw that her face was shining with defiance. "Just for the night. So I can do this."

Lacey handed over the fifty dollar bill and the girl hit a few more buttons on the register, nodding slowly.

"Your total is actually fifty-five dollars and thirty-two cents," she informed Lacey apologetically. Lacey turned to me, eyes wide with panic.

"Which thing should I leave behind? What if we need money for something later? Like food or something? Should I leave the boots?"

I held out Lacey's extremely well-worn and never-very-stylish sneakers. The blue-haired girl frowned and looked from Lacey to me to the shoes to the number on her register.

"Wait," she said.

The girl pulled a wad of dollar bills from her own back pocket and stuffed them into the cash register drawer. When we protested, she shrugged.

"Can't have a soon-to-be-famous American poet in an unfinished outfit on such a big night," was all she said. Lacey thanked her profusely, glowing with shock and embarrassment. As we made our way toward the door, the cashier called out, "Wait, you forgot your receipt!"

"I'll grab it," I said to Lacey, tossing her the keys to the van. I rushed back to the counter and saw with surprise that the girl was writing something on the receipt. She slid it across the countertop to me with a serious look on her face.

"That's my phone number," she said quietly. "Just in case you guys get into—any trouble while you're here."

"Okay," I said, a little confused as I folded the receipt and tucked it into my back pocket. As I looked up, I noticed the small rainbow pin on the collar of the girl's denim jacket.

## CHAPTER TWENTY-SEVEN

### *Lacey*

Spider House was like nothing I had ever seen before. People in outfits much more edgy and cool than anything I was wearing milled around holding beers and cocktails under a web of string lights that gave the whole space a dreamlike glow. Inside the ballroom itself, all the lights were tinted red, adding to the air of unreality that had followed me ever since we got into the van. A mirror ball hung in the center of the ceiling made everything look like it was vibrating.

As I stepped inside, I felt my excitement drain into panic. I was grateful that Jo had chosen me a jacket, an extra layer between me and the outside world. Now I tucked my black notebook under my arm and shoved my hands into the pockets, looking around for a sign or an official-looking person. A bearded man in a button-down approached me with a roll of pink tickets in one hand and a clipboard in the other.

"Are you one of the contestants?"

"Yeah," Lacey said. "How did you—"

"You've got a notebook and you look scared." He laughed. "First time?"

"First time," I repeated, and I really, really meant it.

"Okay," the man said, businesslike. "We start in fifteen minutes. I'm Mike. I'll do intros and announce the winners of each round. We'll have three rounds total, and you'll need new verses for each round you perform in. I'm gonna let you know when you're next, and I want you to wait in the wings of the stage and be on deck for when it's your turn to go when the person before you is performing, okay?"

I felt like I had just stepped under a heavy waterfall of words and somehow come out completely dry. Nothing he said had made sense to me. I could feel my palms starting to sweat.

"Okay," I responded blankly. I looked around and saw Jo, nodding carefully. The man handed us two pink tickets.

"Each performer gets two drink tickets," he said nonchalantly. "But if you're gonna get one now, be quick. We start soon."

He walked away with a determined step, too busy to ask if either of us had any questions. I looked at Jo, a wild fear sweeping over me.

"Was this a horrible mistake and we should just turn and go and pretend this never happened?"

It felt like all of the words came out at the exact same time.

"No," Jo murmured, grabbing my elbow, and steering me back outside toward the parking lot. "Just take a deep breath. Remember—the stakes aren't that high. It's just a poetry contest—the first of many more."

"I mean, they're pretty high, given that I *ran away from home* to do this."

"You did not run away from home," Jo chided gently. "You snuck out to go on an adventure—that's a normal thing for a teenager to do."

I looked around me, taking in the crowd with their easy laughter and confident gestures. They all looked like they belonged here.

"I have no idea what's normal," I said.

"That's what I—that's what makes you, *you*," Jo said.

"That's what you—what?" I asked.

Jo opened her mouth to answer, but before she could, a lanky young man with dark hair approached us so closely that both of us turned instinctively to look at him.

"Excuse me, sorry," he said, "but—are you Lacey?"

Jo watched me as I realized who was standing in front of me.

"Yes…" I said cautiously.

"It's me! Moon Boy Eleven!" The boy put a hand on his chest in a self-reflexive gesture.

"Oh—hi!" I said, gripped by an unrecognizable concoction of emotions. I turned toward Jo and gestured at the guy.

"This is—oh my gosh, I just realized I don't even know your real name."

"Jason." The guy smiled and his eyes lingered on me as he spoke.

"This is Jason. We've been chatting on Slant for, like, months at this point. He's the one who first told me I should perform! Jason, this is Jo." I offered no other qualifiers.

Jo looked the guy up and down and held out her hand for him to shake.

"So formal," he joked.

"Well, you're a stranger," Jo said wryly. He held up his hands defensively.

"Well, hopefully I won't be soon! Would you ladies like a drink?"

"We're seventeen," Jo said shortly. Jason smiled and pulled out his wallet.

"That's why I'm buying," he said smoothly.

"I'll have a drink," I cut in. "A martini, please."

Jo's jaw dropped.

"And for you, madam?"

"Make it two," she said curtly.

Jason disappeared into the interior of Spider House and I turned toward Jo, feeling sheepish.

"Sorry I didn't tell you about him," I said. "I honestly didn't even think he'd come."

"So you came here because of him?"

Jo's voice and manner were icy.

"No," I said defensively. "I came here to actually do something with my poetry. To try something different and not just—stay trapped in my tower or whatever."

"Do you want me to just go, so you can be alone with him?"


## Jo


I knew that I was being petty, but the betrayal by omission when it came to male attention was soaking me in a déjà vu that clouded my judgment. "I just don't want to intrude," I said coldly.

"I don't want to be *alone* with him," Lacey said. I could hear the hurt in her voice, but I didn't care.

"So you brought me as a chaperone?" I asked.

"I asked you to drive me here…"

"So you brought me as a *chauffeur*?"

"Are you serious? That's why you think I asked you?"

Lacey crossed her arms tightly over her chest and took a step backward.

"Well, what—" I started. My whole body felt aflame with frustration. Before I could finish, Jason returned with three cocktail glasses. He handed one to Lacey and one to me and kept the third for himself.

"What did you get?" Lacey asked politely.

"Whiskey neat," Jason said.

I let out a slight scoff, before thinking better of it. Lacey took a step forward, focusing her attention on Jason, who was wearing a wrinkled blue button down over a gray T-shirt and black jeans.

"Your verses are amazing," Jason said enthusiastically. He took a sip of his whiskey. "It's been such a thrill watching you flourish as a poet over the last few months."

"Thank you," Lacey said, looking at the ground as he showered her with compliments. "Actually, Jo has—really challenged me and encouraged me to try new things with my writing."

She glanced at me for a response, but I gave only a tight-lipped nod. Then they were calling the performers into the ballroom to give them the rundown before the slam started.

"All right, I gotta go," Lacey said nervously to Jason and me. "I'll see you guys in there?"

Jason took a step forward and put a hand on Lacey's shoulder, looking into her eyes. "You are a marvelous poet," he said rapturously. "You're going to be amazing."

Lacey let out a nervous laugh and cut her eyes over to me, but I was looking resolutely away. "Wish me luck?" she asked quietly. Jason turned to look at me.

"Good luck," I muttered, still avoiding her eyes. Lacey turned and rushed toward the ballroom door with the other contestants. With his primary object gone, Jason turned his attention toward me.

"So," he started amicably.

"I need to use the restroom." I turned away from Jason and strode into the Spider House bar. I made a beeline for the bathroom, martini in hand. The bathroom was lit with the same red glow as the ballroom and for a moment, I reeled. I braced myself against the bathroom sink and stared at myself in the mirror, grimacing at the features I had encountered there countless times—oversized brown eyes, a scattering of freckles just a few shades darker than my skin, a crop of wavy, dark brown hair. I thought about the tall, masculine stranger nursing his whiskey outside the ballroom, waiting to ply Lacey with alcohol and a bouquet of hollow praise.

"Don't be a fucking baby," I muttered aloud to myself.

"Girl troubles?"

I whirled around to see a girl emerging from the bathroom stall. She had blond hair, dark eye makeup, and a septum piercing. She was dressed head-to-toe in black—a thin tank top, a short A-line skirt, fishnet stockings, and heavy black boots.

"How'd you know?" I asked, taken aback with embarrassment and exposure.

"Just a guess." The girl's mouth quirked to one side and I watched her appraising eyes as she looked me up and down. "Can I buy you a shot?" she asked, with all the smoothness and twice the charm Jason had applied mere minutes ago.

I gestured to my drink. "I've got this," I said vaguely, wondering what 1940s movie had inspired Lacey to ask for a goddamn martini.

"From the look on your face, you need something faster."

The girl reached out and grabbed my hand, dragging me out of the bathroom and toward the bar.

"Two tequila shots, chilled and dressed!" she called to the bartender, holding out a credit card. I set my martini on the bar and leaned against it. I did not want to admit to this pretty stranger that I had, in fact, never taken a shot in my life. The only time I had tried liquor before now was at Natalie's house when we had raided her parents' liquor cabinet and mixed vodka into our Gatorade. The girl handed me the tiny glass rimmed with salt and garnished with a lime. I must not have been able to conceal my nerves, because the girl leaned toward me and said, "Take a lick of the salt, drink the shot in one go, and then bite down on the lime."

I straightened up and clinked my glass against hers.

"To shitty girlfriends," she said with a laugh. Then she licked salt off the rim of her glass, tapped the bottom of the glass lightly against the surface of the bar, and threw it back gracefully. I imitated her, praying that I wouldn't do something embarrassing like choke or spit.

It was like taking cough syrup, I thought, as I squeezed my eyes shut and made a wry face.

"Good girl," the girl said. Then, "My name's Savannah, by the way."

"Jo," I said in a hoarse voice. I looked at my watch.

"It's starting," I said, grabbing my cocktail glass off the bar. Savannah followed behind me. When I opened the door to the ballroom, the first round had already started. I saw no sign of Lacey, but observed with a stab of irritation that Jason had somehow found a seat in the front row. I made my way along the back wall until I found a good place to stand, with a view both of the stage and of Jason. I leaned back against the wall. The movement of the red lights, the adrenaline, and the tequila created a sickening formula that made everything waver. Savannah settled in beside me, letting her shoulder brush mine ever so slightly. I stood perfectly still, trying to take no notice of the panic buzzing inside me.

Then I began to listen.

I listened as poets of every description stood on the stage and unleashed their passion on an enraptured audience. Some were more polished than others, but not, I thought, necessarily better. Some were passionate, but not more convincing. I found myself wishing that Lacey was beside me so that I could nudge her when someone said something provocative or poignant, and could share whispered appraisals with her at the end of each performance. I stole a glance at Savannah, who, I realized with a jolt, was already looking at me.

"Which one is she?" she whispered. I shook her head to indicate that she hadn't performed yet. Lacey was last in the first round. She stepped out onto the stage, her black notebook grasped tightly in her hand. I saw that her hand was shaking a little. I straightened up and took a deep breath. I let out an almost involuntary whisper.

"That's her."

## CHAPTER TWENTY-EIGHT

### *Lacey*

The lights onstage were so bright that I could make out hardly anything beyond the edge besides an amorphous swell of red. Still, I managed to catch sight of Jason beaming at me from the front row. He gave me a cheerful thumbs-up. I had all of my verses memorized, but now it felt like the air was leaking from my lungs and my mind was going blank. My fingertips felt sweaty as I clutched the black journal. I couldn't remember the first line. I cracked open the journal with trembling fingers and looked for the poem I had planned on reading first. It felt like I had taken fully half an hour to find it, although in reality it had probably only been a few seconds.

I took a deep breath and glanced up, scanning the room for Jo's face the way that Jo had done when she played guitar on worship night, but I could not find her. I wondered if Jo had decided not to come in, or worse, to leave me here. I wondered why Jo had been so angry at me for not telling her about Jason. I wondered—

"You got this, girl," came a stranger's booming voice from the crowd. I realized that I had been standing still on the stage with my journal open for far longer than I should have. I looked down at the page and started to read. My shaking voice sounded small in the crowded silence.

*You said, you need this. You need us.*
*You need to be—to do—everything we tell you to.*
*But I won't. I can't. And none of that was planned.*
*It's just a fact.*

*Pull my hand back from the flame, and see it doesn't look the same.*
*But it sure feels better now. How?*
*One day I know—the wound will close*
*because I chose—to let it heal.*
*I choose not to feel*
*the way I did before. Not anymore.*
*You want me to come crawling back now. How?*
*I watched the door swing shut on me when you said,*
*Not now, honey. Maybe later.*
*And now I'll have to make do on my own—go it alone.*
*Lay down the bricks for a new home.*

*You said, you need this. You need us.*
*We're the ones that you can trust.*
*You said, you said, just stay in bed—and dream*
*until your dreams are dead.*

*One day, you'll say—come back.*
*But there's nowhere left to go, except slow*
*slow, slowly forward*
*until I'm someone new*
*and maybe she'll know what to do.*
*No more frozen feet, she'll move*
*forward, onward, upward.*
*You'll say, it's such a shame.*
*She used to be noble, she used to be pure.*
*You'll say, I wonder what happened to her?*
*And I wonder what I'll say.*

Applause filled the room. No one laughed. No one scoffed. No one shouted at me to go home because I was just a stupid little girl. And that was more than enough. I took one more look out at the crowd and finally spotted Jo, standing against the back wall next to a girl I didn't recognize, who was whispering into Jo's ear. I retreated to the back where the rest of the poets were in a makeshift green room crowded around a couch that looked like it had been retrieved from a house fire. One of the other poets clapped me on the back.

"How was that, newbie?"

"Terrifying," I said, laughing at a high pitch. The others laughed alongside me. I was surprised at the warm, open atmosphere of this place. I wasn't sure what I had been expecting, but not this genuine display of camaraderie to someone who was clearly an outsider. When Mike came backstage to announce who would continue to the next round and I was among them, even the contestants who had been eliminated cheered me on. I felt my heart race, but not with the same sickly terror I had felt when I entered the building. This time, it was something new—something good. It was a thrill of recognition, of affirmation, of knowing that someone besides me and a handful of people on the internet had heard my words and had felt something.

It was more than enough. And I wanted more.

Now there were six contestants instead of twelve. Someone made room on the couch for me and I began to page through my notebook, making sure that I had chosen the right verses for the second round. Suddenly, I remembered my martini. It sat on a crate next to the couch, right where I had left it. I wasn't sure what had made me agree to it, but something in the air that night made me feel like anything was possible. I picked it up and took a deep breath, not exactly sure what was even in a martini. Probably liquor of some kind. But it was one of the only cocktails I knew the name of and it sounded sophisticated enough for a poet to drink. And it was something I had seen Katharine Hepburn drink in the movies. I took a sip and winced at the strange taste. One of the other poets, a woman in a flowing green tunic and tight braids, smiled at me.

"You good, kiddo?"

"It's like...drinking a rolltop desk," I sputtered.

"Yeah, vermouth is disgusting." The woman laughed. I wondered what it must be like to be an adult like this—to live in Austin and perform poetry and have fully formed opinions about adult things like vermouth. I wanted to ask each of the other people in the room exactly how they'd gotten here and where they were going next and what they did when they weren't at poetry slams. They all seemed impossibly poised and self-possessed, like they had long ago figured out how to style their hair and clothes and lived in resolute freedom from the rigid expectations that may or may not have been laid upon them in childhood.

I had finished my drink before the second round. I wasn't sure I would feel different until I stood up from the couch and realized that there was a soft blur around my eyes and a glow of confidence in my chest that hadn't been there before. I smiled to myself, thinking of my plea to the heavens at the beginning of the summer. I had begged for something different—and here it was. I had made it happen. Jo and I had made it happen.

I stepped out onto the stage with my head held high and this time there was a murmur of encouragement from the crowd. I had no idea that slam poetry was such an interactive experience—the crowd snapping and vocalizing in real time as the performers struck a chord within them. This time, I used my finger to keep my place in my notebook in case I forgot the words, but I looked out at the crowd as I spoke.

*I shook you by the shoulders—screaming, begging*
*wake up, please, before I freeze.*
*I'm out here all alone.*
*I'm cold and the light of the stars is fading.*
*I don't know how long I can keep waiting.*
*Holding the door, but my muscles are shaking,*
*my tendons are breaking. It swings shut.*
*Now I'm not cold anymore,*
*I'm numb and it feels more like warmth*
*than anything before—cools the burn, puts out the flame*
*the landscape doesn't look the same.*
*I hear the heavy sound of latch and bolt, last one locking*
        *with a jolt*
*I feel the shudder of the frame*
*I hear you calling out my name.*
*a muffled sound of the word WAIT*
*my love's no clock; it can't be late.*
*But my heart is buried in the snow; I'll dig it out before I go,*
*take it with me, dust it off, keep it safe before it's lost.*
*The door to heaven shut and locked, heart skips a beat but*
        *now I'm off.*
*And on the other side, pride, and love,*
*and a little bit of hate, empty echoes of verse eight.*
*You know I wanted to believe, now tender spots, sore as I*
        *grieve.*

*Maybe there's something wrong—with me.*
*Perhaps I can't see past my pride—or greed*
*wrath, envy, sloth, gluttony, lust*
*Just close your eyes and jump and trust.*
*Or maybe, just maybe, it was meant to be*
*maybe the broken thing isn't me.*
*Maybe I woke up, stiff and sore*
*and I remembered that there was more,*
*something I knew in times before.*
*Now I'm awake and I'm alive, ready to be free*
*You don't need me. Hush.*
*Go back to sleep.*

The claps were quieter this time. I retreated to the green room, breathless with equal parts nerves and exhilaration. If I made it through this round, I would be one of three finalists. Even if I didn't, I had still performed two poems onstage to a real, living audience. I clasped my fingers tightly together, hearing the murmur of the last performer in the second round and trying to gauge the enthusiasm of the crowd from their muffled murmurs and applause. Finally, all six performers were huddled in the green room, and I noticed that the chatter and joking had slowed. The air was thicker. Mike came backstage after talking to the judges.

"Amazing job, poets," he said. "You've all done great work here and made Spider House proud. Here are the three finalists: Cameron Lasseter, Shanitra LeBlanc…" He looked down at his paper and back up. "And Lacey Heller."

## *Jo*

"So is that, like, her thing?"

Savannah and I were waiting at the bar for vodka sodas during a short intermission between the second and third round of performances. I had abandoned my martini in the women's bathroom and had no intention of retrieving it, secretly pleased with myself for wasting even a tiny fraction of Jason's money.

"What?"

"Like…the whole sad girl thing. Is that what all her poetry is about?"

"I mean, I haven't read all her poetry," I started, "but I think it's pretty good for someone who is just starting out."

I hoped Savannah didn't think I sounded defensive. Anyway, why *was* I defensive?

"Oh for sure," Savannah said quickly, "I just wondered if she writes about other stuff, or if it's all that same style."

"I think she's just writing about what she's been through," I said, keeping my tone measured. "And she really hasn't been through that much yet. Her parents have basically kept her locked up her whole life and haven't let her out into the world, so she doesn't have a lot of experiences to write from yet—but she will."

"Is that what happened with you two?"

Savannah's voice was casual, but I could feel her eyes on me as she handed me a vodka soda and guided me back toward the ballroom.

"What?"

"Her parents were too involved?"

"What—no."

"Oh, so you aren't exes?"

I shook my head, surprised by the bluntness of the question. Savannah found two seats that had been abandoned and gestured for me to sit next to her. She took a sip of her drink and leaned toward me conspiratorially.

"I bet I know what it is," she said, her eyes twinkling with mischief. I took a long sip of my drink, feeling my nerves starting to rise.

"What is it?" I asked, careful to keep my tone playful.

Savannah leaned in close enough for me to catch a whiff of her perfume; it was spicy and floral. "You fell for a straight girl," Savannah whispered.

I leaned my head back and let out an overly loud laugh. "I didn't fall for anybody."

"Okay," Savannah replied, putting her hand up defensively. "If you say so."

I took another long drink in lieu of a reply. The red lights dimmed, flickering softly in the reflection of the mirror ball spinning lazily around. I didn't see Lacey anywhere, so I figured she must be backstage, which meant she must be one of the finalists. Pride blossomed in my chest like a flower. I wished that I had said something encouraging. I took another sip of my drink. I wished that I had said something inspiring. Another drink. I wished that I had said something honest. I looked around for Jason. He was still in his place in the front row. I studied his features. He certainly wasn't bad looking. I wondered what he and Lacey talked about on Slant. Did they talk about poetry, or other things? Did they talk about the same things that she and I had talked about in the chapel, on the lake, on the picnic table under the stars? I reached into the pocket of my hoodie and fiddled with its contents. I should have given my gift to Lacey before she had performed, but things hadn't gone as I had planned.

The first two performers were, in my opinion, very talented, but not as talented as Lacey. Lacey went last. When she came onstage, I saw that she wasn't holding the notebook anymore. I smiled to myself, knowing that Lacey must have felt confident that she would remember her verses—that she wanted to show her prowess to the audience in the final round. She had refused to tell me which poems she was going to use at the slam. I had heard iterations of each of the previous ones during our workshop session at the chapel, but I had no idea what was coming next. With a jolt, I realized that Savannah had stretched her arm across the back of my chair, her hand resting lightly on my shoulder. I sat still, hoping that Lacey wouldn't look out at the crowd.

But she looked right at me. I could not read the look in her eyes or tell whether she had registered the girl sitting next to me. When she spoke, her voice was stronger and clearer than it had been before. She held my eyes while she spoke.

*We were writ large in the stars.*
*We were the water on Mars.*
*Everyone knew we were there,*
*but nobody knew what it meant.*

*We were sojourners in the wide night sky*
*looking for something we were frightened to find.*

*We were spirits crashing in the sand*
*the only way we knew how to land.*

*We were opportunity in swirling dust*
*waiting for someone to rescue us.*

*We were curiosity on uneven terrain;*
*we roamed the desert and waited for rain.*
*We were the rock and the hard place*
*out in space, and the atmosphere was thin.*

*Everyone tried to reach us, but no one could get a signal.*

*The heart is deceitful above all things;*
*let's cut it open and count the rings*
*let's take it up to the highest point*
*and watch it get struck by lightning.*

*If it falls and breaks, we'll do what it takes*
*to get it working again.*

I sat frozen in my chair. I felt surprised that not everyone in the room had turned to look at me, so enormous was the swell of my feeling and so thunderous the beating of my heart. I jumped up from my chair and started clapping furiously. A few of the audience members glanced at me and smiled, but for the most part everyone was shifting around in their seats waiting for the judges to determine the winner. I pushed my way out of the row I had been sitting in, only vaguely aware of Savannah calling after me. I found my way backstage. The two other contestants were sitting on the couch, making tense small talk, but Lacey was pacing around the room, absentmindedly twirling a curl around her finger. When she saw me, her eyes were alight.

I rushed over to her and shook her by the shoulders.

"What was that! What was that!" I kept repeating breathlessly.

Lacey let out a manic laugh. "You liked it?"

"I *loved* it," I said. "You never—we never worked on that."

"I wanted it to be a surprise."

"When did you learn the names of the Mars rovers?"

Lacey could not take her eyes off of mine; they shone with pride and with something deeper—something enamored. She shrugged, but she could not resist the smile overflowing her face.

"I looked them up."

I took a step back and shook my head slowly, beaming.

"You were amazing," I said. "You were one of the finalists on your first try."

"I know—I can't believe it."

"I can," I said firmly.

Then Mike appeared. The other two contestants stood up abruptly from the couch as he waved them all onto the stage.

"Stay here," Lacey said over her shoulder as she followed the others out onto the stage.

## CHAPTER TWENTY-NINE

## *Lacey*

I tried to take deep breaths, but they came out more like gasps. I felt sweat bead on my forehead and under my arms under the overpowering stage light. I was dimly aware when Mike announced that Shanitra LeBlanc had won third place. I held my breath as he announced that second place was Cameron Lasseter.

"And in first place," Mike said, turning to beam at me, "is a newbie to the Austin slam scene. Everyone give a big round of applause for Lacey Heller!"

A torrent of applause erupted as Mike patted me on the shoulder and I put both hands over my heart, as if to keep it from exploding out of my chest. Mike handed me an envelope full of cash and a faux gold medal with *Spider House Poetry Slam* etched into it. I stood still under the blinding lights, barely able to process the fact that all of this was meant for me. That I had been seen and heard. That I had made this happen.

That we had made this happen.

As the event dissolved into a shuffle for bags and drinks, I rushed off the stage and back into the now empty green room where Jo was waiting at the back. Jo stretched her arms out in a sign of victory and, bursting with sparkling adrenaline, I ran across the room and leapt into them, letting out a triumphant yell. Jo spun me around and I felt my head fizzing with glory and alcohol and freedom. As Jo set me down, I caught onto her forearms for balance, and before I could think better of it, I caught Jo's face in my hands and pressed my lips onto hers. Jo stumbled backward a step, then wrapped her arm around my waist, pulling our bodies together and pushing deeper into the kiss. In that moment, we were outside time and space, caught in a heady dimension all our own.

It was Jason who broke the spell.

"Wow!"

His booming voice echoed from the doorway of the greenroom and we sprang apart, staring at each other wild-eyed.

"You won!" Jason said, striding across the room and wrapping me in a hug. He seemed equally unaware of his intrusion and of Jo's presence.

"I told you, you were amazing!"

"Thanks," I said, trying to compose myself back into a corporeal reality.

"Let's get a round of shots to celebrate!"

"Yeah!" I was surprised by the enthusiasm in my own voice. Jason caught me by the elbow and steered me forcefully out of the green room and toward the bar.

## *Jo*

I stumbled out of the green room, stunned. For a moment, I thought that maybe I had hallucinated the past five minutes, but I could still taste gin and olive juice on my lips. I put a hand to my mouth, trying to preserve the feeling, and followed the last few audience members out of the ballroom. Outside, Savannah lingered, looking around the crowd. When she caught sight of me, she gave me a lackadaisical smile.

"I saw your girl headed toward the bar with some dude in a button-down," she said.

"She—I don't know what just happened," I said, more to myself than to Savannah.

"That's how it is with straight girls," Savannah said with a kind of self-satisfied sympathy. She put an arm around my shoulder and leaned her head toward me. "Want to make her jealous?"

I nodded dazedly and Savannah tightened her grip on my shoulder. She marched me into the bar, where Jason was waiting with his wallet out, trying to catch the bartender's eye in the midst of the post-performance frenzy. He pointed at me when he saw me.

"Y'all want a shot?"

"If you're paying!" Savannah shouted back. "Come on, let's find a seat."

Lacey looked surprised when Savannah and I approached the rickety metal table where she had settled herself, her face and hair glowing under the constellation of string lights. I had never seen her so beautiful or so reckless. Savannah introduced herself and pulled her chair close to mine, letting one hand rest lazily on my shoulder.

"You know each other?" Lacey asked stiffly.

"Oh, yeah," Savannah effused. "We hit it off in the bathroom right before the show. Great job, by the way. It was nice to see you show your range at the end."

Lacey sat up straighter and I studied the look in her eyes, parsing it for meaning. Jason arrived with four tequila shots and I gulped mine down with the determination of a seasoned drinker. I watched Lacey sputter, but she recovered quickly. Jason pulled his chair close to Lacey's, mirroring the proximity of Savannah to me, and began once again to shower her with compliments. I felt myself starting to go numb as the tequila took hold—I wondered just how much alcohol I could tolerate and guessed that it was probably not much more. I snapped back to an alert state when I felt Savannah's fingertips sliding into my hair.

"You have such soft hair," Savannah said, loudly enough for the other two to hear.

Jason raised his eyebrows and smirked, sitting back in his chair. "Please, go on," he said in a voice that made my stomach churn.

Savannah turned her head sharply toward him. "You like when women touch each other?" she asked, her voice a challenge.

"If I can watch, yeah," Jason replied, his smirk widening.

Savannah jumped up from her chair and grabbed my hand.

"That's too bad," she said. She looked at Jason and then looked at Lacey. "Let's find somewhere a little more private."

She dragged me away toward the bar.

❖

## *Lacey*

Jason looked at me. "What was that about?" he asked.

I shifted in my seat, feeling like a hurricane was tearing through me. "I don't know," I said, keeping my voice casual.

"Whatever," Jason said, returning his attention to me. "I'm more interested in what's happening here."

"And what's happening?" I asked.

Jason grinned and pulled his chair a little closer toward me. The mixture of sweat and cologne stifled me and I leaned my head back.

"What's happening here," he said slowly, placing a heavy hand on my knee, "is that a very cool girl came into town to meet up with me."

I froze, a sickly jolt of realization flashing through me. "I came into town to do this competition," I said quietly.

"Right," he said dismissively, "And you were amazing up there. Also, you look amazing—especially in these jeans." He ran his hand a little farther up my thigh.

"So what did you think?" I asked tensely. "About my performance."

"Oh it was great—so good," he said absently.

"That's it?"

He narrowed his eyes, looking a little annoyed. "It was fantastic," he added, as if trying to land on an answer that would conclude this part of the conversation.

And perhaps it was the adrenaline, or the alcohol, or the agony of wondering what was happening inside the bar, but something that had been sleeping inside me abruptly awakened. I looked Jason squarely in the face.

"You know that I don't want to have sex with you, right?"

Jason sat back in his chair and crossed his arms. "Well that was blunt," he said petulantly.

"Is that what you wanted?" I asked. Jason held up his hands in defense.

"I thought we had a connection," he said. "You seemed pretty into me when we were having all those conversations at two a.m. every night."

I stared at him, considering this claim.

"Well, I guess I'm not," I said. And the simple truth of the words sent me out of my chair and into the bar.

## *Jo*

"How was that?" Savannah asked, smiling.

"Good—great," I said, a queasy feeling overcoming me. I leaned my back against the wall by the door, trying to catch my breath. Savannah seemed to take it as an invitation and took a step closer.

"I don't know what's going on with you and that girl," she said, "but you are very cute in a baby butch kind of way."

As she leaned closer to me, something in me snapped. I ducked under Savannah's arm, muttering an incoherent excuse, and rushed into the bathroom. I took as deep a breath as I could, wrapping my hoodie around me tightly. I stared at myself in the mirror, wondering at the way my reflection looked blurrier than it had earlier in the evening. This must be what drunkenness really felt like. The door of the bathroom opened and Lacey appeared in the reflection behind me. Her eyes were aflame with anger.

"What the hell is going on?"

Her voice was shaking. I stared at her in the mirror for a moment, then whirled around to face her. "You tell me," I said sharply.

"Who's that girl?" Lacey demanded.

"Who's that *guy*?" I fired back.

"I told you—I've been talking to him on Slant."

"And he invited you here, right? And you wanted to come see him?"

"What? I wanted to come *perform*!"

"And you just wanted me for—what? A ride and moral support?"

"You're my friend," Lacey said defensively.

"And that's why you kissed me backstage?"

The silence fell like an anvil. Lacey deflated slightly. "I—I don't know," she admitted. "I just—"

"You just what?"

"I just wanted to—"

"To what? To celebrate? Because a hug or a high five would be fine for that."

"I just wanted to know—"

"*Please* don't say you just wanted to know what it felt like," I cut her off. Lacey pushed her hands into her pockets and looked at the ground. I took a step forward.

"You may not know this since you've been locked in a tower your whole life." My voice was low and hard. "But there are plenty of girls who like to kiss other girls *just to see what it will feel like*. And it's not cute. And it's not funny. And I don't want to be your experiment while you flirt with some douchebag you met on the internet."

"That's not fair," Lacey said quietly.

"Maybe it's not," I said. "But I—but you—"

"What?" Lacey looked up sharply.

"You know what," I said.

"Just say it. Please."

"I fucking *like* you, Lacey. I think you know that. And if you don't know who you are or what you want, that's just fine. But don't drag me into it."

Lacey took a deep breath and asked her next question with her eyes fixed on the floor. "Do you think I'm good?"

"What?"

Lacey looked up. "Do you think I'm good at writing poetry and performing and all that, or did you just think I was cute so you told me what I wanted to hear?"

"Are you joking?"

Lacey shook her head. I grimaced and took a step toward her. I put a hand on each of her shoulders and looked up into her face.

"Lacey," I said with a kind of calm heat, "I want to be very clear. I like you. Yes, as more than a friend. But that's not why we're here right now. I agreed to come with you because I believe in you. You are… surprising and sharp and the most unique and intuitive person I've ever met. You can do whatever you want to do if you just believe in yourself. I just wanted to be…to be part of it."

Lacey took a step to close the distance between us, but I backed away until I was leaning against the sink. "I'm sorry—I can't," I said.

Lacey nodded, defeated. Then a strange look came across her face. I watched the color drain from her face until it was strangely white, sweat standing out on her forehead where it hadn't been moments ago. As if in slow motion, I watched Lacey sway forward. I held out my arms just in time for Lacey to collapse into them, heaving. I dragged her into a stall and sat her on the cold ground. Lacey crawled forward to the edge of the toilet, gripping the edges, as vomit poured out of her in an unending torrent. She looked up at me with desperation and panic in her eyes. She could only get out two hoarse words.

"I'm drunk."

My mind raced as I pulled Lacey's curls back from the edge of the toilet bowl. She was draped over the bowl retching. I was only about one drink behind her and in no condition to problem solve.

"Are you going to be able to make it to the van?" I asked in a low voice. Lacey shook her head miserably. I looked around, trying to figure out what I was supposed to do next. Lacey let out a soft groan. I sank to the floor and felt a soft crunch in my back pocket. I reached into it and pulled out the receipt from Uptown Cheapskate—with the cashier's phone number on it. I stared at it, wondering if calling a stranger for help was a wildly irresponsible thing to do. Then I glanced back at Lacey. Her head was resting on her arm, her face the kind of white that almost looks transparent.

"Stay here," I said. "I'll be right back."

I jumped up and pushed out of the bathroom and up to the bar. "Do you have a phone I can use?"

"There's a payphone outside," said the bartender—then, seeing the look on my face, "You in trouble?"

I gave a short nod. "My friend is really drunk and I...I need to call someone."

The bartender gestured for me to come behind the counter. "You can use the bar phone, just be quick."

My hand shook as I punched in the numbers written in blue ink on the back of the receipt. I held my breath as the phone rang twice, three times.

"Hello?"

"Hello—hi—I'm sorry—"

I wasn't sure what words I used or whether I explained myself coherently, but I explained something, because the girl told me to wait with Lacey in the Spider House bathroom until she got there. I took a sharp breath of relief and spluttered a series of thank-yous and I'm-sorrys before hanging up the phone. I repeated the words to the bartender, who gave me a nod, still busy pouring drinks for other customers.

I should have headed back to the bathroom then to find Lacey, but

I happened to look out the window and I happened to see Jason still sitting at the table, waiting for Lacey to return.

Everything went as red as the lights in the Spider House ballroom. I pushed past the bar crowd and ran down the upside steps and up to Jason's table.

"Were you trying to get her drunk?"

Jason looked up, insincere confusion plastered over his features. "What the hell?"

"She's never had alcohol like that before. You were buying her shots."

Jason held his hands up in defense. "Look—don't pin this on me. If she can't handle her liquor, that's not my fault."

"Of course she can't handle her alcohol—she's *seventeen*," I spat out.

"Is that why you've been cockblocking me all night?"

"What did you say?" I took a step closer, but Jason only leaned back in his seat with a smug expression on his face. I could tell from the way that his words bled into each other that he had reached the stage of intoxication that had led to his uninhibited answer.

"I said you've been *cockblocking me all night*," he repeated loudly. A few people at nearby tables turned to look at us. Jason made a show of spreading his legs to either side of his chair and relaxing into it.

"It's always the same with you lesbos," he said, and the word made my blood go cold. "But guess what—whatever you can give her is never going to be as good as the real thing." He laid a hand over his crotch.

Before I could think better of it, I lifted my foot and placed it squarely on Jason's crotch. With all of the force I could conjure, I shoved him backward. His chair hit the ground with a thud and he fell backward with it, cursing while he scrambled to get up. I was vaguely aware of a few people standing up from their chairs as I turned on my heel and marched back into the bar.

It didn't take long for the girl with blue hair to show up. Without asking any questions, she ordered me to help her stand Lacey up and carry her out to her tiny Honda. Lacey hung her head onto my shoulder as we helped her lie down in the back seat. I sat with her, putting a bracing hand on Lacey's back as she heaved and moaned. The blue-haired girl got into the front seat and pulled out of the parking lot.

"What the hell happened?"

"She drank way too much," I said, not bothering to mention Jason.

"Fuck," the girl muttered under her breath. "I'm Maddie, by the way," she added, looking at me in the rearview mirror.

"Jo. This is Lacey."

"Did she make it through the poetry slam?"

"Yeah," I said, brightening a little. "She won."

Maddie grinned. "Good for her. And good for you for calling me."

"I shouldn't have brought her here," I said, more to myself than to Maddie. "I should have known better."

"Hey," Maddie said sharply. "This isn't your fault."

"But—"

"It's not your fault," she repeated firmly. "It happens. You're just trying to take care of your—"

"Friend," I said.

Maddie gave a short nod. She pulled into an apartment complex and the two of us helped Lacey out of the car and into her apartment. It was tiny—just one room, divided into a bedroom and living room by only the placement of the furniture. There were plants everywhere, lit by the soft glow of a floor lamp in the corner of the room. We deposited Lacey on a small couch against the wall next to the kitchen. I watched as Maddie spread a blanket over Lacey, then moved to the kitchen and poured three glasses of water. She brought one over and set it on the end table next to the couch. She dragged a trash can from the kitchen next to the couch.

"In case she needs it." Maddie gave me a long look. "It's going to be a few hours. Maybe you should lie down too."

I considered this offer. My mind spun like a dark whirlpool.

"Drink this first." Maddie handed me another glass of water, and I drank the whole thing in one go. Maddie watched me watch Lacey, who was now breathing softly.

"She'll be okay," she said gently.

I shook my head, feeling tears of exhaustion well up in my eyes. "I just…"

"I know." Maddie put a hand on Lacey's shoulder. "You did good. I'll stay up with her. Why don't you lie down and I'll wake you up in two hours? Then I'll get you back to your van and you'll be back before anyone notices you're gone."

I took in a sharp breath. "They know," I said, resigning myself to whatever that would mean.

Maddie pursed her lips. "Well there's nothing to be done about that now. Might as well get a little rest."

I nodded, defeated, and sank onto the edge of Maddie's bed. The quilt on top of it was soft and worn, the kind that looked like it was handmade by a grandmother. I lay sideways across the bed and trained my eyes on Lacey until they finally closed on their own.

# Chapter Thirty

## *Lacey*

I sat up with a start, gasping in panic as I looked around the strange apartment I found myself in.

"It's okay," said a soft voice. "You're okay."

My head whipped around and I saw a girl I vaguely recognized standing in the kitchen, scooping coffee from a bag into a filter. The girl pointed across the room and I followed her gesture. Jo was at the foot of the bed, her face covered by her arm, sleeping.

I stood up slowly, swaying a little, and taking in my surroundings. The water. The trash can. "What happened?"

"You blacked out."

I put a hand to my forehead, which felt as if it must have swollen to five times its normal size. "Did I really drink that much?"

"Just sit. Let me bring you some more water. My name is Maddie, by the way."

Maddie hit a button on her coffee maker, which started gurgling pleasantly. She brought over a new glass of water and sat down on the couch next to me.

"Your friend called me when you were throwing up in the bathroom. She was too drunk herself to drive you home. I came and got you both."

A new thought shot through my mind.

"What time is it?" I asked, looking around for a clock.

"It's about two thirty a.m."

I covered my eyes with my hands, trying to think, trying to make sense of what had happened and what was going to happen. Maddie said nothing, waiting patiently until I took the glass of water out of her hand.

"Is it going to be bad?" she asked.

I nodded. "Really bad," was all I said. It was all I knew.

Maddie let out a knowing sigh. "What about her?" Her eyes cut to Jo, sleeping soundly on the bed.

"What do you mean?"

"What's going to happen to her?"

My eyes rested on Jo. Her dark blue hoodie lay in a pile on the floor next to her. "I'm not sure," I said, realizing for the first time the stakes of what I had asked Jo to do for me. "She's going to be in trouble too."

I stood up from the couch and retrieved Jo's hoodie, holding it in my lap as if it were a pet. I felt something hard in the front pocket and let my fingers wander to it. I pulled it out. It was a bracelet with light green, dark green, and black beads—the same one I had seen Jo making in the arts and crafts cabin. But now, in the middle, were white beads with black letters on them. I held the bracelet taut in my hands, lining up the letters. *Rapunzel.*

"She was going to give this to me," I said aloud, "before the competition."

Maddie leaned over to look at the bracelet. "What happened?"

"What happened was…was…I think I was an asshole."

Maddie nodded, but did not ask any follow-up questions. I slipped the bracelet over my wrist, letting the elastic expand and contract. I looked down at it, then back up at Jo. When I turned my eyes back to Maddie, I realized that we had been sitting this way for quite some time. Perhaps it was the bizarre nature of the evening, the absurdity of the current circumstances, or the exhilarating anonymity that comes with talking to someone you don't know, whom you may never speak to again, but everything swelling inside me began to spill out.

"I think I might love her," I said. "Is that possible?"

Maddie laughed quietly. "Definitely," she said. Then, more seriously, "Have you ever loved a girl before?"

I felt my face heat up. "I don't think I've ever loved anyone before."

We sat in silence, disrupted only by the percolating coffee pot. I looked down at my hands when I finally broke the silence.

"Do you think it's wrong?"

I looked sideways at Maddie, not knowing why I would ask a stranger to provide a moral compass in a matter of the heart. Something about the lateness of the hour, the dim light, and the strange circumstances made me feel awake in a way that I never had before.

"What do you think, Lacey?"

Jo must have told her my name. "I don't know what to think," I confessed quietly. "But I know what my parents would say."

"What would they say?"

I sighed. "They would say that it's a sin," I said simply.

"And what do you think?"

"I don't know what to think," I confessed.

Maddie got up and poured three cups of coffee into different pastel-colored mugs—yellow, green, blue. She handed me the green one and cupped the yellow mug in her hands. I watched the steam rise from the mug, obscuring Maddie's face ever so slightly. She did not offer any cream or sugar, but I took a sip and let the bracing, bitter liquid warm my throat. I was starting to feel like a person again.

"It's okay not to know," Maddie said. "It can take a long time to figure it out."

"It didn't take her a long time," I responded, looking at Jo. "She knows who she is. She knows what she wants."

Maddie tucked her feet under her and leaned against the back of the couch. "It's different for everyone," she said.

I put a hand over my face. "I feel like everything I knew has been turned upside down," I said, my voice cracking a little. "Tonight was so wonderful—and so awful. And when we get back—I just don't know. I don't know if I'm going crazy or if I'm—sick somehow."

"You're not sick," Maddie said firmly. "But the world is sick, and it's always going to be."

I took another sip of coffee.

"Just don't let her be a casualty," Maddie said, gesturing toward Jo with a tip of her head.

Jo began to stir. She sat up, bleary-eyed, taking in the scene. "How do you feel?" she asked me.

"Better," I said.

"Should we go?"

Jo's clothes were wrinkled and her hair stuck straight up. Looking at her, I felt a strange rush of affection and a desire to protect her from whatever was going to happen next.

"Drink this first." Maddie handed Jo the blue mug. Jo took a sip of it and her eyes widened.

"That's strong."

"Well, you're going to have to drive in the middle of the night, so you're going to need it."

Maddie asked more questions about the poetry slam while the three of us drank our coffee and I described the evening—the excitement of the competition, what the other poets had been like, what winning had felt like—leaving out the part about Jason, the fight in the bathroom, and the kiss. Maddie listened and laughed and asked questions until all of our cups were drained. Jo got up off the bed and stretched. She walked over to the kitchen and put her mug in the sink, then walked over to me and held her hand out for her hoodie.

"Not gonna let you steal this again."

I handed it back with a laugh, suddenly wanting to snatch it back and wrap it around myself. Maddie drove us back to the Spider House parking lot, where only the white van was left.

"You girls be careful out there," she said as we climbed out of the car. "And keep my number for your next emergency."

"Thank you," Jo said sincerely. "I don't know why you helped out some strange teens, but I have no clue what we would have done without you."

Maddie shrugged. "You're not strangers," was all she said.

She did not pull out of the parking lot until Jo and I were safely in the van.

## Jo

I put the radio on as soon as we were on the highway. I glanced over at Lacey, but she was curled up in the seat, leaning against the door and staring out the window. I would have given anything to know what she was thinking. Were we still fighting? Were we still going to be friends? Were we ever going to talk about what happened in the green room? Weariness settled over me and I turned the radio up, letting the indie station fill the silence that spread through the van and beyond. We were alone on the highway nearly the entire way back to Camp Lavender.

When we pulled back onto the camp grounds, I felt dread beginning to spike in my chest. Lacey guided me back to the parking lot outside the dining hall. I put the van in park and then we sat in silence for what felt like a long time.

"Thank you," Lacey said quietly.

"For what?"

"For taking me—for taking care of me."

I gave a dismissive wave of my hand. "Anytime."

Then something caught my eye. The bracelet around Lacey's wrist. I pointed to it and Lacey pulled her hand up to her chest.

"Sorry, I...found it in the pocket of your hoodie. I thought it was for me."

"It was. It is."

I held my hand out and Lacey laid her hand gently on top of it. Our fingers twined together and I ran my fingertips over the letters on the bracelet. Lacey shivered slightly.

"You should be proud," I said, almost in a whisper. I looked up and saw that Lacey was looking directly into my face for the first time since we had fought in the bathroom.

"I'm sorry," she whispered.

I squeezed her hand. "Don't be."

## *Lacey*

When I got to the door of our cabin, I started to shake. I had never done anything like this before, and there was certainly no reality in which my parents had not noticed my absence. It was my father who was sitting up at the kitchen table, open Bible in front of him, reading in the dim light shining over the stove. When I closed the door behind me and entered the kitchen, he looked up. I didn't think I had ever seen this look on his face before. I had seen disappointment and disapproval, but this was much colder. My dad had never yelled at me, but I half expected him to do it now. He didn't.

"Where were you?" was all he asked.

"I went to a poetry slam."

"With whom?"

"By myself," I lied.

My father sighed and shook his head. "Do not lie to me, young lady. I know that Josephine Delgado was missing from cabin six this evening."

I feigned a look of surprise as best I could and shook my head. "Missing?"

"Do not lie to me," my father repeated, "I know more than you think I do."

I felt my skin go cold. "What do you mean?"

My father's face looked almost statuesque in its stillness. His voice came to me distant and tinny, as if broadcast over a radio. "I know that Josephine is a homosexual," he said. "Her aunt told me before she arrived. She was here to seek counsel and correction, not to lead my own daughter down a path of folly."

My heart pounded. "Dad, I don't know what you're talking about, but I just went to see a poetry competition and I was by myself and I'm sorry and—"

My father stood up from his chair and drew close to me. "Did she initiate sexual contact with you?"

"*What?*"

"Did Josephine Delgado try to defile you and compromise your purity?"

"Dad—what—no—"

"Did she try to engage you in any kind of sexual relations?"

"*Dad.*"

"Did she tell you she loved you?"

Some kind of desperate fury had shaken me out of my fear and I stood my ground. I spoke calmly. "I do not know where the missing camper was," I said, "But if you want to punish me for sneaking out, go ahead. Don't take it out on her."

My father scoffed. "When I find her, I am sending her home."

"What? Why? She didn't do anything."

"She missed curfew."

"That's happened before, Dad—she probably got lost and—"

"Lacey, if you are trying to rebel against my authority because I decided to postpone your college experience, engaging in homosexual experimentation is extremely dangerous and damaging both to you and to everyone around you."

I threw my hands up in frustration. To my surprise, my father grasped me by the wrist and spoke in a hiss. "You will not be leaving this house until the end of camp."

"FINE."

I did not bother to keep my voice low as I ran up the stairs. I ran past my mother, who was standing tensely at the top of the stairs, and into my room, slamming the door shut behind me. As soon as it was closed, I collapsed against it and pulled my knees to my chest, shaking. I wondered if Jo had been able to sneak into cabin six—if she was going to get caught and expelled from camp—if something worse was going to happen.

But there was no way for me to know.

# CHAPTER THIRTY-ONE

## *Jo*

I had managed to slip into cabin six in the dark and creep into my bunk without disturbing Funfetti or any of the other campers. It was almost daylight by the time my eyes closed. It felt as if I had just shut them when the lights in the cabin snapped on. Funfetti told the campers to get ready and at first, it felt like any other day. Then I noticed that the other girls were glancing at me furtively, and giving each other meaningful looks. I wondered where the gossip had landed. As we trailed to the dining hall, I fell back to wait for Hayley.

"So where were you?" Hayley asked, a cold edge in her voice.

"I—I snuck out."

"Yeah, we know."

Hayley sped up her already long stride and I jogged to keep up.

"What are people saying?"

"I mean, we looked everywhere for you, Jo. You didn't tell anyone where you were going, so we were all pretty worried that you, like, drowned in the lake or something."

"I'm sorry," I said, my body aching with exhaustion.

"Whatever."

Then Funfetti fell into stride with me. "Mr. Heller has asked that you stay after breakfast," she said in a neutral tone, averting her gaze. She did not comment on my absence or ask where I had been.

"Okay," was all I said. I looked at Hayley, but she had sped up to talk to Kristen.

Breakfast dragged on slowly. I tried to swallow a few bites of grits, but my throat felt like it was completely solid. All I wanted was to go to sleep, or leave, or simply disappear into the ragged carpet of the dining hall, but I thought about what I was going to say to Mr. Heller. The girls chattered in their usual rhythm, as if they had all been told not to address my absence. Mr. Heller announced that this week, the last week of camp, everyone should be preparing for the talent show on Friday night.

"Sing, dance, juggle—show us your secret skill!"

As the campers all filed out for Bible study, I sat in my seat, staring at my still-full plate and trying to avoid making eye contact with anyone. Mr. Heller was talking to a counselor as the crowd made its way toward the doors, but at last, it was just the two of us alone among the scatter of round tables. He made his way over to the cabin six table and sat down opposite me, as if he did not want to be close enough to breathe the same air.

"I am going to give you a chance to explain yourself."

He folded his hands and waited. I had been in a lot of bad situations with adults before—there had been yelling, cursing, even hitting once. I had learned to stand my ground and stand up for myself and others. This was the first time I felt utterly cowed by the anger of an authority figure. But something had told me that this was going to happen. I had only one shot, and I took it.

"I went to the chapel," I said, gambling on the fact that no one had looked for me there. "Across the lake."

I saw Mr. Heller's stone face flag for a moment in surprise. I leaned forward, clasping my hands, and speaking with an earnestness that would have made the theater kids in my school back home proud.

"I heard the still, small voice," I continued, "and I went to talk to God."

Mr. Heller pursed his lips.

"I lost track of the time," I went on, starting to feel the passion increase as I spoke. "I prayed through the night. I heard him and I felt his presence. I was utterly enraptured. Being at Camp Lavender has caused a transformation in my heart and I think I finally understand what it means to have a true spiritual experience. He forgave me. And he made me new."

I held my breath, afraid to say more. I had rehearsed this speech in my head all through breakfast. After a few agonizing moments of silence, Mr. Heller nodded slowly. He stood up from his chair and came around the table to sit beside me. He reached out and took my hand and I felt a small shudder echo through my body.

"He forgave me too, Josephine," he said. "I know that he can forgive you. Hearing the still, small voice will change you forever. But you will have to carry it back with you when you are no longer surrounded by spiritual warriors to lift you up."

I nodded solemnly.

"Let's pray together."

Mr. Heller put a hand on my shoulder and prayed aloud for me— prayed that my soul would be transformed and that I would be free from the shackles of sin and from the stronghold of Satan forever. I flinched a little at the grip of his hand, but I sat completely still, my eyes closed, as he spoke the words over me. When he finally said *amen* and released his grip, I felt like I had just come up for air after being held underwater for a few seconds too long.

"Thank you." I took a deep breath.

Mr. Heller's eyes were full of tears. "Welcome," he said, "daughter of Christ." He stood then, and I stood with him.

I pointed toward the door. "Should I go join the Bible study?"

He reached out and gave my arm a gentle squeeze.

"Go."


## *Lacey*


I woke up feeling like I had died and been brought back to life against my will. My head pounded and my throat was dry. I dragged myself into the bathroom and ran cold water from the shower over my head until I felt alive again. Then I stepped quietly downstairs, unsure of whether I was alone in the house. My mother was sitting at the kitchen table, reading. She looked up when I appeared, giving me a small smile.

"Are you hungry?"

I nodded, pacing over to the refrigerator and pulling out a slice of cheese. I grabbed a box of crackers from the pantry and paused at the bottom of the stairs.

"Listen, Mom, I'm—"

My mother looked up with a smile that chilled me to the bone.

"We don't need to discuss it," she said brightly. My mouth dropped open slightly. I stared at my mother. She met my eyes, but I felt that she was very far away somehow.

"Okay," I said quietly and made my way back up the stairs. I had spent many days like this—in my room, with only my books and my thoughts. For many of them, I had felt perfectly content, even blissful. But this one felt different.

It was nearly evening when I heard a quiet knock on my door.

"Dr. Dan has asked to see you."

I looked up from my notebook, surprised. "Oh," I said, unsure of how I was meant to respond.

"You can go," my mother said. "But I have told him to tell me when you arrive and when you leave. You will go straight there and come straight back. Do you understand?"

"I understand." I jumped up and pulled on a pair of basketball shorts. I grabbed my notebook before leaving the room.

Dr. Dan leaned back in his chair when I entered the infirmary.

"Well, well, well—" he began.

"Don't," I said. "I know."

Dr. Dan shook his head, smiling. "You know, when I told you that you should try to branch out this summer, I didn't mean that you should steal a van and run away from home."

I let out a mirthless laugh. "I guess I misunderstood the instructions."

Dr. Dan tilted his head to the side, looking at me intently. "And Sidewinder got you to Austin?"

"What?" I snapped my head toward him.

"Yeah, she said she was making a trip in for supplies and she took you along."

"Right. Yeah…" I said absently, wondering why on earth Sidewinder had chosen to save me not once, but twice, this summer.

"Hey," Dr. Dan said. "It's going to be okay, you know."

"I guess so."

I dropped into the chair on the other side of Dr. Dan's desk. I put my chin in my hands and gazed at him, suddenly wondering new things about him that I had never thought to ask.

"Why do you work here?" I asked.

Dr. Dan shrugged. "Because it's a fun time and decent money."

"But like—is it because you like that it's a Christian camp?"

Dr. Dan eyed me, appraising. "Why do you ask that?"

"I don't know," I said. "I'm just…working through some stuff."

"Does this *stuff* have anything to do with your little friend?"

"Who?"

Dr. Dan gave me a reproachful smile. "C'mon," he said. "I'm talking about the short-haired kid you brought in here after she fell off the blob."

"Oh, her," I said, suddenly unable to meet his eyes. "Yeah, I mean, she's very different from most of the people who come here, you know?"

"Oh yes. I know," Dr. Dan laughed. "I like her."

"You do?" I imagined that my dad must have come to the infirmary looking for me. If Dr. Dan was still here, he must have told him everything. Dr. Dan folded his hand on his desk and narrowed his eyes at me.

"You know," he said slowly, "Not all Christians think the same way about everything. Some might really surprise you."

I couldn't tell whether he was speaking vaguely on purpose, so I just nodded.

"I know your dad probably has strong feelings about certain things, but you're your own person, Lacey. You get to make your own decisions. You're a smart young lady. You'll figure things out."

I looked at him, seeing a kindness and knowing in his eyes that I had never seen there before. Suddenly, an idea struck me.

"Can I ask you a favor?"

## CHAPTER THIRTY-TWO

### *Jo*

"Get in line for the blob!"

Hayley was in front of me, just as she had been that first day. She was still giving me the cold shoulder, but everyone else was treating me relatively normally. I gazed out at the blue, yellow, and red striped inflatable pillow floating on the greenish lake. I looked down at the cut on my knee, which had already begun to turn into a scar. At least I'd have something to remember all this by. My mind wandered to Launchpad—I wondered what those kids had done all summer, if they were all going to list Launchpad as one of their extracurriculars on their college applications.

Then Hayley was climbing up the ladder in front of me and I was climbing after her. She was wearing a black one-piece swimsuit this time. When the counselor said the word, Hayley leapt gracefully onto the blob, which reverberated under her weight. She crawled out to the edge and looked back at me defiantly.

"Now," said the counselor before I jumped, "You want to land as hard as you can, and aim for the *middle* of the blob."

"Got it."

I looked down. It seemed like a longer way down than I remembered it being. I took a deep breath and backed up a few steps. Then, with a running start, I leapt into the air, landing with a thump on the center of the blob. I couldn't help myself from laughing as Hayley shot into the air, limbs flailing, and landed with a splash in the lake. I crawled to the edge and waited for Lindsay to jump. Lindsay was heavier than me and when she landed, I felt myself launch into the air. For a moment, I felt suspended in both the air and in time, taking in the brightness of the sky, the darkness of the trees, and one deep breath of the scent of pine before I plunged into the cold of the lake. It had all gone right this time.

I reveled in the cool darkness of the water as I felt myself float back up toward the surface of the lake. As I made my way back toward the ground, I saw Hayley sitting on the bench where I had waited with my bleeding leg on the first day of camp. My T-shirt clung to my body as I climbed up the short ladder and made my way to the towel I had tossed onto the bench. I sat down and wrapped the towel around me, squinting in the bright midday sunlight.

"How did it work out?" Hayley asked suddenly, her eyes fixed on the shining lake.

"What do you mean?"

"I mean," Hayley said, turning toward me. "Did you get what you wanted? Does she like you back?"

My mouth opened, searching for a response.

"Don't worry," Hayley said, "I'm not going to get you in trouble. But yeah, I saw you leave. I know you were with Lacey. So can you just tell me?"

"I don't know," I said, and it was the truth.

Both of us turned as we heard the crunch of gravel. When the golf cart rounded the corner, my heart jumped. But it wasn't her. It was Dr. Dan. I stood up, somehow knowing that he had come for me. He braked the golf cart and pointed at me.

"You're due for a follow-up appointment," he announced. I turned and looked at Hayley.

"Will you let the others know where I am?"

"Sure," Hayley said.

"Hey, listen," I said, "I'm sorry I didn't tell you."

"It's not that," Hayley said, her voice fiery.

I raised my eyebrows in genuine surprise. "Well what is it?"

Hayley rolled her eyes. "I really liked you," she said. "You idiot."

She turned and walked back toward the rest of the group as I slid into the seat next to Dr. Dan.

"I've got a message for you," he said as the golf cart zipped through the pathway in the woods. My heartbeat stuttered. "I don't really know what it means, but apparently you're going to need to use my computer."

"What's the message?" I asked, embarrassed by the eagerness in my voice.

Dr. Dan used his hand to emphasize each word. "The message is *check Slant.*"

# CHAPTER THIRTY-THREE

## *Lacey*

Nothing interesting ever happened at Camp Lavender. Of this, I had been completely certain. Six weeks at camp always ended with a talent show—exhausted, sunburnt teenage girls piling into the rec room ready to play piano or show off the dance they had choreographed with the new best friend they had already made promises to write to every week until next summer. This year, I had barely managed to get permission to attend the talent show. It had taken a week of meek obedience and many assurances of good behavior in the future, but I had been allowed to go since my father would be there for the entire event and would walk me both to and from the rec room where it was taking place.

After a few hours of agonizing, I had decided that wearing a black T-shirt and denim shorts was the only real option to satisfy all parties involved, since I had carefully hidden my distressed jeans and bomber jacket in the bottom drawer of my dresser under piles of pajamas with adorable micro prints splattered all over them. I made polite conversation with my father as we walked the path to the rec room—there was a tension between us that was utterly unfamiliar to me. I was unsure whether it was the result of the events that had transpired, which had not been directly spoken of since the night in the kitchen, or a fundamental change within myself that would put distance between us long before I ever moved out of the house.

I tried hard not to be too obvious when I scanned the room looking for a particular face. It wasn't a hard one to find. Jo was sitting with the rest of the cabin six campers, wearing black jeans and her usual dark blue hoodie. When my father left me on my own so he could help a camper drag the electronic keyboard to a different part of the stage, I pulled my green and black bracelet from the pocket of my shorts and slipped it over my wrist, feeling suddenly and acutely nervous to see and be seen.

Trainwreck played the part of emcee, introducing the girls one by one and letting each one of them drag out their display of talents, such as they were. The caveat for performing in the Camp Lavender talent show was that you had to give a small speech. You were expected to explain the high of your camp experience and what you were going to take with you back to your secular life, before presumably returning to Camp Lavender the next summer. Unless you were going to college, in which case you were presumably going to evangelize everyone on your campus within an inch of their lives.

I wasn't sure why I had wanted to come to the talent show. I felt certain that there was no way I would even get to speak to Jo, but the promise of being near her one last time, in the same room experiencing the same absurd phenomenon, was enough. I watched the profile of Jo's face as the lights went down and the first camper performed a sign language version of "Be Thou My Vision." I noticed with a guilty sense of satisfaction that Hayley and Jo weren't sitting next to each other. The event dragged on for almost two hours, and I started to regret begging to come. But parents would be picking up the campers first thing in the morning. Then it would be over. I would be here, living the same life, as if nothing different had happened this summer.

My heart jolted against my chest when I heard Trainwreck say Jo's name. It pounded furiously as I watched Jo stand up from the audience and walk toward the stage and across it, picking up one of the acoustic guitars from its stand. She carried a microphone over to the center of the stage and adjusted it to her height.

"Hi," she said into the microphone, testing it. The campers stirred restlessly, ready for their late-night snack of cookies and chips awaiting them in the dining hall upstairs.

"Um, okay, so I'm not really a great singer," Jo said, "But I had a life-changing experience here at Camp Lavender. And I can tell you all, I'm definitely going to go back to my regular life completely changed."

Jo directed a broad smile toward my dad.

I held my breath.

Jo began to strum, taking a step back from the microphone. When she sang, her voice came out in a soft alto that made me feel like my skin was glowing. I recognized my own words, layered over the chords Jo had chosen.

*Never have I ever—felt this way before*
*I never thought an angel would show up at my door.*
*I could sit here forever, in this wooden pew*
*I could sit here forever, talking to you.*

*I whispered a prayer, I whispered a word*
*but I never believed that you would have heard*
*and now you're here, and now you see*
*the best and the worst, duality.*

*Never have I ever, because I never knew how*
*never have I ever known what love felt like*
*until now.*

As she played the last few chords, Jo looked up and ran her eyes across the room. When they found me, a faint smile played across her face. When she finished, the audience erupted in whoops and cheers. My father strode onto the stage and clapped a hand onto Jo's shoulder.

"That's the power of the Lord," he declared, "And it can and will change lives."

I hung back as everyone shuffled to grab their water bottles and backpacks and make their way upstairs for their late-night snack. I saw my dad leaning in and speaking earnestly to Jo and my stomach twisted. How Jo had managed to escape punishment or expulsion, I could not fathom. But my father seemed pleased with Jo, speaking easily to her as if he were closer to Jo than I was.

It was the rumble of thunder that made us all look up.

It happened fast, the way it does in Texas. Most of the campers were still outside on the dock, and chaos arrived as quickly as the storm. The clouds broke and the rain fell hard. Lightning flashed over the lake and a few of the campers shrieked. My father ran out of the rec room and started helping the counselors herd the campers up the stairs and into the dining hall. I did not lose a moment. I dashed out the door and ran toward home where my backpack was waiting for me.

## *Jo*

I searched for Lacey as I stepped off the rec room stage, but I could not spot her in the crowd. I had seen her lurking at the back of the room during the talent show. Part of me had been afraid that the Hellers would not let Lacey out for the talent show and that the song I had been working on every afternoon that week would be for nothing. But I had known that those words were meant for me. I had read them and read them on Dr. Dan's office computer until I had them memorized. I had hoped desperately that Lacey would be in the rec room that night—and she was. But where was she now?

Funfetti was gathering all the cabin six girls and pushing us up the stairs, where we would all wait and eat cookies until the storm died down. I glanced over my shoulder, looking for any sign of Lacey, but saw none. I stood by the door in the dining hall until every camper was inside, but there was still no sign of her. Had Mr. Heller sent her to walk home by herself in the storm? I stared out the window at the pouring rain, and thought about the fact that when I had first arrived, all I had wanted was for it to storm.

And now it was.

My head shot up and I was overcome with the conviction that I knew where Lacey was. But surely not—how would she even know what to do? I stole a glance around the room and saw that everyone was occupied with the chaos that the sudden storm had created. I pulled my hoodie over my head and slipped out before anyone could ask me where I was going.

If I was wrong, then those few moments of eye contact in the rec room were probably the last time I was going to see Lacey Heller. I pushed the thought out of my mind as I pulled my hoodie tight around my face against the slant of the rain. I tried to reassure myself that this was definitely the right path and I definitely wasn't going to get lost in the woods in the rain in the dark. I stepped off the path exactly where I had remembered stepping off it before. I made my way across the field, but the zipline tower was a blur on the other side.

When I got to the bottom of the steps, I hesitated. If I was wrong, then I would be climbing up these slippery spiral steps for nothing, not to mention having to go back down. I gritted my teeth and gripped the wet railing as hard as I could. One step at a time, I made my way to the top of the zipline tower. At the top, I stopped to catch my breath. And there she was, crouched over a crudely made version of the electroscope I had placed at the top of the tower my first night here.

"Lacey!"

She jumped at the sound of her name.

I held out my hands in a gesture of bewilderment. "What are you doing here?" I shouted over the pounding of the rain against the wood and metal of the tower.

"It's the highest point at the camp!" Lacey shouted back. I let out a laugh.

"I know!"

I sank to my knees and crawled across the platform to where Lacey was fiddling with the electroscope.

"How did you do this?" I asked.

Lacey smiled. "I've been really, really bored," she said. "Try it."

She pointed to the switch. I crawled forward and examined the contraption. If it worked, I would really believe in miracles. I grabbed Lacey's hand, wet with rain, and flipped the switch.

It worked.

I let out a victorious yell. I sat down hard, stretching my legs out in front of me and letting the rain fall on me, soaking through my pants and socks.

"Did it work?" Lacey asked.

I put a hand over my heart. "It worked."

Then Lacey was on top of me, straddling me, pushing my hood off my face, and letting the rain fall on both of us as she put a hand on the back of my neck. Our faces were both wet from the rain as we pressed into each other. Lacey sat, wrapping her legs around my waist, and we sat together, entangled at the top of the zipline tower, ignoring the lightning and thunder raging around us. When Lacey finally pulled back, I pulled her back in, pressing my forehead against hers.

"I can't believe you did this," I said, laughing as the rain dripped from my hair into my eyes.

"I had to finish your experiment. Lacey said. "I can't believe you climbed all the way up here. I thought you were afraid of heights."

"I thought there was a chance you might be here," I said.

"I didn't know if you wanted to see me," Lacey admitted.

"I didn't know if *you* wanted to see *me.*"

Lacey looked down, then back up at me. "So you got my message?" She put her hands in the front pockets of my hoodie.

"Yes," I said. "I got your message. It was perfect."

"I can't believe you sang in front of everyone."

"I was only singing to you."

We stayed there until the storm had passed, wrapped up in each other, soaked in the rain, in a state blissfully free from the constraints of linear time, until the stars appeared once again.

## CHAPTER THIRTY-FOUR

### *Lacey*

When I woke up on July sixteenth, I felt an unfamiliar ache inside me. This was not the hollow, predictable feeling I usually had on the last day of camp, knowing that the campers were going back to their normal lives, and that I would stay here, suspended in place, until the next set returned. Ordinarily, I also felt a sense of relief, knowing that my territory's invaders would soon disappear, vanquished by time, and that I would once again resume my uninhibited reign across the spaces they had temporarily occupied.

But today was different.

Today I found myself aching to go with them—to crawl into one of their trunks and stow away in one of their cars and be carried away to whatever part of Texas they had come from. I pictured myself lying curled up in the back seat of Jo's mom's car, being carried away from Camp Lavender, never to return. But I knew better. I dragged myself out of bed and put on my faded Camp Lavender T-shirt and khaki shorts so that I would blend in with the counselors.

My parents were not downstairs this morning. Perhaps they had decided to give me a reprieve, or that my sentence was over, since there was not much trouble I could get into once the last of the cars had ground out of the orange dirt and out onto the main road. I wandered toward the dining hall, feeling the wet heat from last night's storm form a sheen on the back of my neck. Today I would help the counselors break down the cabins, stripping beds and spraying down mattresses, setting everything up to be preserved until next summer.

Next summer. When I would still be here.

I stopped in the dining hall only to grab a cup of coffee. I did not add anything to it—I had started drinking it the way Maddie had served it to me. I took a sip of the bitter liquid and immediately thought about the small couch and the soft light in Maddie's tiny apartment—of the secret adventure I had dared myself to take. Already, it felt as though it was fading into the unsaturated color of a dream. I headed toward the infirmary. Dr. Dan was there, organizing the shelves and drawers and closing everything into boxes. He smiled broadly when he saw me push through the door.

"I have some news for you," he said.

"Shoot."

"Don't be so excited." He laughed. "I had a little talk with your parents."

I froze. "That can't be a good thing."

Dr. Dan laughed. "Don't be such a pessimist. I convinced them to let you enroll in community college classes and start getting some college credits. I told them that I thought that you were ready and that branching out into new environments would be an important part of your spiritual journey."

"No way." I was incredulous.

"I know it's not NYU," Dr. Dan added, "but you can go next year—or even maybe transfer in the spring."

I sighed. "Thank you," I said sincerely.

"And I told them I would come visit and teach you how to drive so you could take yourself."

My jaw dropped. "And they agreed to that?"

"Everybody trusts a doctor," Dr. Dan said with a grin. I laughed.

Jo was waiting with the other campers near the front entrance, holding her duffel bag. I stopped when I saw her, taking her in one last time. I had told myself that it would be better not to come here today, that it would be better to leave us both with the memory of our rainy night on top of the tower—that seeing her one more time would just make my ache that much sharper.

And I was right.

But it was worth it.

❖

## *Jo*

I felt a tap on my shoulder. I turned around and saw Lacey, wild hair and shining eyes, dressed in the same faded purple T-shirt she had worn the first time I had laid eyes on her. She threw her arms around my shoulder and I dropped my duffel bag into the orange dirt. I put my head on Lacey's shoulder, breathing her in. I wanted to stand just like that as long as I could, but all too soon I recognized the honk of my mom's car horn. I heard Rudy's voice.

"Jo!"

I turned around and waved at Rudy, who waved both hands enthusiastically and leaned out of the passenger side window. I leaned down and unzipped my duffel bag. I pulled the dark blue hoodie out and tossed it to Lacey.

"Aren't you going to need this?" she asked.

I shrugged. "Something to remember me by."

Lacey rolled her eyes.

"Hey," I said, a sudden urgency taking me over. I took a step forward and put a hand on Lacey's arm. Lacey waited for me to speak, but I couldn't find the words I was looking for. At last, I just said, "I had a much better summer here than I thought I would."

"Me too," Lacey said quietly. I took one step closer and raised my lips to Lacey's ear. In a quiet voice just above a whisper, I said, "You don't have to have everything figured out right now. If you want to forget about this and just go back to the way your parents do things, that's okay. But if not…"

I hesitated, running my hand down Lacey's arm and grabbing her hand. "If not," I said again, "come find me, okay?"

## *Lacey*

Jo turned and picked up her duffel bag. I slipped the dark blue hoodie over my shoulders and zipped it up. I watched as Jo opened her mother's car door and tossed her duffel bag into the back seat. With a sudden and desperate rush of feeling, I ran the few steps over to her. I brushed my lips against Jo's ear and whispered, "I will."

I watched the Delgados' car pull across the orange dirt and out onto the main road, and when I turned to walk back into Camp Lavender, I couldn't stop myself from smiling.

## *About the Author*

Elizabeth Bradshaw is a late-blooming queer millennial who spent most of her growing-up years with fictional friends for company. She writes herself through her questions about the nature of life, love, and the pursuit of meaning. She lives in Austin, Texas, with her partner and her two cats, where she spends most of her evenings consuming snacks and discussing TV characters as if they're real people.

# Books Available From Bold Strokes Books

**Good Christian Girls** by Elizabeth Bradshaw. In this heartfelt coming of age lesbian romance, Lacey and Jo help each other untangle who they are from who everyone says they're supposed to be. (978-1-63679-555-3)

**Not Just Friends** by Jordan Meadows. A tragedy leaves Jen struggling to figure out who she is and what is important to her. (978-1-63679-517-1)

**Proximity** by Jordan Meadows. Joan really likes Ellie, but being alone with her could turn deadly unless she can keep her dangerous powers under control. (978-1-63679-476-1)

**A Talent Within** by Suzanne Lenoir. Evelyne, born into nobility, and Annika, a peasant girl with a deadly secret, struggle to change their destinies in Valmora, a medieval world controlled by religion, magic, and men. (978-1-63679-423-5)

**Take Her Down** by Lauren Emily Whalen. Stakes are cutthroat, scheming is creative, and loyalty is ever-changing in this queer, female-driven YA retelling of Shakespeare's *Julius Caesar*. (978-1-63679-089-3)

**Two Winters** by Lauren Emily Whalen. A modern YA retelling of Shakespeare's *The Winter's Tale* about birth, death, Catholic school, improv comedy, and the healing nature of time. (978-1-63679-019-0)

**Boy at the Window** by Lauren Melissa Ellzey. Daniel Kim struggles to hold onto reality while haunted by both his very-present past and his never-present parents. Jiwon Yoon may be the only one who can break Daniel free. (978-1-63679-092-3)

**Three Left Turns to Nowhere** by Jeffrey Ricker, J. Marshall Freeman & 'Nathan Burgoine. Three strangers heading to a convention in Toronto are stranded in rural Ontario, where a small town with a subtle kind of magic leads each to discover what he's been searching for. (978-1-63679-050-3)

**#shedeservedit** by Greg Herren. When his gay best friend, and high school football star, is murdered, Alex Wheeler is a suspect and must find the truth to clear himself. (978-1-63555-996-5)

**The Infinite Summer** by Morgan Lee Miller. While spending the summer with her dad in a small beach town, Remi Brenner falls for Harper Hebert and accidentally finds herself tangled up in an intense restaurant rivalry between her famous stepmom and her first love. (978-1-63555-969-9)

**Bury Me in Shadows** by Greg Herren. College student Jake Chapman is forced to spend the summer at his dying grandmother's home and soon finds danger from long-buried family secrets. (978-1-63555-993-4)

**I Am Chris** by R Kent. There's one saving grace to losing everything and moving away. Nobody knows her as Chrissy Taylor. Now Chris can live who he truly is. (978-1-63555-904-0)

**The Dubious Gift of Dragon Blood** by J. Marshall Freeman. One day Crispin is a lonely high school student—the next he is fighting a war in a land ruled by dragons, his otherworldly boyfriend at his side. (978-1-63555-725-1)

**Jellicle Girl** by Stevie Mikayne. One dark summer night, Beth and Jackie go out to the canoe dock. Two years later, Beth is still carrying the weight of what happened to Jackie. (978-1-63555-691-9)

**All the Worlds Between Us** by Morgan Lee Miller. High school senior Quinn Hughes discovers that a broken friendship is actually a door propped open for an unexpected romance. (978-1-63555-457-1)

**Exit Plans for Teenage Freaks** by 'Nathan Burgoine. Cole always has a plan—especially for escaping his small-town reputation as "that kid who was kidnapped when he was four"—but when he teleports to a museum, it's time to face facts: it's possible he's a total freak after all. (978-1-163555-098-6)

**Rocks and Stars** by Sam Ledel. Kyle's struggle to own who she is and what she really wants may end up landing her on the bench and without the woman of her dreams. (978-1-63555-156-3)